SHIRA

An Urban Fantasy

ANN GIMPEL

CONTENTS

SHIRA

CIRCLE OF ASSASSINS, BOOK ONE

Urban Fantasy

By
Ann Gimpel

Tumble off reality's edge into a twisted world fueled by lore and magic

Copyright Page

BOOK DESCRIPTION, SHIRA

If they had one of those anonymous rehabilitation programs for folks like me, my introduction would be, "Hi, I'm Shira, and I kill people." Except rehab suggests killing people bothers me. It doesn't.

Neither am I particularly committed to anything other than not being caught. That sounded a shred on the hard-hearted side. I'm not. I'm a lot like you. I get up every morning, clean myself up, and check my phone to see what I have cooking.

Everyone has a job. Mine happens to be ridding the world of people who shouldn't be here. Not that I'm making those decisions. People hire me, and I trust they've done their homework.

I've always been...different, never had a close circle of friends or even associates. Once I discovered I could do unusual things, I kept to myself. Those rare skills make me a perfect choice because I kill from a distance and leave no evidence. What I do is lucrative. I'm pretty much set even for my rather long lifetime.

In theory, I could quit anytime.

I say that after every job. That I should walk away, except I don't. Tell you what. Don't judge me, and I might spare you if your number comes up on my dance card. Deal?

BOOKS IN THE CIRCLE OF ASSASSINS SERIES

Shira, Book One
Quinn, Book Two
Rhiana, Book Three
Kylian, Book Four

AUTHOR'S NOTE

Between Covid-19 and the California fires, I've had a lot of time to dream up ideas for books. Watching too much *Blacklist* and *Warehouse 13* and *Stranger Things* probably didn't help. And the last season of *Supernatural*. I will miss Sam and Dean...

Meanwhile, a concept shaped up for me. Assassins have always held a fascination factor. Death is a job for them, but what kind of people are they beneath their knives and guns and poison? Toss a few bond animals into the mix, and the bones for a darkish urban fantasy series took shape.

Within its pages, you'll ride alongside men and women who found their way to an age-old profession. Every king worth his salt had a court assassin, and so has every ruler from olden times to modern. If you're shaking your head saying such things can't happen today, take a look at "suicides" that are swept under a whole bunch of rugs. Oddly enough, all those suspicious deaths had stories to tell, stories someone wanted silenced—forever.

Shira would understand completely. I can't wait for you to meet her.

CHAPTER 1

Neon flickered, casting garish lights over the alleyway beneath me. Water ran down gullies in the cracked pavement. Every now and again, a flash of red from rodent eyes was accompanied by the squeals of rats squabbling over a prime piece of garbage.

I pushed straggling bits of hair under my hood to keep them out of my eyes. I'd been here for longer than was prudent, but my target hadn't shown. A pounding, punishing rain had soaked me all the way to my skin. Was this a setup? Or had the nameless faceless ones who employed me screwed up?

It happened, and more often than I'd like.

I work through a dark web registry. In theory, I have no idea who hires me. On the flip side, they don't know me, either. Anonymity is a gift in the assassin trade.

I gave it another fifteen minutes, but the only life forms in the alley were rats and the occasional feral cat. Every once in a while, a cat made a move, but they usually backed down. Not much bigger than the king-sized rats, they usually thought better of the proposition. Cats are scrappy fighters, but rats pack up and are totally unprincipled and lethal as all get out.

Time to go. Past time, actually.

Unwinding the spells I'd swathed around myself so I wouldn't be quite so exposed on the narrow wrought iron balcony where I'd settled in to wait, I took one last look around. Still no one. I grabbed hold of the pole I'd used to slither into position. Whatever magical talents I possess are self-taught, so they leave a lot to be desired, but what the hell.

It's not as if I can google witches or magical instruction and come up with anyone other than total charlatans. The Internet wasn't even a gleam in anyone's eye when I was born, but once it hit its stride, I did make a good faith effort to find a teacher. What joke that turned out to be.

My hand slipped on the pole. Ninety minutes ago when I'd shown up, it had only been sprinkling. I'd been on time, even a few minutes early. This job was supposed to be a slam-dunk. Easy in, fast out. But my target, who supposedly took this route every night after leaving his favorite watering hole, had either changed his routine—or someone had tipped him off.

I took a few deep breaths. I was overreacting all over

the place. He could have hired a hooker, or a boy-toy, or fallen face down dead drunk.

I make a point of getting as little information as possible about my hits. That way, they're more like jobs and less like people, maybe people with lives and homes and kids and families. I also don't give a flying fuck why someone thinks the world would be better off with them dead.

Above my paygrade and not my call.

I do require a JPEG, but only to make certain I kill the right person. My night vision is impeccable; it's part of my magic, and I'm conscientious about shredding the photographs once a job is done.

I made a full commitment to the pole I'd planned to climb back up. Once I hit the roof, the fire escape offered an easy out. Taking a firm hold, and wrapping all my limbs around the slick pole, I tried to shinny.

And slid right back down.

Oops. Two more tries convinced me I'd never manage it. Not without ropes and a grappling hook. I hadn't counted on the rain cutting off my exit route. The balcony was really only a cage around windows that were probably locked. Was anyone inside? I'd scoped out this perch for a few days before I selected it. In all that time, I hadn't seen the drapes shrouding the windows so much as flicker. Before I added a potential B&E to my rap sheet—and yeah, I do have one—I peered downward.

A good hundred feet separated me from the pavement below. Made sense since I was eight floors up. Too far to jump. My handy-dandy pole extended downward as well. It was probably some sort of drainpipe from the roof, but it stopped maybe twenty feet from the bottom.

Twenty feet was manageable. I could twist a bit of magic into a cushion to break my fall. It would work for twenty feet, but not for a hundred. I hunched my shoulders against the downpour. It was raining harder, if that was even possible, and I longed for my cozy home and a hot shower. Usually, I make quick decisions, but for whatever reason I looked from the window to the alley a few times. The window route was simpler—so long as I didn't run into whoever liked living in the dark.

This was an upscale neighborhood in a renovated area of downtown Seattle. My odds of running into dead bodies or decaying skulls were thin, but most people didn't keep their curtains closed all the time, either. The Pacific Northwest was gloomy enough without exacerbating the problem.

Splaying my palm across the glass, I snaked a thread of power through it and pulled my hand back as if I'd been burned. What in the hell lived inside? I cursed myself for retreating before I'd gleaned much except a growing sense of unease. Black magic has a particular zing to it, and if some iteration didn't live inside that apartment, I'd eat raw brains.

Footsteps and drunken voices sounded from the far end of the alley. Shit. Could things get any worse?

Um, of course they could. Lots worse. I was pretty exposed since I'd dismantled my *don't look here* spell.

Mortals wouldn't notice if I resurrected it, but what if whoever was lurching my way had power of their own? Magic calls to itself—I'd found that out the hard way—so I had to be careful.

What were the odds this was my target?

Not good since three men were closing the distance between us, and I'd only been expecting one. In my line of work, it's best not to leave witnesses. My exit from below had just been cut off. The window route was viable—so long as I was prepared to fight my way through whatever lay on the other side of the glass.

I took a chance, did a sloppy job dragging my concealment spell back into place, and waited. The men's slurred words were in Russian. My target was Russian, so maybe he was down there after all. While I recognized a word here and there, it's not one of the languages I'm fluent in.

My cell phone vibrated against my chest, but I couldn't take my attention away from the tableau unfolding beneath me. The men were close enough for me to see their faces. Sure enough, my target was in the middle. Burley with slicked-back dark hair and Slavic features, he was ripe for the plucking.

Or he would have been if he'd been alone.

Should I make it a clean sweep? Or come back and try another day?

I was edging toward shelving tonight—since nothing was coming together and I didn't have good feelings about any of it—when the man on the right end of the group pivoted. When he came around, a gun was in his hand.

Bullets splattered too close for comfort.

Fuck. Who'd set me up? When I found out, I'd cut the balls out from under him and stuff them down his throat.

More bullets. They knew I was here somewhere, but they couldn't see me. Nothing magical about this batch. They were using the scatter technique, figuring if they took out the sides of a few buildings with ammo, they'd hit me. Sure enough, the next round peppered the building next door. I made a full commitment to shielding myself.

Adrenaline coursed through me, leaving a metallic taste on my tongue. My heart shot into triple-time rhythm. Fight or flight is a bitch when there's nowhere to run to. More gunfire lit the night. Where in the fuck were Seattle's finest? Someone must have dialed 911 by now. No love lost between the cops and me. I'm on a first name basis with a few of them, and I've spent the odd night locked up.

Someone beneath me had switched to a semi-automatic weapon. The *phut-phut-phut* of bullets releasing every couple of seconds was unnerving. I laid a hand on the window again, determined to ride it out this time. Didn't take all that long before I had my answer. Vampires lived within. I'd thought they went to ground during the day in caskets, but this batch lived on the eighth floor of a spanking new condo complex.

The blood business must pay well.

I'd almost decided to jimmy the window with magic when I realized at least two of the Undead were inside.

Nighttime was their time, but what was the worst they could do to me? I didn't care for the answer. They could turn me. I'd heard they liked magic-wielders. Apparently, we didn't have quite as rocky a transition as mortals to the blood-sucking life.

I'm not immortal, and I had zero desire to turn into one courtesy of dying.

Welp. My choices had thinned considerably. Sirens wailed in the distance, but they might not get here soon enough. In one of the split-second decisions that have made me one of the most sought-after killers on the West Coast, I threaded power through the eye of a magical needle and split it three ways.

Shouts were replaced by gasps and mumbled curses as three hearts stopped beating. My favorite method to kill involves poisons of various natures, preferably tailored to my marks, but what I chose in this instance was quick. A shot of power to the aorta rips it in two, and my victims bleed out. All without a visible mark on them. The ME will cite heart attacks, albeit under suspicious circumstances. Since when do three relatively young men have cardiac events at the same time?

I surveyed the wreckage and would have dusted my hands together if they weren't soaking wet. Would my employer triple my take? Ha. More likely, they wouldn't pay me at all because I'd drawn undue attention to what should have been a quiet little operation. Sirens warbled. Car doors slammed. Shit. Crap. Fuck. Past time to leave.

What in the hell was I doing still crouched in this wrought iron trap?

Grabbing hold of the pipe, I rode it to its end, dropped to the ground, and faded into the cramped space between two buildings. Something stinky squished under my feet. Probably human shit. Or maybe something even more ominous like an entire body. This part of town had been sketchy before an urban renewal project rescued it from the homeless.

Sheer will and adrenaline propelled me forward. I hadn't researched exit venues nearly well enough; the way my luck had been running tonight I might end up with concrete walls all around and have to backtrack. Except the alley was crawling with boys in blue. I pressed forward, willing my path to lead somewhere. The slender space widened and spit me out on First Avenue not far from the Pike Place Market. Since I don't require weaponry, I was safe enough. Even if someone stopped me for questioning—and why would they?—I wasn't carrying anything that would label me a suspect.

Remembering the message that had come through on my phone, I dragged it from an inside pocket. Luckily, iPhones are impervious to water. Despite being as drenched as the rest of me, its display lit like always. The rain had slacked off, but it still sluiced over my head. At least it was cleaning the muck off my boots.

One word flashed across my screen: *Abort*.

I'd have laughed, but I didn't want to draw attention to myself. Aborting hadn't been on the table. Not after the trio began shooting at me. The message suggested someone knew I was in danger. It had to be my anonymous employer. If they were warning me, they probably hadn't sold me out.

No guarantees on that one, though. People do a lot of strange things to create the illusion of innocence. I glanced at my display again. The text had come in half an hour ago, just after the three men entered the alley.

Running on autopilot, I circled around to where I'd left my nondescript Ford. An older beat-up Explorer, it was ubiquitous enough to escape notice. Thousands of white SUVs traveled the highways, many of them old Ford Explorers.

I hit the clicker to open my door and then hesitated. If I sat on the upholstery, it would take days to dry. Snagging a towel from the back, I draped it over the driver's seat. It would absorb some of the moisture drenching my garments. After pulling the door shut and hitting the central lock button, I grappled for my keys.

The mournful sound of a pack of wolves howling filled the car. My phone must have been shunted off silent when I was reading the text. I glanced at the screen. Private Number flared across it. Screwing my face into a grimace, I punched accept.

In my business, all incoming calls originate from private numbers.

"Shira," a man's deep gravelly voice said.

"What's it to you?" I replied. In a surly mood, I wasn't

in a hurry to mitigate it. My windows started to fog from my soaked hair and clothing.

"Did you get my message?" he asked.

"Maybe—depends who you are and what the message was—but the one I got was too late."

A long breathy sigh rustled against my ears. Christ, I loathe men who are drama kings. "But you got it," the man pressed.

"After my position had been compromised." I gave up on being coy and stopped to suck in a breath. "It's been a long night. I'm off duty. Unless there's something specific you need, this call is over."

I started the car, turned the defroster to high, and rolled into light traffic. I'd drive around a bit to make certain no one was tailing me, and then I'd go home.

"You didn't do as we requested, and—" the man went on.

"Your intel was fucked," I spoke over him. "I expect to collect at the usual location."

"Expect all you want. It's not going to happen. No money when you blow your assignments."

Even though I'd expected something like this, the adrenaline already humming through me turned into rage. My hands were shaking, so I pulled over in front of an all-night market and reached through the cellular web with an experimental strand of magic.

Bingo. It connected. Depending on a whole lot of factors I hadn't been able to identify, sometimes I could kill remotely with the assistance of electronic toys.

Winding cords around the man's neck, I snugged them, gratified when I heard a cough.

I could just picture him massaging his windpipe and wondering what in god's name was going on.

"Not paying me would be a huge mistake," I purred. Holding the connection open with magic—so even if he hung up it wouldn't make any difference—I added, "Feel that?" and pulled my noose in a few more notches.

"That can't be you. You're nowhere near me," he wheezed.

"When logical explanations fail to explain unusual circumstances, it pays to widen your net," I crooned and added more pressure. What I was doing was downright stupid. I'd painted myself into a corner. If I didn't kill him, he'd tell everyone not to touch me with a million-foot pole. So even if I got paid for this job, the next one would be a long time coming.

If I killed him, my threats about payment would have been for nothing. No one would understand why he was dead.

"Way to go, Shira," I mumbled.

"Stop that," he gasped.

An idea bloomed. It might or might not work. If this dude wasn't the money man, I'd be nattering on for nothing. "Pay me. Transfer the funds. Do it now."

"I can't."

"Try harder," I suggested and brought up the screen for one of my many offshore accounts, the one I'd used for tonight's escapade. No one was more surprised than me when $50,000 rolled into it.

As soon as the transfer was complete, the man said, "There. Check your bank."

I smiled. Who says you can't have your cake and eat it too? I released enough magic to romp through our connection and strangle him. At least he had the good grace—or maybe it was dignity—not to spend the last of his air pleading for his life. It wouldn't have done him any good, and it might have made me feel bad.

Or not. He wasn't worth wasting any of my limited compassion stores on. He'd threatened to stiff me. I'd been a bit on the heavy-handed side. Probably, I should have reminded him of the contract I have all my employers sign. Especially the clause that addresses unforeseen circumstances and allows me latitude to proceed as I see fit.

Eh, no reason to second-guess myself. My instincts were generally sound.

Once I was certain the guy was dead, I severed the link, gathered my power back into me, and started for home. My number would be the last one on his cell, but I wasn't worried about it. His associates would think he'd called to tell me I was shit out of luck.

I shook my head. I'd set out to kill one and netted four. Granted I dealt with bottom-feeders, but tonight was over the top even for me. Before I threw myself a genuine pity-party, I cleared my mind of everything. I never revisited jobs. Why would I? Once they were done, I moved on to whatever came next.

Live in the moment was one of my few mottos, but I knew the truth. The only way I could keep doing what I did was if I never dissected any of it.

CHAPTER 2

Sunlight, a rare phenomenon, streamed through my bedroom curtains. I have blinds but rarely use them. From the angle of the rays, it might be midafternoon. I didn't remember much of my drive last night because the adrenaline had retreated leaving me worn out and shaky. I'd had the presence of mind to drop my wet clothes over hooks in the mud room, though. From the looks of things, I'd taken a quick shower as well.

I'd purchased this home a few years back. Located in a gated compound on Mercer Island with half a mile of private beach, it was my retreat. No one had ever associated its owner, Suzanne Teague, with me, Shira Teague the assassin.

It's ridiculously simple to mislead people, and Teague is a fairly common name. My cover story pegged me as a rich, eccentric widow who preferred to be left alone. After a few attempts to stop by with cookies and casseroles, my neighbors gave up. None had made it past the front door.

I stretched, extending my arms over my head and breathing deep. The trashed feeling from last night had retreated, so I'd gotten enough rest. It surprised me. Lately, my dreams had been graced by a dragon. At first, I'd thought it coincidence. Lots of people dream of dragons, except the same dragon showed up over and over again. Or maybe all dragons had silver scales, reddish wings, and forked tongues.

Tough to tell since I've never met a real one. If you'd asked me many years back, I'd have pooh-poohed the existence of any supernatural critters. But that was before I understood I was one. And before I'd run into a pack of Vampires. At first, I thought they were a bunch of dicks playing at Halloween off-season. They'd set me straight damned quick. And if I hadn't been quicker than them, I'd have joined their ranks and found out way more about the Undead than I ever wanted to know.

It had been the beginning of a spotty education. Like I said, finding someone to teach me had proven impossible. I'd given up after the sixth googled shaman turned out to be just as bogus as the first five.

Back to my dream dragon BFF, I had a dream interpretation book stashed somewhere, but I didn't put much stock in it. After I'd first begun turning my proclivity to end people into a profitable venture, my dreams had been off-the-charts bloody. Before that, I'd killed to survive. If anyone thinks killing is the same across the board, they're dead wrong. Not to make a pun or anything.

Ending someone who had me in their gunsights was a necessity. Killing because someone hired me is an entirely different animal. I swallowed a snort. Last night held elements of both. It was what had made doing away with the ones shooting at me a no-brainer.

I swung my legs over the side of the bed and padded into the bathroom. My hair was the same tangled fright it always turned into when I washed it and fell into bed. Because it was easier than dragging a comb through my thick, unruly locks, I washed it all over again and slathered a giant blob of conditioner into the worst of the snarls.

Later, standing in front of the steamy mirror with my hair dripping all over the floor, I forced myself to take a good look. By some twist of fortune—maybe the same bit of luck that powered my magical ability—I still appeared to be in my thirties. My features were nondescript, except for my hair. I should have left it dirty blonde. Instead, it's a whole bunch of colors that change from time to time. At the moment, pink is the leading shade, but I've had it purple and blue and green.

My eyes looked tired, their clear-blue color marred by a fine web of capillaries that made it appear I'd come off a several-day bender. With my not-quite-six-foot height, relatively slender build, and girl-next-door looks, I was eminently forgettable—so long as I slouched—which was how I liked it.

I called it my any-girl-USA costume. It had fooled a

whole lot of people into underestimating me. In truth, I was closer to eighty than thirty. When I passed fifty it dawned on me I wasn't going to age like normal folks. Took me a few years to come to terms with that part of things.

Because I live in an era when women have lots of work done on themselves, I figured I was good for another decade or so at my current location before I needed to move and redo everything from my name upward. Knowing criminals comes in handy. Several forgers will be a good match for the task when I get to that point. If they're dead by then, a new batch will have cropped up.

Wrapping a towel around my head, I left the bathroom and hunted down something to wear. Once I was dressed in my usual jeans and stretchy top, I checked in with my phone. Sheesh. Twenty messages had come in between when I'd turned it off last night and now.

They'd wait for me to brew a pot of coffee. Once it was in process, I hesitated in front of the refrigerator door willing food to magically appear inside. Didn't work. When I pulled the door open the same containers of too-old-to-eat Chinese takeout hadn't moved.

My freezer yielded bread. Peanut butter and honey were in a cupboard. After toasting the bread, I made a sandwich. It would have been better with cream cheese and bananas and raisins. Eh. Maybe I'd make it to the store today. I'd just poured myself a cup of coffee, black because I didn't have any cream, and settled in with my sandwich when an outraged squawk told me Reggie had figured out I was not only home but awake.

The large African grey parrot swooped into the room and landed in front of me, pecking at my sandwich with great enthusiasm. "Honey is bad for birds," I told him and received a louder squawk for my troubles. Maybe honey wasn't bad for him, but I had a list somewhere of things I shouldn't let him get into.

A quarter of my sandwich had disappeared. I laid a hand over the rest of it and yelped when Reggie pecked it to get me to move away from what he now viewed as his breakfast.

"Shira," he cawed. "Shira. Shira."

Blood flowed from multiple places on the back of my hand; I held my ground. "Go eat your food," I suggested, but he skewered me with his intense avian gaze and didn't show any sign of budging.

If I hadn't been so hungry, I'd have just given him the sandwich. Staring back at him, I said, "Trade ya."

It was a game we often played when he got hold of something I didn't want him to have. He fluffed his wings and repeated, "Trade. Trade."

"Over there." I pointed at a granite counter next to my empty cookie jar.

After a lengthy hesitation, the bird fluttered to the indicated spot, but never took his gaze from the sandwich. I grabbed the peanut butter jar and slopped a glob of it onto a plate.

Seemed to do the trick because Reggie hunched over his find. I returned to my decimated sandwich, my cooling coffee, and my neglected phone. I'd been right about the time. It was three thirty. I skimmed the messages. Half of them were about last night's fiasco. One said I'd been paid before they realized I'd screwed up.

No one mentioned the dead guy. The one I'd strangled via my phone.

The rest of the texts were about other jobs. Enough so I could cherry-pick what I wanted. I'd done that with last night's assignment, though, and look how it turned out. Some of that was the fault of defective intel, but the rest was on me. I'd been stupid not to check what lay on the far side of the glass next to my perch.

I drained my cup, and got up to pour myself another one. It took a lot of caffeine to get me going. Phone in hand again, my first reply was to the text about being paid by mistake. *"Sorry you feel that way. The dude who called me wired the money. Not inclined to return it."*

Should be the last of it. That's the thing about dirty money. There's no bank or credit card company or PayPal to arbitrate. Ignoring the rest of the texts about the previous evening, I scrolled through new job offers. Reggie had left, but the plate where I'd dabbed peanut better was pecked clean. At least, he hadn't made an end run to nab my sandwich.

I'd wanted a pet, but nothing requiring me to be here often enough to provide daily food and water. Reggie hunted to supplement what I kept out for him. Sometimes a week or more passed when I didn't see the bird. Not the closest relationship, but it worked for us. I'd picked him because he was long-lived and independent.

In his own way, he'd picked me too. He didn't have to come back from his hunting jaunts, but he always did.

None of the jobs rang my chimes, but I kept coming back to one. Travel involved, it said. Maybe putting some distance between me and Seattle wasn't a bad idea. By the time I got back, whoever had ordered last night's hit would have moved on. Nothing is static in the criminal world. It changes from moment to moment.

I finished my second cup of coffee and got to my feet. I really needed food, but after I got back from the store I'd look a little deeper into the job requiring travel. My cup and dish and knife went into the dishwasher, and I walked out onto my little-used deck with its view of Lake Washington. Small boats bobbed on its waters, probably hobbyists thrilled it wasn't raining. My outdoor furniture was tucked under waterproof covers. I was never out here long enough to rescue so much as a chair.

Back inside, I stuffed my feet into trail runners and grabbed my purse and keys. I'd bought the house semi-furnished and never added to any of it. The white-on-white-on-white motif was incredibly boring, but I'm a street kid. Or I was one. Having a roof over my head, and nice digs, was more than enough. I'd never felt the need to piss in all the corners and stamp mine all over everything by customizing the place.

The things I checked had nothing to do with fancier furniture. I made certain none of the markers I'd left had been disturbed. It was unlikely anyone would find me here, but I couldn't afford to become complacent. Sloppy got you killed. I could have installed an upscale surveillance system—the one I had was cheap and outdated—but they can be disabled. My process was undetectable.

Satisfied I'd made it through another day without unforeseen visitors, I nosed the car out of the garage and nodded at the gatekeeper as I drove past the entry kiosk. I hated shopping. It was at the bottom of my list of chores. I'd rather scrub floors—or toilets—than shop. Telling myself I needed an attitude adjustment, I covered the mile to a big chain supermarket, parked the car, and got moving.

An hour later, I was back home, schlepping sacks inside.

Unlike me, Reggie adored it when I went to the store. He flew around the kitchen like a bat on crack, poking his beak into all the bags.

My phone vibrated before it began to howl. I really needed to change my ringtone for something quieter. Private number flared across the screen. So, what else was new?

"Yes?" I waited, expecting some thug threatening me if I didn't return yesterday's fifty grand.

"Is this Shira?"

I didn't recognize the voice, so I made a noncommittal grunt.

"I, uh, met you about a week ago. It's Jay. We traded numbers, and—"

"Hold it right there, buster. I'm not in the habit of trading anything."

He must have intuited I was about to hang up because

he said, "Wait. Please. You were in that little bar next to Ivar's. I bought you a beer. We talked."

I culled through my memory banks. And disconnected. I hadn't been in any waterfront bars in months. My phone rang again; I let it drop through into voicemail.

If the mystery caller hadn't had access to my uber private cell number, I'd have chalked it up to mistaken identity. He'd run into someone, thought it was me, etc. etc. The only way he could have accessed my phone was via underworld connections. It meant I couldn't trust him, no matter how benign he'd sounded.

Glad that was settled, I put the groceries away, made tentative plans for what I'd have for dinner, and brought up the registry where I find jobs. Funny how dark web sites are faster and better organized than mainstream ones like Linked-In and Google.

The info box popped up right away. The way things work is I check a bunch of parameters that live with my profile. Any jobs that hit two or more of my requirements are forwarded to my in basket. I studied the assignment. Much of the information was purposely vague. Usually, I steered clear of jobs with so little data.

I'd found out the hard way when I'd walked into situations far worse than last night's had been. Of course, I'm smarter than I was. And not as hungry. Thirty years doing my thing coupled with a lifelong aversion to wasting money had set me up nicely.

Many people who come into unexpected riches squander them. Not me. I know what it is to be hungry, to not have anywhere to crash. It's been years, but I still remember the creepy feel of men's hands all over me and waiting them out so I'd get paid. That phase was short-lived once I discovered it was simpler to pick their pockets while they rooted around on top of me.

It also avoided the problem of them underpaying me. Or not paying at all.

Talons closed around my shoulder, and I stroked the parrot's neck ruff. He squawked. I cooed. We did that for a while.

"Dinner," he cawed. "Dinner."

"Nice try, bud. It's at least two hours from now. Want to hunt?"

Launching off my shoulder, he flew toward the window I habitually opened for him. A judicious shot of magic slipped the locking mechanism. The French leaded glass pane flew open, and the parrot shot through. I used to worry about him in the great outdoors, but he always comes back.

I picked up my phone and looked at the job specs again. They were skimpy, but I (or whoever) needed to be on tonight's redeye for LAX with a connecting flight to Havana. The plane would arrive at eight in the morning, and apparently the mark would be at the airport. The big glitch was then I'd be stuck for the next several hours until I could catch a flight out.

Presumably, the place would explode into action once the hit was discovered.

I set the phone down on the table with a *clunk*. Why

was I even considering it? I didn't need the money. Cuba is a real shithole. I've never cared for the tropics. Yeah. The list was long, so where was the appeal?

Phone back in hand, I scrolled through nine other potential jobs. None held the slightest temptation. It was either Cuba or nothing. I tapped a foot. "What in the hell is wrong with taking a few days off?" I asked myself.

When the answer came, it both shamed and humbled me. I'd been comfortable for a long while, but the gutter-girl who'd eaten out of garbage bins wasn't all that far beneath the surface. The life I'd lived meant there couldn't ever be enough creature comforts to assure me starvation wasn't lurking around the next bend in the road.

Raised in a series of orphanages and homes for wayward youth, I had no memory of my parents or why they'd abandoned me. My earliest recollections are of sleeping in barracks with whatever I didn't want to lose beneath my body. Other kids stole from me anyway, but not after I got bigger.

And especially not after I discovered I could hurt them with my thoughts. That had been the end of the last children's home. It had been around 1941, in the middle of the second World War, and I'd been on the edge of being sent to a labor camp for blinding a boy who kept jamming his dick into my ass after I'd gone to sleep. I'd been maybe ten at the time.

The first year on my own had been a total shit show, but things got better. I'd expected the authorities to come after me when I ran away. They never did. One less mouth to feed was a plus in their book. Lone children weren't uncommon. Every large city had a contingent of feral youth. My first gang turned into the family I'd never had.

A glance at the clock on the microwave told me if I was going to go to Cuba, I needed to pull it together. Hell, I hadn't even been hired yet. For all I knew, someone else had snapped up the job. Still telling myself I was making an unbelievably bad decision, I clicked through my display and said I was interested.

Less than a minute later, a message came through, followed by several more. I clicked and signed and forwarded bank info. And had them sign my agreement. My gambit to add a private jet to the deal didn't merit so much as a, "You've got to be joking." They ignored it and sent my itinerary. Apparently, my flights were already booked, and they gave me an address I was familiar with to pick up a phony passport and matching driver's license.

Suddenly, the dinner I'd planned was the last thing on my mind. After changing into traveling duds, I grabbed one of my go-bags, stopped by the open window, and whistled for Reggie.

When he didn't come, I closed it. He had his own way inside via a ducting system that didn't compromise my security. A quick check of my go-bag—aka carry-on luggage—yielded a flurry of "oh fuck" moments as I added to it. Finally ready, I locked up the house, set the alarm system that was more for show than anything else, and headed for the bogus passport pickup point.

CHAPTER 3

My flight to LAX ran two hours late, so late I checked into changing to another one. The harried reservations counter person reminded me I'd bought rock-bottom price tickets and exchanges weren't allowed. Unless a flight actually cancelled, which mine hadn't.

At least I had plenty of time for a decent dinner with a nice bottle of twenty-year-old cab. I slept most of the way to LA, and the flight crew finessed one of those maneuvers where they shooed me off the plane first so I could head for my connector at a dead run.

There are solid reasons I never wear heels. This wasn't one of them, but I was grateful for my trail runners. They fit right in with my usual travel garb consisting of cargo pants topped by a nondescript shirt and an equally unmemorable fleece jacket and watch cap.

The only part of me that sticks out like a sore thumb is my pink-streaked hair. I really should dye it mouse brown and be done with it, but I haven't. My inner wild child drew the line at totally blitzing out every shred of who I am.

They were just closing the plane's door when I squeaked through and hustled down the aisle to the only empty seat. I'm sure some standby bum was pissed I'd made it. Several were milling around the gate, and I overheard the dude manning the entrance to the jetway telling them I was on my way.

I travel light. Big surprise. What wasn't was not finding space for my carry-on—not much more than a glorified shoulder bag—in the crowded overhead bin. A flight attendant took it from me and told me to collect it in Havana. Nothing I couldn't replace, but my extra clothes and a few first aid supplies came in handy from time to time. I'd tucked the cash and ID in pockets during my uber-long layover.

After a round from the drink cart, the cabin crew doused the lights. Havana is three hours later than Seattle; it runs on the same clock as the East Coast, and this wasn't a very long flight. Under four hours assuming we didn't run into problems.

Naturally, I was squished into a center seat. A tired looking woman, her brown hair going gray, had the window, and a seriously overweight man sat in the aisle seat with his bulk taking up half my spot. He gave me a dirty look when

I claimed it. I ignored him and closed my eyes, reviewing my moves once I was on the ground.

A lot of folks would have jumped at a chance to escape the perpetual gloom of the Northwest at the tail end of November. But I'm not them. Shorter days mean longer work hours for me. I've killed in broad daylight. In fact, I'd be doing it very soon in Cuba, but I prefer shrouding myself in darkness. Clouds and nighttime have always been my friends.

Ha. Maybe that vampire nest had more in common with me than I'd thought.

Winter weather aside, I hate the holiday season. All those cushy memories most of you cherish haven't been part of my life. Ever. I'm always grateful when January first rolls around. A brand new year. A clean slate. Maybe one where I'll take a long-promised break from slicing and dicing.

Yeah. Right. Call me sick. Call me twisted, but I was exactly where I belonged doing what I was destined to do. If I'd been born in the Middle Ages, I wouldn't have had to hide my light under a barrel. I'd have been quite the hot commodity since the regent with the most effective assassin almost always came out on top.

The idea brought a smile to my face. I blessed my lucky stars—and the unlucky ones too—mortals can't read minds.

Eyes shut, head leaned back, I reviewed what little I knew about my target. His picture was on an encrypted file in my phone, but I'd memorized his stark features. A fall of blazing red hair touched his shoulder blades, and his face was arresting with a square chin and pronounced cheekbones. When I'd studied his likeness, dark-blue eyes had stared back at me, almost as if he knew I was looking at him. A slight shiver ran through me. I was being stupid, a ninny. Even if he had magic of his own, there'd be no way he knew I was studying him. Not from thousands of miles away. According to the registry, he was six foot five, give or take, with a rangy build.

I'm tall, closing on six feet, but he probably outweighed me by a hundred pounds. Or at least eighty. A remote approach to the task at hand was my best bet. One clean kill shot from across the terminal, and then I'd go about my business. Maybe take a cab into town, be a tourist for a few hours, and then back to Jose Marti International.

I really prefer poison. It's challenging to mix up a draught specially tuned to someone's physical weaknesses. But for that, I needed to be home with access to my basement laboratory. And I required something from my victim to pull their DNA from. Eh, wasn't going to happen for this assignment.

Decisions made, I shut off my thoughts. Not much reason to second-guess my plan. I might switch things up if something intervened, but for now I'd done all I could. My thoughts wandered from this to that. Mostly inconsequential items. I'd slept enough on the flight from Seattle, and I was relaxed, ready for the next few hours.

With no warning, the dragon I'd seen in my dreams filled my mind. Literally. Its wings stretched from one side of my visual field to the other in all their red-and-silver glory. My tendency was to shake my head to dispel the image, but this was the first time the dragon had shown up when I wasn't dead to the world.

I've always favored a direct approach, so I asked, *"Why are you here?"* And projected an astral impression of myself in front of him (her?).

Eyes spinning like pinwheels latched onto me. They were red with golden centers. Spines protruded from the creature's neck and shoulders, and his scales were the size of dinner plates. I felt him studying me, certain it wasn't the first time.

For some bizarre reason, not coming up short was important to me. I wanted him to view me as worthy. Weird, huh? I've never given a rat's ass what anyone thought about me. Not since I was a small child when it sank in no one else's opinion mattered a twit.

Steam mixed with smoke puffed from his partially open jaws. Why did I keep calling it a him? Did dragons even come in genders? I could have sworn I smelled smoke and felt the warmth of steam enveloping me, but I had to be imagining it. The whole scenario was playing out inside my head. Neither of my seatmates had flinched. The woman was working on a tablet, and the man snored in gasping pants. Hopefully, he wouldn't have a cardiac event. Depending how bad it was, the flight crew would reroute the plane to the nearest airport.

That could really screw up my plans. But I was

borrowing trouble. The likelihood of him keeling over in the next couple of hours was thin.

Almost as if it recognized my attention had wavered, the dragon lumbered closer to my astral self. I locked gazes with it—not an easy task—and repeated my question. *"Why are you here?"*

It vanished as quickly as it had shown up, the place it had stood an empty stage in my head. I must have startled because the woman next to me turned and laid a hand over my arm. "Are you all right?"

I opened my eyes. "Yes. Thank you. Just a..." A what? Not a nightmare. Mentioning visions and astral projection in polite company was frowned upon. Not in countries like India where soothsayers still commanded followings, but we were winging over the U.S.

"It's all right." The woman removed her hand from my arm. "I do the same thing sometimes. I'm not asleep, but neither am I awake. It's an in-between place, and it's weird." She gave a little shrug. "Happens when I fly too much."

"How much is too much?" I turned the conversation away from me.

Another shrug. "It's a good month if I'm in the air for less than ten days."

"Wow." I didn't have to feign surprise. "What do you do?" I held up a hand. "No need to answer. It's none of my business."

She offered me a smile that shaved ten years off her appearance. "It's okay. I work in commercial real estate.

Large projects like malls and urban renewal. I suppose I could do more on the computer, but there's no substitute for actually seeing something. That way I know if it has potential."

"I get it," I murmured. One day those of us who predated the digital age would die out, but until then we'd never be entirely comfortable with remote depictions of anything.

"I'm Muriel." She extended a hand.

I shook it and murmured, "Suzanne," while I girded myself for the next, inevitable question. Muriel didn't disappoint.

"What do you do, dear?"

I didn't have to work very hard to look chagrined. It's an act I've perfected over the years. "I'm widowed. I manage my late husband's interests, mostly in banking."

"You poor dear. You're young to be a widow. I'm sorry."

"Thank you."

As I expected, she retreated to her tablet. Death makes people uncomfortable. Imagine how she'd have reacted if I'd told the truth about who I was and what I did for a living? On my other side, the heart-attack-in-waiting slept on, oblivious.

I must have dozed because when one of the crew announced we were on our final descent into Havana, it jarred me. I did as good a job as I could stretching in the narrow seat. Sheesh. Considering how much they were paying me, my employers could have sprung for first class.

"Why Havana?" Muriel asked.

My turn to shrug. "Vacation. Seattle gets mighty gray this time of year."

She laughed softly. "It does, indeed. I live in Arizona. Love the heat and sunshine."

Peering around her, I watched the runway rise up to meet us. The day was blindingly bright, and I braced for a blast of humidity. I didn't have to wait long. The minute they opened the plane's doors, the fetid heat common to all tropical locales wafted through the cabin.

No jetways here, or not for this flight. We all lurched to our feet when the crew said we could. I checked my phone for any last-minute messages that might have come in while I was in the air. I didn't mind aborting this assignment, but my screen didn't hold any such instructions. Plenty of messages, though. The ones who'd paid for the last fuckup still wanted their money back.

Fat chance.

They'd give up after a while. They might even hire me again. After all, the one they'd wanted out of the way was deader than dead.

After collecting my carry-on from a pile near the door, I strode down rusty stairs and onto the tarmac. The black asphalt was already radiating heat at eight in the morning. After gathering a few unobtrusive strands of deflection around me, I wandered into the terminal and stopped at a Starbucks.

Gods they were ubiquitous. Find me an international airport, and I'll pay you ten grand if it doesn't have a Starbucks somewhere in the terminal. And a McDonalds.

I bought coffee and a greasy-looking pastry and was on my way to a seat off to one side when Muriel hurried up to me. "Want to share a cab into town?"

Oh-oh. Just like when she'd inquired how I earned my keep, I needed to come up with an excuse. All I'd said was I was on vacation, which left many open pathways. I turned a sunny smile her way. "I'd love to, but I'm waiting for my, uh, vacation partner."

Her dark eyes developed a knowing look, and she smiled conspiratorially while handing me a business card. "That's my cell, Suzanne. Feel free to call. Maybe we can plan dinner since we're both here." Her grin widened. "I'd love to meet your boy toy."

I grinned back. "How do you know it's not a girl?"

"I just do. I like girls, and I'm good at picking up vibes." She waved and trotted toward a luggage carousel where bags were beginning to clunk onto the conveyor belt. So, she was good at reading vibes, huh? It had been so long since I'd taken off my clothes in front of anyone except my parrot, I scarcely remembered what sex felt like. Sometimes I missed the feel of a hard-muscled body stretched full-length against me, but not enough to hunt down a one-night stand.

I settled into the chair I'd originally headed for and scanned the terminal. It was a few minutes past eight. Where was my mark? I'd been paying attention and hadn't seen anyone even close to his description. My hand closed around my phone, but I didn't pull it out. No need to take another look. Even if my target had dyed his hair, anyone that tall would stick out like a cornstalk in a wheatfield.

I sipped my coffee. Vintage Starbucks. French roast tasted the same no matter which country I was in. The pastry was cloyingly sweet. I dropped it back into the bag after a couple of bites and settled in to wait. When half an hour had passed, I did look at my phone.

No new messages.

What in the fuck was going on? This was beginning to feel like a replay of my last job when I ended up stuck on a balcony eight floors up. At least it wasn't raining here, but the terminal was hot and humid and stinky. All that heat and humidity makes everything either rot or rust.

Nine o'clock came and went. Unsure what to do next, I picked up my carry-on and slung it over a shoulder before heading for the restroom. I couldn't leave, not until my job was done. I had until two when my flight back was due to board. Even if it was late, I'd have to go through security and sit near the gate.

I'd have loved to splash cold water on my face, but it wasn't a good idea. Tap water wasn't safe here. Not to drink or for anything else, either. It also wasn't particularly cold, more in the tepid range with a brownish tinge that had left stains in the sink. After taking care of business, I walked back into the terminal and scanned it for my mark.

Whoa. There he was. His JPEG hadn't done him justice. He had the kind of face and body that made women stop dead in their tracks and stare. His hair held a luminance that reminded me of liquid fire with red and copper and bronze tones woven into it. And it didn't stop at his shoulders but cascaded down his back. His face was all planes and angles with a chiseled mouth that made me wonder what it would feel like traveling up and down my body.

Damn my eyes. What was wrong with me? Sex had never gotten in the way of anything, so why was I fantasizing about how well he had to be hung and what said appendage would feel like jammed up inside me?

I'd been staring. Of course I had. I yanked my gaze away from his Adonis good looks before I concluded killing the most perfect masculine specimen I'd ever seen was tantamount to sacrilege.

Do the job, my inner drill instructor snarled. *Never think about any of it.*

I pretended to walk toward the rental car kiosks and plotted my next move as I gathered power into a lethal arc. Mortals can't perceive magic, so no one else saw the barbed strands as they pulsed wickedly between my hands. In one smooth practiced motion, I pivoted and loosed my power while still angling toward the Hertz desk. Bending to retie a shoe should cover my sudden shift in body posture. After fumbling with the laces for a few seconds, I continued my trajectory toward the rental car counter.

My work was done. I waited for screams and squeals and grunts, but nothing materialized. I'd almost made it across the large room before I turned to figure out what had happened.

The man, my target, was not only still on his feet, he

was about ten yards away and angling right for me. Aw shit. Fuck. Crap. He must be some kind of mage who'd sensed my blow and deflected it. No wonder he was so striking. It must be a glamour. No one looked that good all by themselves.

I needed to vanish and damned fast, but there were a whole lot of people around me. Someone would notice if I warded myself and disappeared. Besides, if he had magic of his own, he might be able to see right through any warding I cobbled together.

Switching directions, I picked up the pace and aimed for the nearest door leading outside. I'd have more options than I did in here. I doubted I could outrun the dude I'd just tried to kill, but at least I could go to ground. Maybe wait him out.

If the last blast of power hadn't done it, I was out of tricks. Unless we ended up eyeball to eyeball. I'd have an edge if I didn't have to project power across an entire airline terminal. I passed through the circular glass door with him too close for comfort.

Heat and humidity hit me like a wall. It had felt like the terminal didn't have air conditioning, but once I left its bland interior, I may as well have been breathing through a hot, wet mop.

Luck was with me because a cab was steps away. Tossing myself into the back seat, I slammed the door shut and told the cabbie to take me downtown and to hustle because I was late.

As we screeched away from the curb, I caught a

glimpse of my mark standing where I'd been seconds before. Would he grab a taxi of his own? He stared after me out of eyes as blue and hypnotic as they'd been in his picture. Eventually, he turned away.

He'd been ready for me. Had he known I'd be there? Either that or he possessed exceptionally quick reflexes. Some mages were extraordinarily old, like thousands of years. If he'd been a warrior, he might operate on full alert all the time.

I rubbed my forehead. Would he be gone when I showed up for my return flight? What would I do if he wasn't? Havana had a few small, private airports. I could try one of them and book myself a charter to Miami.

The cab rocked on worn shocks as we careened around turns in between globs of stalled traffic. A good little assassin would be sneaking back to the airport and tracking her target. So what the fuck was I doing?

Running wasn't like me. At all. Had he rattled me so much, I'd put my tail between my legs and rabbited out of there?

"Apparently so," I mumbled.

"Senora?" The cabbie flicked me a look over his shoulder.

"Nothing. Hey. You can drop me anywhere."

"But you said downtown," he protested, his English highly passable.

"Changed my mind," I said brightly, stuffed a five spot across the divider, and got out the next time the taxi rolled to a stop. I half expected the driver to yell after me I owed him more, but he didn't.

U.S. money is always worth more than either of Cuba's currencies, even though one of them is pegged to the dollar. My cab continued on without me.

I spied a sidewalk café and walked toward it, intent on plotting what to do next. Not that I had many options. Either I killed time until my flight and hoped to hell my mark wasn't still at the airport and out for blood. Or I returned to the terminal, used magic to track him, and finished the job I was being paid for.

Sweat dripped down my forehead and slicked my sides as I sat under a striped umbrella and waited for the hot tea I'd ordered to materialize.

"Mind if I join you?" a deep voice rumbled from behind me.

Startled, I jumped to my feet, knocking my chair over in the process, and gaped like a landed fish. The dude, my mark, was five feet away, a genial smile on his knock-your-socks-off face. My knees felt like jelly; a blow to my solar plexus would have had a similar effect.

His smile widened. "You can run, but you can't hide, so you may as well hear me out," he said, walked to the other side of my table, and took a seat.

CHAPTER 4

How had he found me? Eh, scratch that. Now that he was close, I felt the pulse of his power. Having him behind me was even weirder than facing him, so I righted my chair and dropped into it. I've never been one to avoid the hard shit, so I stared at him.

"Who are you? What do you want with me?"

"Good starter questions. Do you usually get to know your"—he lowered his voice—"victims?"

I tossed my head. "I don't have to answer that. Besides, you hunted me down. Why?"

My tea arrived. I ripped open a packet of sugar and poured it into a cup before adding tea from the small ceramic pot. I'd just taken a sip of the scalding liquid when he said, "Shira."

Good thing I had a firm grip on the mug, or I'd have dropped it.

"Yes, I know your name." He nodded pleasantly. "Other things about you too. Want to come with me to somewhere more conducive to talking?"

I set the mug on the plastic tabletop. "Whatever you have to say will happen here. I'm not going anywhere with you."

"Fine, but if anyone nearby holds even a modicum of power, they'll sense our discussion." His rich voice reverberated through my mind, laced with such strong compulsion I opened my mouth to say I'd go anywhere with him. Before something ridiculous spewed out, I clamped my teeth together and looked away. The mesmerism sheeting from him didn't go away, but it was slightly easier to resist.

"I'll take my chances," I replied in kind. Two could play this game, although I hadn't ever spent time around anyone even remotely like me. Until I'd begun researching mages and magic back in the days when libraries were the go-to spots for information, I'd thought maybe I was the only one.

He rested his chin on an upraised hand, regarding me. The weight of his gaze was unsettling as he ran what felt like a lightning rod from the top of my head to my toes and back again. Power fairly crackled through me, meeting his head on. He reminded me of a feral beast sharpening its claws for a kill. It should have scared the crap out of me. Instead, I was fascinated in an eerie, macabre kind of way.

I arched a brow and shelved telepathy. "Did I pass inspection?"

"Maybe."

"What's that supposed to mean?" I spread my hands in front of me, splaying the palms on the table, my tea forgotten. "I came here to do a job, and—"

"I placed that notice in the registry, hoping to draw you out. Tried phoning too, but you hung up on me."

My eyes widened. Out of anything that could have come from his mouth, I hadn't been expecting that. No wonder the job had looked so attractive, despite its obvious drawbacks.

"Baited the hook, did you?" I inquired.

"You might say so."

"Why Havana? You could have set this up in a more commodious location."

"Gateways exist here." He was back to mind speech.

"So?"

"I'm hoping we'll travel through one of them."

I'd taken another sip of tea, mostly to unravel the knot in my throat. Swallowing was suddenly impossible, so I spit it on the ground. It was either that or choke. "You went to a lot of trouble—and expense—for nothing." I got to my feet and made a grab for my carry-on. "We're done here. I'm not going anywhere with you. What I am doing is going home."

"Why?" Both his hands were on the table, and he angled his head. Power wafted from him, wrapping around me.

I batted the strands aside and built a ward, although I doubted it could keep him out. "Stop that," I hissed.

To his credit he didn't ask, "Stop what?"

"Please," he said. "Sit down. Give me five minutes. At the end of that time, if you don't like what you've heard, you can leave."

The dregs of his compulsion spell still lingered in the air. I narrowed my eyes to slits. "Five minutes on one condition."

"What is it?"

"Sheathe your power. If words don't convince me, I don't want to get suckered in by a stray spell."

"That's fair."

Usually, I'm decent at ferreting out lies. He seemed to be telling the truth, so I perched on the edge of my chair, bag across my lap, ready to bolt if need be. Toward that end, I readied my own magic. I can't exactly teleport, but I could move a few feet away. Enough to give me a head start if I needed one.

Surely, he sensed what I was doing, but he didn't object. Instead, he tipped his chair back on its two rear legs, crossed one of his long legs over the other, and regarded me. His clothes almost matched mine. Khaki trousers, a tan linen shirt, and a windbreaker tucked under one arm. My fuzzy jacket was in my carry-on. I knew I wouldn't need it here. A pair of stout, battered boots graced his feet. They looked like they'd seen hard times.

"How about your name?" I asked. "Since you know mine."

"Grigori."

"All right, Grigori. Your five minutes starts now." I

folded my arms under my breasts. I'd hear him out, and then I'd leave.

"I've been watching you for a long while now. Years. You have the raw material my group is looking for."

I started to ask what raw material. Instead, I inquired, "Am I the only one under consideration for whatever this is?"

My question earned me an approving nod. "At the moment, yes."

"What did you mean by 'your group'?"

Another nod, and then telepathy. *If I tell you, there will be only two ways out. You will join us—so long as you pass our tests.*" He paused and regarded me with the same speculative aspect he'd adopted earlier. *"If you don't sign on willingly—or if you do and don't make it through our training— your memories of me and everything about my circle will be modified."*

I snorted. "You mean obliterated. How careful are you? Can you guarantee only the parts you want to wipe out are affected?"

"No."

Mmph. At least he was being honest. I chewed my lower lip, no longer concerned about cutting this off after five minutes. "All right, then. Tell me the parts you can without requiring Draconian measures at the tail end."

He steepled his fingers together. A heavy gold ring set with an unusual deep blue stone circled the middle finger of his left hand. Pale tattoo markings wound around the finger, across the back of his hand, and disappeared beneath the cuff of his sleeve. Either they'd faded, or they were purposely obscure, but I made out animals and birds.

"I am part of a group," he began. "We do the same type of work as you but in a more organized fashion."

A protest rose that I was plenty organized, but I was smart enough to sit on it. I waited to see what he'd say next.

"All of us have some type of power," he went on in mind speech. *"And we work in concert with various animals. The bond with our animal companion is the first test. Once it's been established, the other trials include both of you since you will always work as a team."*

"Where are you based? Who hires you?"

Grigori shook his head. "Answers to question like those will land you in the center of a place you said you didn't want to be."

I was back to chewing my lower lip, a nervous habit left over from when I was a kid in orphanages. "What can you tell me?"

"If you join us, the commitment is for life."

Breath whistled from between my teeth. "That's a long time. Particularly if things aren't going well."

"It is." He unlaced his fingers and balanced his hands on his thighs.

"How many of you are there?"

He shrugged. "Enough to get the job done. We don't keep an exact count. It isn't important."

"Would I ever work with any of you?"

He nodded slowly. *"Sometimes. Depends on the task. We are*

careful, though. No stray links to backfire. Or lead someone to us. We've escaped discovery for an exceedingly long while, and we aim to keep it that way."

I shelved the back and forth from talking to telepathy, opting for the latter. *"Define long while."*

"Our association goes back a thousand years or better."

I whistled long and low. *"Jesus. Are any of you that old?"*

"Some."

"Would I be able to stay in my home?"

"If you wished. We have a guild house, several actually. Many of us shuttle between residences. You will want to spend time with your bond animal, and it could be difficult where you live."

Alrighty. He knew where I lived. He said he'd been watching me for a while. The next logical question was, *"Why approach me now? If you've been keeping an eye on me for some time, why not months ago? Or years."*

"We had to make certain you were ready. I'd have waited even longer, but your bond animal lobbied for us to move forward."

I swallowed hard. The lump was back in spades, so I gulped cold tea as my dreams and visions rose to taunt me. *"It wouldn't by chance be a dragon?"* If I'd been talking, I'd have choked on the words.

Grigori didn't say a word. He didn't have to. I read the answer in his eyes.

"But how could I work with anything that big?" I stammered. Success hinged on me remaining unseen, hidden.

"Earth is far from the only world."

All of a sudden, everything was too much. "I— I have to think about this. How can I contact you?"

"You won't have to. I'll find you." He rose to his feet, towering over the small table.

I shot upright. "This training. How long does it take?"

"Depends on you. Think it over, Shira." Turning, he hurried down the boulevard. The overheated day turned cold without his presence. More empty than cold, actually. When he'd been sitting across from me, every one of my nerve endings had ignited with possibilities. I'd never felt more alive. It took everything in me not to race after him and say yes. Just so I could spend more time with him. Never mind I had no idea what I'd be agreeing to, other than a radical shift in my entire existence.

I grinned ruefully. The feral beast had sharpened his claws all right, and sunk them into my psyche.

Phooey. I was being stupid, acting like a besotted fool. Not that I was in love with him. I've never been in love with anyone. Sad, huh? The love factor aside, something about him drew me in, rendered being alone unpalatable, which made zero sense. I'd been alone my entire life. For it suddenly to be found lacking was absurd.

What would it be like to hang around with others like me? Would it be a relief to finally stop hiding what I was? Or would I constantly be comparing my magic with someone else's and feel bad because I came up short? These were mages who'd been practicing their trade for centuries. I was a neophyte by comparison. Did any of the others have a dragon bondmate? Was the fact a dragon wanted to work with me significant? Did it mean I was stronger than I thought.

I squeezed my hands into fists to shut off my thoughts. I couldn't stand by the table much longer. A couple of waiters had already stopped to ask if I needed anything further.

The street had grown busier during the time we'd been at the café. I'd already paid for my tea, so I hefted my carry-on over a shoulder and walked back toward the airport. It couldn't be more than a couple of miles, and I desperately needed to clear my head. A quick glance at my phone confirmed it was ten thirty. I hadn't spent more than three-quarters of an hour with Grigori, but it felt as if we'd been together forever.

There I went again. Making more of this that it would probably turn into. My life was fine as it was, thank you very much. Satisfying work that paid well. Reggie for company. Birds and dinosaurs were distantly related. Did it mean birds and dragons were too?

"For Christ's sake," I mumbled as I loped along. "Give it a rest."

Yeah. In a pig's eye. What I really wanted to know was if the dragon was available as a standalone. Could I get to know him without the rest of the package? I suspected the answer was no, but it was something I should have asked. Maybe I still could. The next time it showed up in my dreams, I'd ask him if we could meet, and—

"I'll do no such thing," I said firmly. Talking out loud earned me a few interested stares. Most people here speak

English, but it's not their first language. Spanish is with Creole a close second. Even if the dragon agreed to a meet and greet, what the hell would I do with him?

Virtually all my jobs held a stealth factor, something I'd lose entirely showing up with a dragon who looked as if he were seven feet tall, not counting his wingspread.

The airport came into view, but I'd been expecting it from the persistent roar of jets overhead. I had three hours to kill, and I could do it on one of the benches outside or I could go in and take my chances with lunch. So long as it was well-cooked, I'd probably be all right.

Wind had been gathering velocity, and more clouds rushed by overhead. Havana was gearing up for an afternoon thunderstorm. It would cut the heat for a short time. I settled on a concrete bench under a couple of palm trees. I didn't have to decide anything. Not today. Not tomorrow, either.

From the sound of things, Grigori had been watching me for years. It meant I could mull over my response, do a thorough job of thinking it through. I licked my lips, noting the bottom one was sore from me chewing on it. No matter how much thinking I did, a sudden burst of clarity was unlikely.

For one thing, I wouldn't suddenly be privy to more details. I knew everything I was going to until I gave a firm response that I was willing to explore Grigori's offer. A large, fat raindrop splatted on my head, followed in quick succession by several more.

Bolting to my feet, I made a run for the terminal door.

Storms in the tropics can form from nothing; skies going from blue to gray-black in a matter of minutes. From the sound of the wind, a humdinger was on its way. Luckily, it should blow through long before my plane was due to depart. Of course, my flight had to get here. If the weather turned to shit, it might not be able to land.

Rain pounded on the terminal's roof, sounding like shrapnel. I stood by a window and watched golf ball-sized hailstones leave dents in cars and planes. An ominous sizzling sound was followed by the lights first flickering and then dying completely.

It took a few minutes before the comforting hum of generators signaled the return of electricity. I pulled out my phone. Just shy of twelve. My flight was due to leave at two. A quick glance at the board told me it hadn't yet departed from Miami.

Should I get a motel for the night? It beat sleeping on the terminal floor, which was none too clean. Or outside in the rain. I've done my share of outdoor adventures, but I had no reason to be outside tonight. No targets to stake out. No activities to monitor.

Mind halfway made up, I walked to the ticket counter for American Airlines and waited patiently for my turn. When I got to the head of the line, I inquired about Flight 892.

The counter person didn't even have to consult her computer screen. "It's been delayed," she said.

"I know that. When do you think it will show up?"

This time, she clicked a few keys and scrolled through

screens. A small frown formed. "Not until tomorrow at this time. You see, it flies here and then back to Miami, and then to LAX. Soon, it will be time for it to depart Miami for Los Angeles."

I flashed my e-ticket on my phone display. "Any chance of getting me back to Los Angeles tonight?"

She glanced at my ticket and launched into the no exchanges lecture I'd heard once today. Or maybe it was yesterday.

"I know." I cut her off. "I can pay for different tickets."

She brightened. "There is a flight leaving here at twenty-three hundred tonight. It arrives at LAX shortly before midnight. The only problem would be your connecting flight to Seattle. That will not happen before six in the morning. Would you like me to put the change through for you? It will be $1562."

I blanched. Not that I don't have plenty of money, but I hate spending it unnecessarily. Poor childhoods do that to you. "Why so much?"

She shrugged. "Last minute tickets always cost the most."

"But I already have a ticket," I pointed out.

She consulted her screen again and offered a disingenuous smile. "Sorry. My error. The total comes to $843. Would you like me to process it for you?"

Her error my ass. She'd have pocketed the extra $700 with no one being the wiser. Particularly not me. I gave her credit for chutzpah.

"Is the flight out of here full?"

She shook her head. "Nope. Lots of time for you to decide."

"Thank you." I walked away from the counter and heard a bevy of disgruntled sounds from others in line behind me. Ha. They should be cheering I was finally done hogging the clerk's time.

I settled in with my phone and checked room rates at a few hotels. Apparently, they all subscribed to the last-minute-prices-are-higher theory. I really should travel more. If I did, I'd know these things. The $800 price tag for different plane reservations didn't seem so outlandish balanced against $500 for a night in a decent hotel. Havana has a lot of crime. I could find something cheaper, but not if I wanted to get any sleep.

A quick glance at the ticket line told me I didn't want to wait through it again. Not right now. I got a coffee and a grilled sandwich, mulling my options as I inhaled the food. I really was hungry. Big surprise. I hadn't eaten in hours.

Distilling my choices was simple. I had three. Motel for the night and flight tomorrow afternoon, flight tonight, or let Grigori know I was ready to move forward. I'm not a big believer in coincidences. My flight had bombed out for a reason, one potentially deeper than bad weather.

I've never been a woman to wallow in indecision, but no one was more surprised than me when I visualized Grigori in my mind's eye and invited him to find me. What had happened to caution? To making certain I was ready for such a monumental change.

Before I came up with even a single answer, he was striding toward me, a genuine smile on his gorgeous face.

"What made the difference?" he inquired once he got within earshot.

I grinned back. "They cancelled my flight."

He chuckled. "Are you always such a cheap date?"

"Only with men I like," I joked back.

He turned back the way he'd come. I drained my coffee, picked up my carry-on, and trotted after his disappearing back. He'd wait for me. No worries on that front. The question was who'd pick up the pieces when I discovered I'd made the biggest mistake of my life?

No longer bothering to wait until I was asleep, the dragon bounded into my mind trumpeting like a mad thing. Fuck me. What kind of crazy-upside-down world was I walking into?

CHAPTER 5

We interrupt this novel because the dragon became unmanageable, and the poor author had a book to finish...

Bugles, trumpets, fire, and fanfare!

Aidyrth here. You haven't met me yet, but that's about to change. It's time for me to say a few words of my own, clarify any misperceptions. I wanted to stake a claim to this book and describe my role at the very beginning. But I was overruled. Authors can be unreasonable, but she finally capitulated. Sort of. More likely, she was sick of me nattering in her ear, or she recognized I couldn't jump into the action without some explanation.

I'm the dragon in Shira's dreams, but ever so much more than that. I'm one of the creatures who willingly joined the Circle of Assassins in its earliest days. Life was simpler then. No one flinched when I winged through the skies. Quite the opposite, they left offerings. Sheep. Goats. Cattle. I ate every last one.

I prefer my food alive, but freshly killed runs a close second. So long as the blood is still warm, we're good, but I'm getting sidetracked. Food has that effect.

I'm here to tell you why I picked Shira over Grigori's protests, but I'm getting ahead of myself. More on that in a little while.

Grigori is a werewolf who runs the Circle of Assassins. Back in the day, every nobleman employed assassins. Some were more competent than others. The lack of consistency annoyed Grigori. More than annoyed, it offended him. He took his work seriously, and shoddy jobs gave all of us a bad name.

After one particularly badly botched poisoning incident, he made a point of meeting each assassin—back when we were all still in the Old Country— vetting them, and inviting some to work with him. It was good business for Grigori because he made it widely known he was the principal point of contact. If someone wanted a job done, they contacted him, and he provided an appropriate mage for the task.

His only requirement was that each mage forged a lifelong bond with an animal. The pair would work together, augmenting each other's efforts. I'm certain he orchestrated things that way because of his dual nature. Nonetheless, it was a damned fine idea. Creatures like me don't bat a scaled eyelid about killing. We welcome it.

Sometimes beings who wear mortal forms have second thoughts, attacks of conscience.

It was why creating working pairs was so valuable.

Years passed. Times changed. Suddenly, those like me weren't in demand. No one believed in dragons any longer, so mages all wanted wolves or birds or big cats as partners. I'm the only dragon left in the Circle. Along with a unicorn, we're the exception, the sole legendary animals still standing.

Eventually, there were so many mages in Grigori's employ he instituted rules, and a kind of training protocol. Generally, his system worked well. He'd honed it through the centuries, making adjustments as the world shifted around us. The advantage for those working for him was it inserted a protective layer. Irate kings—and now dictators—were as likely to turn around and murder their pet assassin as they were to hire them for another job.

Mages are tough to kill, but it isn't impossible. Dead men tell no tales. If someone wanted to ensure secrecy regarding who'd ordered a particular death, the very best approach was to silence them. Permanently.

My first bondmate died. An enchantress with flawless power, she chose her own death when illness ate away at her insides, outstripping magic's ability to forestall the inevitable. Concerned when I moped about disconsolate, Grigori selected my next bondmate. It didn't go well. I tried, but there's only so much I can do with a mage whose cruelty is stamped into their bones.

The Circle has ways of dealing with assassins who don't

make the cut, and after a few grim years they got rid of my problem. Grigori knew better than to pair me up with anyone else.

Thanks for putting up with such a long lead-in. We've finally almost made it to how I found Shira. After the disaster with my last bondmate, I left the guild house where I'd taken up residence. For a while, I moved from world to world telling myself I was on the hunt for a new place to call home.

Never found one. Residents in some locations figured I was a new breed of hallucination; others welcomed me warmly. One place, a pack of giants tried to turn me into dinner. Ha. Bet I'm the last dragon they try that with. I ate plenty of them, and burned a whole lot more. After years of wandering, I returned to Fire Mountain. For those of you who don't know, it's the dragons' home world.

While it was comforting to return to the spot I'd been hatched, and heartening to renew old acquaintances, I'd become somewhat of a pariah among my own kind. One of the precepts dragons live by is noninterference. We hold ourselves aloof from other magic-wielders and mortals. For obvious reasons. Our magic is superior to anyone else's, so the Circle of Assassins felt perverse to most of my dragon kinsmen. Joining our magic with anyone other than another dragon ran counter to the precepts in our covenant.

We've never been fond of mortals, especially since they quit leaving offerings to appease our fiery natures. Worse, they not only stopped believing in us, they added things with engines to the skies. I wasn't in a hurry to share my flight space with jets.

I could have remained in Fire Mountain, but I felt like a woman without a country, and so I returned to the guild house. Grigori greeted me warmly. He didn't grill me. Quite the opposite. He didn't ask a single question about where I'd been. The next day, while flying over familiar terrain, I began hunting for someone to bond with. I'll spare you the details, but I returned to my cave not far from the guild house—and my hoard—and walked the dream paths.

There's a dream guardian. I had to bribe him with a few choice gemstones, but he allowed me unlimited access to the dreamworld. It's simple to pick out those with magic. Their dreams are brilliant and multifaceted compared with mortal night wanderings.

From there, I selected a few possibilities. It wasn't as simple as it might appear. I needed a mage who wasn't adverse to killing. After all, it was what I did. And I needed to find a woman. There are no cross-sex pairings in the Circle. Shira was perfect in so many ways. Gutsy and determined, she was already an assassin.

That part was dialed in. The only downside was she slopped magic around like a neophyte. Either she didn't believe in her power, or she'd never had any training. Maybe a bit of both.

When I presented myself in her dreams, I expected her to leap at the opportunity to get to know me. She treated me like any other dream image: interesting, but not real.

After several tries, I went to Grigori and asked if he could help me. At first, he was pleased I was willing to try again, but after he checked up on Shira, he told me I could do better.

That conversation did not go especially well. Amidst fire and ash and smoke, we argued. He even took his wolf form, which while far from dragon-sized is still substantial. I'm not certain quite what turned the tides in my favor. Maybe it was reminding him just how badly his choice for me had ended up, and all the years I'd wasted trying to rehabilitate a damaged mage.

"Shira is too young," he'd argued. "She won't want to leave Earth. Hell, I bet she doesn't even know there are other worlds she could visit."

"But you will help me," I'd persisted.

Finally, after I'd been certain he'd refuse, he capitulated. I'd poked into her mind as she flew to her meeting spot with Grigori. She might have been more receptive; it was tough to tell. I have to offer Grigori credit. He put his best foot forward. He was gentle, not overbearing like he usually is. After all those years he's put in running the Circle, he doesn't put up with garbage from anybody.

Despite his efforts, including going to the trouble of running her down after she snubbed him, her position was she had to think about it.

Smoke whooshed from my mouth. What in the Great Dragon's name was there to think about? She understood I would be her bond animal, and she hadn't leapt at the chance.

I'd been standing by, waiting on the sidelines just past the first gateway, so I wouldn't miss a thing. Maybe Grigori had been right this time. Occasionally, he missed the mark —like with my last bonded one—but not often.

I shook myself, listening to the comforting rattle of scales. There'd be someone out there for me. I wouldn't give up. I'd keep looking, and—

Shock rolled through me with Grigori's magic stamped all over it. Mingled with disbelief, the unexpected emotion snapped my attention away from planning to resurrect my search for a partner. I'm excellent at reading emotions, and Grigori was with Shira again, talking with her.

Even better, she was following him out of an extremely poorly built building. If it were located anywhere other than a tropical island, it would have fallen down. Might still happen if enough storms loosed their fury.

I straightened, made myself tall, and prepared to meet the woman I'd elected to spend all the years of her life with. Grigori had interpreted her relative youth as a drawback. For me it was a plus. Losing my first bondmate had nearly broken me. I aimed to keep the next one by my side for as long as possible. Once she was no more, I'd leave the Circle and live out my immortality on Fire Mountain. Some of the animals associated with the Circle moved from mage to mage as they died. I didn't have it in me to bond with more than two—and I'm not counting the failed one in that number. It made Shira more important than she could imagine. If I had my way, we'd make history, cherry pick our assignments, and become the stuff legends are spun from.

But first, she had to see the advantages.

That was more my task than Grigori's, and I was ready for it. My first move was a proper greeting, and I bugled as warmly as I could right into her mind.

CHAPTER 6

Grigori was easy to follow. I never exactly caught up, but neither did I lose sight of him. The streets of Havana flashed past as we set a course roughly northwest. Finally, when it became clear he wasn't going to slow until we reached wherever this gateway spot was, I called, "Hey. Wait up."

He turned and called, "Walk faster."

I broke into a run. Even at a full out gallop, it took me a couple of minutes to reach him. "Your legs are too long," I panted, wheezing in the humidity.

"No one's ever complained before."

"Not a complaint. Merely an observation. Tell me about this gateway thing. Where will we be on the other side of it, and—"

He did stop then, and turned to me. The folds of a

privacy spell settled around us before he said, "Ssht. You'll feel the alteration when we pass through."

"What's on the other side," I persisted. I may have gone off half-cocked, but now that I'd chosen a path, I needed information. Lots of it.

He shook his head and narrowed his eyes. "Do you wish to rescind your choice? There is still an opportunity, but in a few minutes that door will be closed. Permanently."

Awk. There it was. The forever part of this. I hadn't forgotten, not exactly, but it had paled balanced against the thrill of the unknown. The dragon had long since quit making a racket, but I felt him watchful and waiting.

"If I do this, I'll never be alone again, will I?" I wasn't exactly looking at Grigori, but I felt the weight of his full attention. And the dragon's.

"Alone is relative," Grigori said slowly, "but you won't be by yourself in the same way you are now." His lips thinned to a disapproving line. "I've watched you for a long time. Your only companion is that bird."

"So?" I settled my hands on my hips, letting the carry-on dangle from a shoulder.

He mimicked my posture. "Most mages interact with others like themselves."

I rolled my eyes. "Most mages probably are indoctrinated into magedom—or whatever—when they're children. I didn't have a childhood. Not much of one. I didn't even know the things I could do were weird until I was maybe ten or so. And then, they weren't anything I wanted to flaunt." I blew out a breath. "Every kid wants to fit in. Magic is pretty unfitinable."

"It does tend to alienate those who don't understand it." He frowned. "So you are self-taught. I assumed as much."

I waited. No point responding since he already had my number. When he didn't say anything, I asked, "Is there a problem with that? I've done as much as I could, but I'm still learning."

"You wasted a lot of time, but that's not the issue here. Are you coming with me to meet your bondmate, or not?"

I furled my brows, surprised events would progress so quickly. "Is that why the dragon's been in my mind?"

"Of course. She picked you, and she's eager to meet you."

"She?"

He nodded. "We pair with same sex animals."

I cocked my head to one side. "What animal is yours?"

Power flared around him, and the outline of a wolf took shape. When he smiled, his incisors had lengthened, and his flame-colored hair looked more like a pelt. Breath caught in my throat. I was looking at a living breathing werewolf. Much like vampires, I'd never believed they were real—until I ran into a pack.

"You have come to a crossroads," he informed me in solemn tones. "Will you step through?"

"If I don't?"

"I will vanish, but not before making certain you forget this meeting."

I'd known that part. "What will happen to the dragon?"

Approval softened the harsh cast to his features. "Aidyrth will be disappointed, but she will manage. You won't be the first setback in her long life. Dragons are truly immortal. A few of the rest of us are too."

"Is this how it always happens?" I asked. "The animal picks the mage?"

"Sometimes they pick each other," Grigori replied. "But that was before magic took a back seat to science." He gripped my forearm. Prickles powered by his magic jolted through me. "Enough. You're stalling. Do you want this enough to proceed?"

I studied the dusty tops of my trail runners. It was the question of the hour, and no matter how many ways I sliced and diced it, I wasn't certain. But I was intrigued. The dragon had drawn back, become more shadows than visible edges. She'd picked me, huh? Why?

"Ask me yourself," echoed through my head.

It might have decided me. When I dissected this moment later, trying to lay my hands on exactly what flipped the switch and moved me past my ambivalence, I never came up with an answer.

I looked up, latching onto Grigori's direct gaze. "Yes. Let's do this."

A small smile played around the edges of his mouth. "I'd have been disappointed if you'd said no. I never pegged you for a coward."

"I'm not," I bristled.

"For a while there, it could have gone either way," he

said bluntly. Keeping the sound screen around us, he changed up his hold on my arm, and we resumed walking in the same direction. In less than five minutes, something jabbed me from every side except the one next to him. I figured it was the gateway because Havana's trash-choked boulevards dropped away. We walked through a whitish mist that smelled like wildflowers. It was a welcome change from the stench of tropical rot and urine.

"Where are we?" I asked.

"The place between."

"It tells me less than nothing," I informed him tartly and waited for a brisk reminder of how lacking my magical education had been.

"Those with magic who know the proper frequency can travel from world to world using the in between," he explained. "It's a vibrational interdimensional phenomenon built long ago by the gods to facilitate movement from place to place. If you teleported away from Earth, you'd use these channels."

"I can't exactly teleport," I admitted, and then asked, "How come I never stumbled into the in between place?"

"Not the kind of place anyone, magical or otherwise, stumbles into." The corners of his mouth twitched as he rode herd on a smile that wanted out. Or maybe it was a critical glare. I didn't know him well enough to read his expressions.

"How many of these other worlds are there?"

"I have no idea," he replied. "Many, but not all of them

are...pleasant to visit. You have to plan your excursions, though, or you risk never returning."

"Why?" Images of monsters and medieval torture devices floated across my mind.

"Aidyrth can help you with that type of thing," Grigori said.

We rounded a corner about the time I realized we were floating more than walking, and that gravity wasn't the same here. A dragon popped into view out of literally nowhere. One minute, the corridor ahead of us was empty. The next, there she was.

Breath whooshed from me. Jesus. She was huge. Maybe seven feet tall, but broad too. Red wings folded across her back. Silver-gray scales covered her body. When she focused her red eyes on me, their golden centers took on a luminous aspect as power flowed from her enveloping me.

I should have been terrified—concern did nag at the edges of my mind—but mostly I was fascinated.

"You took a chance," she said in a surprisingly soft voice for such a large creature.

I couldn't take my eyes off her. "That would be me. The original risk-taker. You're unbelievable, amazing," I blurted and hoped I hadn't offended somehow.

"Aye. Good you recognize it." Steam curled from her half-open jaws.

"I'll leave the two of you to get to know one another," Grigori said.

"Thank you." Aidyrth inclined her scaled head his way.

"What's she thanking you for?" I asked before he left.

It was bold of me, and I expected him to ignore my question.

He surprised me, but then this was a day for surprises, when he said, "She couldn't get your attention in your dreams, so she asked me to intervene." After a pause, he added, "I'll be close." His rangy form shimmered to motes of light. Before he vanished entirely, he became a wolf, albeit one twice as large as normal.

I returned my full attention to Aidyrth. "Why did you select me?"

"You have potential. You're already an assassin, which means you're not squeamish about bloodshed. It's quite the windfall."

I chewed my lower lip. "Erm, don't take this wrong, but the work I do requires stealth, invisibility."

The dragon tossed back her head and bugled merrily. "You're wondering how to incorporate me into your life. Doesn't work that way. All jobs originate from Grigori. He won't send us somewhere that isn't a good fit for our talents."

"Are you comfortable with that?" I asked. "Never selecting your own objectives."

"Aye. It's how the Circle of Assassins works."

"You're all magical?"

Aidyrth nodded. "It would be better for me to start at the beginning. Many of your questions will be answered, but far from all of them."

"All right. I have time." It was true. No one was waiting for me, except Reggie, and it wouldn't matter to him if I showed up tomorrow or next month. I didn't have any job commitments. The neighbors in my gated complex never visited because I'd made it clear they weren't welcome.

The hardline truth was I led a solitary existence. I'd designed my life that way because I couldn't be myself around mortals. They'd be horrified the first time I twitched my nose and someone who'd told a bad joke or offended me keeled over dead. Correction. Only some would be appalled. Others would rush to contact me privately. Even though it's a sore spot for mortals, most everyone has an arch enemy they'd like to see suffer. Or die.

I'd thought I was satisfied with my isolated lifestyle. Had I been lying to myself to make a tough situation more palatable? Aidyrth had begun talking; I gave her my full and undivided attention and pushed the fact I was in a magical land listening to a dragon far to the side. If I got lost in the impossibility of it all, I'd miss some of Aidyrth's tale.

It was important she view me as acceptable. Even if we ended up going our separate ways, I did not want it to be because she'd found me lacking in some regard.

"Like all dragons, I was hatched on Fire Mountain and spent my early years there with my nestmates learning how to manage my power. Dragons are the strongest of all when it comes to magic, and so our elders made certain we recognized the grave responsibilities that go along with extreme ability."

I had a feeling this was going to take a while. Aidyrth

reminded me of storytellers I'd listened to in countries like India as her voice settled into a soothing rhythm. "Why'd you leave?" I asked. I'd have given a whole lot to have had brothers and sisters. And someone to teach me about my nascent magic.

She shrugged amid rattling scales. "Who can predict these things? Some youth are restless. I was one of them. After my mentor allowed me to leave Fire Mountain, I traveled from one world to another hunting for something, but I didn't know what it was.

"I was knocking around the Scottish hill country back in the days when dragons weren't an unusual sight. Villagers feared and revered us both. I was feeding on an offering when an enchantress sashayed up to me and announced she'd always wanted to ride a dragon."

Aidyrth puffed smoke and steam around a merry bugle. "She became my first bondmate. Because she was the local duke's assassin, we began working together. Eventually, Grigori found us and invited us to join the Circle. It was smaller then."

"What happened to her?" I should have kept my mouth shut, but I needed to know if unfortunate occurrences befell the mage half of things. Grigori played both roles— mage and animal—but I wasn't a werewolf.

A muted *clink* was followed by another. It took me a few seconds to understand tears were welling in Aidyrth's eyes and dropping to the ground as gemstones. Bending, she scooped them up, and they vanished into a pouch in her scaled chest. My bet was she'd add them to her hoard. If the lore was correct and dragons possessed such things.

"She was old even by mage standards when I met her." Spinning eyes bored into mine. "Dragons are immortal, mages merely long-lived. I mourned her passing."

Turning over what Aidyrth had said didn't exactly answer my question, yet she seemed genuinely upset. Asking pointblank if she'd been the cause of her bondmate's death would be worse than indelicate. It would be crude, offensive. I selected a different path.

"I've never gotten to know anyone else with magic," I murmured and blew out a breath. "It took me years to understand what I am, and my few attempts to find a teacher turned up phonies. Mortals pretending to wield power."

The dragon nodded. She'd stopped crying, and her expression might have been serious. It wasn't easy to read her. "You're young. It was one of Grigori's objections to you. By the time you were born, magic-wielders had dropped out of common view. A few hundred years earlier would have made a difference. You could have found others to teach you."

"Is it genetic?"

Aidyrth knitted her scaled brows into a thick line. "What do you mean?"

"Magic. Is it passed from parents to their children?"

"Not always."

I waited, but no more words came. "You have to say more than that," I pressed.

"Dragons, unicorns, and other magical animals aside, mortals are a hit-or-miss affair." She puffed smoke, tilting her head so it floated past me. "If your question is whether your parents held power, my guess would be no."

Fascinating. "Why?"

"If they did, they'd have gone to exceptional lengths to hang onto you. Mages aren't exactly infertile, but they produce very few children. The ones they do have are cherished whether they're magical or not. Do you remember your parents at all?"

I shook my head. "Not really." Feeling the same creeping discomfort that always surrounded me whenever I thought about the mother who'd abandoned me, I asked, "What happened after your bondmate died?"

"I mourned. Grigori pushed me to bond again and selected my next companion. It didn't go well."

There it was again. The possibility of failure. "What happened to her?"

I'd been expecting something bland, uninteresting like maybe she returned to her home or her family. I almost choked when the dragon said, "She was dealt with accordingly."

This time, I was done pussyfooting around. "Did you kill her?"

"No. Grigori took care of it."

I took a step back and folded my arms beneath my breasts. "Is that what will happen to me if things don't work out between us? Or between me and the Circle?"

The dragon's unnerving gaze skewered me. "It's an

outside possibility. Normally, we erase memories and return mages who wash out to wherever they originated."

"What made the difference with"—I floundered around hunting for her name before remembering I'd never heard it—"the dead one?"

Aidyrth's jaws parted in an approximation of a smile. "I like you. You're direct."

"You didn't answer me."

"With that one, the negatives far outweighed the positives. She had very few redeeming qualities, and her magic reeked of darkness. Grigori thought proximity to me would rehabilitate her. It didn't."

"I see."

"No, you don't. Not really," Aidyrth countered. "You are concerned the same fate will befall you."

"Anyone would be," I replied. A picture was forming of the Circle, but I was still unclear what my role in it might be. "I asked before, but how did you find me? And why me and not some other woman with magic?"

Aidyrth nodded slowly. "I walked the dreamers' paths. It's the simplest way to search out those with magic."

I wanted details about exactly why that was, but I didn't ask. In the grand scheme of the world, it wasn't especially important. "So you found me on these pathways?" I prodded.

"Your magic shines particularly brightly. After my last experience, I was cautious, so I watched you for a while."

I bristled, not liking the idea of being spied on. "How did you do that? I never saw you."

She didn't exactly answer me. What she said was, "The first order of business will be teaching you about power. Yours and others'."

The notion of finally having a go-to place for my million questions about how magic worked was intoxicating, but I couldn't let it sidetrack me. "I still want to know how you spied on me without me knowing."

"All mages have a particular vibrational field, a magical signature that differentiates them from all others with power. I merely memorized yours and tracked it from a distance." She tilted her head to one side. "Getting yourself stuck on that balcony was sloppy."

Hot words wanted out, but being in a rush to shield the indefensible from criticism was stupid. Even I'd rebuked myself for slipshod work that night. Missing the vampire nest had been particularly egregious.

"Yeah. I know. What's your point?"

"Only that I know where you've been."

I rolled my shoulders back, standing taller. "If I'm so inadequate, why do you still want to join your fate to mine?"

"I never said you were inadequate, only that you'd made an error." This time a tongue of flame joined the smoke as she exhaled. "I wasn't testing your decision-making, or second-guessing it, either. What I was doing was assessing your mettle. Those who kill can go one of two ways."

My ears perked up. I knew exactly what she was going to say, and she didn't disappoint me.

"Being an assassin either strengthens the better parts of

your nature, or it rots your core. There aren't any other options. It all revolves around who you were before you started killing people."

She extended a foreleg. Reaching up, I grasped it. "At first, you killed to survive. Later, you refined your approach, became selective about your jobs."

Untangling my fingers from her claws, I shook my head. "You're giving me too much credit. The sad truth is I don't have to work. I have plenty of money. I've kept killing because it's what I do. I'm good at it, but I do pick and choose my targets."

"Your honesty is appreciated."

I was certain I wasn't telling her anything she didn't already know. She hadn't come out and admitted it, but what happened to her last bondmate hadn't been easy on her. Why else would the killing have fallen to Grigori?

"If I do this thing," I began, "what would happen first?"

"We will travel to the nearest guild house. The Circle maintains several scattered around Earth and a few other worlds. There you will learn about magic, and we will work to blend ours until we work seamlessly together."

"How long would that take?"

"Not more than a few years. We'd take jobs in between lessons."

"Years?" I blurted. "I don't think so. I have a life. A house. A bird." Eh, that was pushing it. I had no idea if Reggie would miss me if didn't come back. He was plenty smart. He'd know I was gone, but the biggest change for him would be no more birdseed and chopped vegetables in his feeder cups.

The dragon's forked tongue flicked out a time or two. "I suppose we could make an exception in your case. You could travel back and forth, but if you breathe a word about the Circle—or skip out on your obligations to us—I will personally hunt you down."

I narrowed my eyes. "That sounded like a threat."

"It was. I take what I do seriously, and loyalty to the Circle must come before all else. You are fortunate to be considered. Anything less than your complete devotion will be a problem."

"I'd be the youngest one there, huh? By a good big bunch."

"Aye, but how would you know?"

"Because concepts like total dedication fell out of favor a few centuries ago. Hell, no one even sticks with the same job for more than a few years nowadays."

"You did," she pointed out.

"It scarcely counts since I work for myself."

The dragon shifted her weight to her other rear foot. "Does that mean I'll be returning you to your home?"

The prick of power bubbled around me, hot and viscous, before I'd even answered. "Are you going to give me a chance to respond?" I asked. "Or will you just assume I'm incapable of sticking with something? Of seeing it through."

"I went to a lot of trouble to finesse this meeting," she informed me. "I will owe Grigori for wasting his time, but it's best we know now before either of us has invested anything beyond a surface exchange of information."

"So? You're going to kick me to the curb because I voiced doubts and said I needed some time at my own house?" Incredulity tinged with anger rolled through me before anger came out on top. "I have to be able to express what I'm feeling. If there's not room for that, then you're right, our partnership is DOA before it even gets rolling."

"What is DOA?"

"Dead on arrival."

After a short pause, Aidyrth hooted what sounded like laughter. It puffed from her along with steam and ash.

"I fail to see what's so funny," I sniped.

"Interesting turn of phrase for an assassin," she managed between fire and smoke. Once her mirth ran its course, she said, "I owe you an apology. I'm edgy because of Grigori's doubts and the fiasco with my last bondmate."

"I was prickly too," I admitted and rushed to add, "But I was serious about spending time at my house. Maybe half my time there and half with you."

"Why can't I join you at your home?"

The logistics were daunting. "Um, you'd have to be invisible."

"I can manage a ward."

"What would you eat?"

Her jaws lolled into a grin. "You? Your bird? Have a spot of faith. I've been feeding myself for millennia."

I relaxed my arms, dropping them to my sides. "This isn't going to be easy," I told Aidyrth. "I will do the best I can, but I haven't answered to anyone in close to seventy years."

"You won't answer to me," she said, "but to Grigori." She bent so her eyes were on a level with mine. "I want this to work, Shira. I do not appreciate failure."

It was a good note to end on. "Me, either," I said. "Let's begin, shall we?"

"Once you enter a guild house, it will become more difficult to unravel your memories," she cautioned me.

I'd already figured that part out. "Thanks for the warning." I grinned. "If I were you, I'd hurry before I change my mind."

The misty spot we'd been standing shattered. When my vision cleared, I stood in front of a medieval fortress complete with turrets, towers, a moat, and a portcullis that happened to be down. Serpents swam lazily through the water.

"Where are we?" I took in trees I'd never seen before, a pale-violet sky, and dual suns suspended overhead.

"Not Earth."

"Yeah. I knew that part. I can't teleport. You must promise you'll help me leave if I ask."

"I will. But focus on right now, not on a future that hasn't yet occurred." The dragon lumbered off at a quicker pace than I'd have imagined her capable of. "Our first stop is the lore room. You have much to learn."

She was being kind. From the looks of things, I had almost everything to learn. I hustled after her and sent threads of power outward. Were we alone here? I couldn't sense anyone, but they could be shrouded with magic of their own. It was simpler to focus on that than the enormity of what I'd just done.

What if I didn't like it here? What if Aidyrth and I ended up at odds like we had back in the in between. If things didn't work out, would I lose everything I'd learned? Probably so. There wasn't a way to leave my soon-to-be-gleaned knowledge intact while stripping my memories of how I'd obtained it.

My heart was beating faster than usual, and my throat felt dry and scratchy as the portcullis creaked upward admitting us to the stone fortress.

<h1 style="text-align:center">CHAPTER 7</h1>

I've never been much for frequenting libraries. The Internet hasn't exactly made them obsolete, but almost. Once we crossed beneath a twelve-foot lintel and went inside, I was far more intrigued by the guild house. The place was not just huge, but laden with expensive-looking furniture, sculptures, paintings, wall hangings, and every iteration of decoration in between. In aggregate, it had a big wow factor. I'd never been anywhere half so grand, and I've toured many of Europe's castles. Well, maybe not toured, not exactly. But I'd chosen a couple of them as sites for jobs I'd accepted. Impossible not to appreciate them as I passed through on my way to set up a snare or poison someone's beverage.

I wanted to stop and examine the thick obviously handloomed rugs and intricately stitched wall panels. Whoever had furnished this place had impeccable taste judging from the sculptures and artwork. Not that I'm much of an expert on such things, but the furniture appeared to date back to the 1800s, when craftsmen used high quality materials and built chairs and divans to last. They didn't have the cush factor of today's couches and recliners, but they'd still be around long after Barcaloungers had hit the landfill.

I wanted to linger and gaze at things, but Aidyrth hurried me along. We ended up in an enormous room with a twenty-foot ceiling. Lined with books from the floor to the roofline, it also had long tables with stained glass reading lamps scattered at intervals. Rather than individual seats, benches sat on both sides of the tables.

The dragon spread her wings, floated more than flew to a high shelf, and plucked a few scrolls from their spots. Was there a resident librarian? There'd almost have to be with this many items to keep track of. Aidyrth thumped down a couple of feet from me and dropped the scrolls onto a nearby table.

"Here you go," she said cheerily. "These should keep you busy for a while." Power shimmied around her.

"Wait," I cried. "Aren't you going to stick around?"

The spell that had been taking shape around her wavered. "Why would I need to?" she tossed my way.

"What if I can't read whatever those"—I flicked a few fingers at the stack of reading material—"are written in?"

"They will adapt to you," she said. In a flurry of flames and whirling dust, she was gone.

Studying has never been my gig. I dropped out of

school about the time I left the last children's home. Even though I predated the Internet by a whole lot of years, I've figured things out on my own fairly well. I may not have hung out in libraries, but I did show up there when I really needed to know something I couldn't track down any other way. Back then, no one cared about serious identification documents. Obtaining a library card was as simple as giving a phony name and address.

My how things have changed, and not exactly for the better. At least no one here gave a rat's ass about who I was or where I'd come from. I blew out a breath. And then one more. I could stand around wasting time, or I could get to it. It wasn't that I didn't want to know more about how magic worked, but I half-resented it being forced down my throat.

"For the love of everything unholy," I mumbled, "get over it."

A few steps brought me to the table, and I unstacked the scrolls. They were old, the vellum cracked and fragile looking. If items like this had been in an archive managed by humans, I'd have been offered a pair of cotton gloves to wear before I touched them.

Being careful, I unrolled the scroll that had been on top. It looked like it was written in runes, but as I stared at them, they sparkled and shifted until a familiar alphabet took shape. Geez, Aidyrth hadn't been joking about them adapting to me. English isn't my only language. I'm pretty decent with most modern ones, but the runes weren't doing it for me.

And there I went off on one more tangent. Determined to plow through the scrolls, I began reading the one in front of me. It was slow going. This one catalogued the various iterations of mages explaining why each type worked magic differently. I was barely a fraction of the way through it when an obvious question rose.

Out of all of those listed, what was I?

Turned out it was simpler to engage in a process of elimination. I might not know much about the magical world, but I was quite conversant with what I could do. If a particular mage possessed a skill that would be beyond my ability, I chalked it off as, "not me."

I longed for a notebook before I realized I had one and pulled out my phone. Naturally, it didn't work here, but the note section was intact. It didn't require an Internet connection.

As interest in my task expanded, I stopped chafing at my enforced assignment. The library lacked windows, so it was tough to judge how much time had passed. I was still deep in the first scroll, making notations on my phone, when Aidyrth's voice jolted me.

"Finding it remarkable, are you?"

I twisted around on the bench until I faced her. "It's dry, like reading a textbook."

"What did you expect? An adventure story?"

I hadn't had any expectations, not really. Raking a hand through my hair, I said, "I've always been more of a hands-on learner."

The dragon nodded. "Me as well. What would you like to practice?"

Something occurred to me, and I angled my head to one side. "I bet you already know."

"Already know what? You're talking in riddles."

"This scroll"—I turned around and tapped it gently —"delineates history and explains the different types of magic-wielders. Do you know what I am?"

Her eyes spun faster; power jabbed me from all sides. "Oh my. You really don't know."

Irritation pricked deep, and I pressed my lips into a thin line. "I'm not in the habit of asking questions I already know the answer to."

"Of course," she rumbled. "Who would have told you?"

"You could," I interrupted her.

Scales clanked as she nodded. "You're a mixture of bloodlines, but the predominant one is dark Fae. It's why being an assassin is a natural pursuit."

What did I know about any Fae, dark or otherwise? A big fat nothing. I rolled the scroll to the part describing the Fae. I'd looked at it and decided I wasn't one. "I'm not certain that's quite right," I told Aidyrth.

"As I noted, you have other magics in the mix. A wee bit of witch, and a smidgeon of shifter, but they're not primary."

"Shifter? What kind?" I sputtered.

She waved a foreleg my way. "Doesn't matter, you don't have enough to change into anything."

"It says here"—I stabbed the scroll with a fingernail

and punched a hole in the vellum—"Fae can bend time. I'm not a time traveler. And my ears aren't pointy." I smoothed over the hole, determined to be more careful.

"Dark Fae have rounded ears. In terms of time travel, how do you know? Have you ever tried?"

"Actually, yeah. I was trying to escape a guy I owed money to when I was about fifteen. By then, I knew I could do things most kids couldn't, and I'd listened to enough radio to understand the gist of time travel. Anyway, I played things this way and that, but never got away from the mid-1950s.

The dragon flapped a foreleg my way. "Not a fair test. You were young and using the scatter technique."

Her words made me smile. "Same way I've characterized a whole lot of my efforts. Toss enough shit at the wall, and sometimes some of it sticks."

Aidyrth made a clicking noise. "By the time we are done, you'll have learned not to waste your magic hoping something works. You'll know ahead of time which avenues to pursue."

The sound of heavy boots in the hallway brought me to my feet. I might be here with Aidyrth, but this wasn't my home. I was an interloper. Two people, one male and one female, sashayed into the library.

"See?" the woman said. "Told you I heard voices."

I tried not to stare. From never being around anyone else with power to it suddenly being the only game in town was a pretty big leap. The woman was maybe five foot eight and round without being overweight. Her ears rose in graceful points, which pegged her as Sidhe or the other iteration of Fae. A cascade of pale hair had been drawn into a queue and hung halfway down her back. Her timeless face was marked by distinct cheekbones; aquamarine eyes studied me.

The man was about my height. Close-cropped red curls fluffed around his high forehead and square chin. Much like the woman, he wore modern garb. Cargo pants and a muted plaid shirt with a jacket slung over a shoulder. One ear had been pierced several times. Gold hoops decorated each hole. Liquid, dark eyes held a somber aspect.

"And you are?" He moved closer. Near enough for me to scent his power. Woods and ocean mixed into a brew that reminded me of every day I'd spent outdoors.

Glad I was already on my feet, I extended a hand. "Shira. And you?"

He ignored my hand. My cheeks grew warm with embarrassment as I dropped it to my side. I'd never fared well in groups of humans. Would this be the same ugly mess where everyone judged me and found me lacking?

Aidyrth puffed smoke over his head. "Be nice, Loren. She will be my new bondmate."

He batted at the smoke and coughed. "Goddammit, Aidyrth. Leave off with the smoke already." The full weight of his gaze settled on me, and I felt him probe me with his power. What the hell? Was he some kind of earth mage? I needed to return to the scroll.

"Stop that." I draped a ward around myself determined not to start out in a one-down position.

The woman turned to Loren. "You're being insufferably rude."

He shrugged. "Concepts like rude only apply to humans. That one—Shira—is not only young. She's untried. I'm appalled you"—he twisted to face the dragon—"would even bother. After your last disaster of a bondmate, I figured you'd select someone seasoned, someone—"

"Enough!" Aidyrth roared. Fire shot from her mouth, and his jacket ignited. Shouting curses, he ran from the room pouring power over the garment to douse the flames.

"No fire in the library," the woman reminded Aidyrth.

"The books were never in danger. Give me a little credit," the dragon huffed.

The woman turned to face me and held out a hand. "I'm Mae. Nice to meet you, Shira. Don't mind Loren. He sometimes has a bad case of better-thans."

"What is he?" I blurted.

"Earth wizard," she replied. "There aren't many like him, so he assumes it makes him special. All it makes him is dick of the year when he starts lording it over us."

I laughed and took her hand, shaking it warmly. "You're funny. Uh, I'm pretty new here, so if something I do or say crosses a line, let me know right away, but where's your bond animal?"

"Hunting, along with Loren's. They make quite the pair."

Curiosity got the better of me. "What are they?"

"Mine is a hawk. Loren's is a wolf. Mine sights the prey

and flushes it out. Loren's kills it, and they share the spoils."

"Figured I'd find you here." Grigori loped into the library. "Are you up for a job?"

No one said anything. I'm not usually slow on the uptake, but it took a moment or two before I understood his words had been addressed to me. I glanced sidelong at the dragon.

"It's up to you," Aidyrth said firmly.

"Baptism by fire. May as well dive right in," Grigori's deep blue gaze bored into me. Sheesh. Everyone scrutinized me so intently, it made me nervous.

"I thought there was some kind of test first," I sputtered. "One between Aidyrth and me."

"You passed. Or she wouldn't have brought you here," he informed me.

Eh. Would have been nice if someone had told me.

The biggest hawk I'd ever seen, with gorgeous mottled brown-and-gold feathers, winged into the library and landed on Mae's shoulder. Its head stood about a foot above hers. Something bloody hung from its beak, but it managed to squawk around it.

"What kind of job?" I asked.

Grigori shook his head. "Not the way it works here. Once I tell you about it, it's yours."

"But what if—" I shut it down there. I'd been about to inquire what happened if I didn't think it was a good fit, or it didn't rise to my level of urgency. Killing someone was damned permanent. I at least tried to ensure my targets weren't worth breathing space.

"See?" Loren bellowed from the doorway. "Aidyrth chose badly. Again. A brand new mage who hesitates doesn't deserve to be part of the Circle."

I forgot all about being the new kid on the block, about being polite and conciliatory. Fuming, I covered the distance between us and stood tall, rolling my shoulders back until I looked him dead in the eyes. "This ain't my first rodeo, bud. I've been killing most of my life. And I've done it on my own, without this"—I spread my arms wide—"cushy organization to shield me or bail me out."

Breath swooshed from me, but I was on a roll, so I kept on talking. "Have I made mistakes? Sure, but I've crawled out from under them and lived to pick one more target. Plus"—I puffed out my chest—"I'm self-taught. And I'm not ashamed of it. Absent the glut of information in this room, I've managed to get by, forced my magic into channels that made my tasks simpler."

"Your point?" Loren gritted.

"Stop looking down on me. You don't even know me, and you've already decided I don't make the cut."

"Because you don't." He glared from beneath lowered brows.

"In case you're thinking Shira jumped at our offer," Grigori cut in, "she didn't. She walked away from me. Twice."

"And she ignored me when I came to her in dreams," Aidyrth added. "She very nearly turned us down because she's used to working on her own, making her own choices."

"Aye, and she'll be a breath of fresh air around here," Mae said, smiling broadly. The hawk squawked agreement. Mae stripped a bit of meat from the chunk hanging off the bird's beak and popped it into her mouth.

A snarl and a growl were all the warning I got before Loren's wolf bounded into the room, hackles at full mast and a mouthful of fangs aimed at me. Supersized like the hawk, the wolf was coal black with shining amber eyes. Before I could react, Aidyrth glided between us. "She is mine," the dragon announced. "Any who dare to harm her shall answer to me."

Fire punctuated Aidyrth's words, but it went out before hitting the floor.

"No fire in the library," Grigori said sternly.

When I looked closer, a corner of his mouth twitched. Clearly, he was fond of the dragon, but upholding the Circle's rules was part of his job. Maybe someday, I'd figure out just how everything slotted together.

The wolf growled again, but softer this time, and padded to Loren's side. Power flickered around them, and I figured they were talking. "We'll take it," Loren said to Grigori.

The werewolf twisted toward him. "It wasn't offered to you," he said.

"She doesn't want it, so we'll do it," Loren insisted. "My bondmate and I are in agreement."

"I never said I didn't want it," I protested. "Shit. I don't even know what 'it' is."

Grigori walked to me. "I'm not in the habit of setting my people up to fail. Your first assignment is critical. It will cement your affiliation to the Circle. Similar to you coming here in the first place, accepting the task I've offered requires trust." He stopped long enough to take a measured breath. "I recognize trust takes time, and you barely know me. Still, you were confident enough to accompany Aidyrth here despite understanding your memories would be wiped clean of everything if you changed your mind."

"Can I know anything?" I asked. "Like where I, er we, will be working?"

"Why does it matter?" Grigori asked.

Loren's wolf growled again as if to punctuate his bondmate's assertion I was damaged goods.

Forgetting about him—his opinion didn't matter a whit—I focused my next words at the dragon. "Are we ready?"

She shrugged. "We'll figure it out as we go."

"I get a voice, though. Right?"

"If by that, you're asking if I will take your opinions into consideration, the answer is yes."

"Why would you do that?" Loren muttered plenty loud enough for everyone in the room to hear.

"Because, unlike you, I respect her," Aidyrth shot back.

It was good enough for me. "We'll do it," I told Grigori.

With a nod and a smile, he wrapped me in power that

was beginning to feel familiar and whisked me from the library. "What about Aidyrth?" I asked.

"She knows where I'm taking you," he replied, adding, "It speaks well for you."

"What does?"

"That you inquired about her first."

"She and I are partners. Not that I'm used to working with anyone else, but it's a logical question." I snapped my fingers. "Aw crap. I should have put the scrolls away."

"No one will disturb them."

A circle of white oak trees shaped up around us. True to Grigori's word, the dragon was already there. "This is where we always receive our assignments," Aidyrth said by way of explanation. "The grove is shielded and linked to Grigori's power. No one can listen in."

Grigori made a wry face. "A real shame I have to go to these lengths, but occasionally another bonded pair will try to poach an assignment, particularly if they thought they should have been chosen."

"Where are we going?" the dragon demanded. "Who is our target, and what's the timeframe?"

It seemed crass, but I added, "How much will we be paid?"

"You won't, not directly," Grigori said. "The Circle will see to all your needs."

"How does that work? I show up and ask for money?"

"Thought you said you didn't need to work," Aidyrth reminded me.

My face grew warm, but I faced the two of them. "I

don't. Today. Who knows what the future will bring. When you grow up the way I did, hand to mouth, never sure when I'd eat next, having a bank balance is important."

Grigori dropped a hand onto my shoulder. "The Circle cares for its own, Shira. Your days of being alone are over."

It sounded good on paper, but I didn't believe it. Not completely, and not yet. To avoid someone skimming thoughts out of my head, I made a come-along motion with one hand. "Sooner we know the details, the sooner we can get moving."

I wished I'd asked about how payment worked before. I hadn't. Damn it. If I was going to back out, now would be the time to do it. Before Grigori sketched in specifics about our job.

"Shira?" The dragon was not just looking at me, but through me.

I reined in my doubts—about everything. Either I gave this 100 percent, or I should call it quits right now. I'd made it this far. Everywhere in the world had its share of Lorens. His disdain wasn't a reason for me to put my tail between my legs.

"I'm good," I said. "Let's launch."

CHAPTER 8

I'd figured Grigori would send us to another world, a spot the dragon wouldn't have to be perpetually hidden. He hadn't. We were in Chicago's interminable railyards skirting skid row. At least the targets had been palatable to me, worthy of killing. Out of all my doubts and worries, that sat at the top of the list. I'd been concerned I'd be ending someone who might have had a shot at redemption.

When I picked my own jobs, I'd factored in many variables. Since that door had closed, I'd have to trust Grigori's judgement. It would be easier after we'd worked together for a while; at least I hoped it would be. I'd been edgy waiting for him to roll out all the details.

He'd given us plenty of time. Two weeks, more if we needed it. What surprised me most, though, was he'd handed me a full complement of phony identification, complete with credit cards and a couple of burner phones. My first task was to book a suite at an upscale hotel, buy some fancy clothes, and present myself at a casino flashing money around. My cover, which would probably fall apart if anyone took the time to check, was I was a bored Russian playgirl with a gambling problem.

"How bulletproof is my cover?" I asked, using telepathy to not draw attention our way.

"It will stand up to scrutiny. Grigori is nothing if not thorough."

I wanted specifics; my control freak genes were leaking out all over the place. Maybe I'd adapt more easily to my new life than I'd assumed, but it wasn't happening yet. Before, it had been me—a regular one-woman show—taking care of everything. Or not, as near misses like the Vampire nest proved.

We stood in the railyards to strategize. It wasn't as if the dragon carried a cellphone. She didn't need one—we'd been working on our telepathy, not so much the mechanics but shielding it in case anyone tried to intercept our communication.

Most of the bums sprawled in the yard were perpetually drunk. If they did notice Aidyrth, they'd chalk her up to a particularly bad case of DTs.

"Book a suite," Aidyrth instructed. *"Get the biggest one you can. That way there will be room for me."*

"You'll have to be careful. You could give some poor maid apoplexy."

"Like Grigori said. Have a spot of faith. I've done this before."

Of course she had. My stint in the assassin trade was a drop compared to her ocean. *"Three targets, right?"*

"Mob bosses. It would be simpler if they were from the same contingent, but they aren't. It's why our timing will have to be impeccable, but that part comes later. First, you must ingratiate yourself so you can get close enough to do some good."

"What do you have in mind?" I had a feeling what the answer was, but I hadn't compromised myself in that fashion in a very long while.

"You will be the point woman. You'll figure it out."

A muted howl from nearby told me some drunk thought he'd just seen the impossible. Time to get moving. *"I'll let you know once I'm settled,"* I told Aidyrth as she faded to a dark shadow. The howling died away. Not the drunk's first hallucination, nor would it be his last. Humans. What in the hell was wrong with them that they had to blot out reality with booze and drugs?

I wasn't likely to come up with an answer to that purely rhetorical question, so I pulled out a burner phone and set about hunting for swanky hotels. It was a departure for me. Usually, I stayed in dives to be as unobtrusive as possible. After a few calls, I booked myself a suite at The Gwen. According to its hype, it was a luxury hotel on Michigan Avenue.

As soon as I requested a fancy room, the desk clerk became far more attentive and sped me through the check-in process. Supposedly, all I'd need to do was swipe the single-use code he sent to my phone by the keypad next to the door. Everything I needed would already be inside the room. Good. It would save explanations about my nonexistent luggage. I still had my carry-on, but it looked more like a large purse than a suitcase.

The day was a brisk thirty-five degrees with an icy wind blowing off the southwestern shores of Lake Michigan. My West Coast clothes weren't adequate, so I decided to shop before I settled into my swanky digs.

For someone who's avoided spending money all her life, it took some modifications to read the menu from left to right instead of considering price first. Surprising how quickly I adjusted to snatching up gorgeous clothing and reveling in the feel of quality fabrics rustling next to my skin.

Grigori hadn't said anything about being careful not to damage most of the clothing, or returning any of it. I'd double-check with Aidyrth to be certain. Obviously, whatever I wore when we finally made our move wouldn't fare so well, but my "bait" garments could probably end up back at the posh shops where I purchased them.

Dropping thousands of dollars takes time. It was full dark by the time I trudged to the hotel laden with bags and boxes. Some I'd had sent ahead because I couldn't carry everything.

A uniformed doorman held the door of The Gwen for me. I smiled my thanks. "Would the lady care for assistance?" he inquired. "Perhaps a bellhop to carry some of that to your room?"

"I'll be fine," I told him and headed toward a blinking sign that announced where the elevators were located. I'd pulled up the hotel layout from the Internet so I wouldn't have to stumble around, arms laden with packages blazoned with labels from Chicago's best shops.

I was on the sixteenth floor in the Gwen Luxe suite. Juggling packages, I finally gave up and set everything down to dredge out my phone. When I opened the door, my chest felt tight, and it took a stern push to propel myself forward. I moved my bounty inside via a combination of nudges from my feet and grabbing bags.

An additional pile of boxes and shopping bags sat off to one side on an ornate antique table made of highly polished wood. The door swooshed shut behind me; I sank to a crouch taking in acres of thick carpet, a sitting room, doors that presumably led to bedrooms—two of them—and a terrace that was supposed to overlook the best of the city.

I live in a nice house, but I've kept its furnishings on the spartan side. The practical part of me believed it was a waste of money to surround myself with comfort, but my frugality ran deeper than that. If you scraped all the layers away, the scared little girl who'd scrounged food from dumpsters wasn't too far from the surface. If you'd asked her, starvation was real, and it could happen again if I wasn't careful.

I worked on autopilot as I unpacked my bounty and put things away in dressers in the bedroom. A king-size bed topped by a thick duvet and many pillows looked inviting. The bathrooms—both of them—were black-and-white marble affairs with sinfully deep tubs. After a token battle with myself—I should be working—I filled one of the tubs, added scented oil to the hot water, and sank into it after dropping my scruffy everyday clothing in a heap on the floor. I'd fold them and put them away, but later.

The water was relaxing, deep enough to cover my breasts. I shut my eyes enjoying a rare moment of not only doing nothing, but also not being on perpetual guard. The hotel had plenty of security. My suite door had double locks. At the very least, I'd have plenty of warning if something unexpected happened.

I must have drifted off because a solid thump from outside my door launched me from the tub. After making a grab for one of the thick terrycloth robes thoughtfully provided by the hotel, I wrapped it around myself and sent a jolt of seeking magic through the door.

Breath rattled from me. Aidyrth. She'd found me, but then she hadn't had to work too hard. Magic calls to its own, and we were bondmates. I yanked the door open; steam wafted into the suite.

"Practicing up to become like me?" Aidyrth grinned, jaws lolling as she displayed double rows of teeth and puffed steam of her own to join the cloud rolling from the bathroom.

I grinned back. "You never know. Did I do okay picking a hotel?"

"You did. This will make a perfect base of operations for us. No cameras in this suite. I checked."

My eyes widened. Sweeping the suite for electronic surveillance had never occurred to me. The fleabag dives I frequented could barely afford maid service let alone electronics. "Do hotels usually spy on their guests?"

"Some do," the dragon said, "but it's more prevalent in other countries than here."

"How about other worlds?" I asked, fascinated by the possibility of seeing what lay beyond Earth.

"Patience," she counseled, followed by, "Show me what you bought."

We spent the next half hour going over my purchases. Aidyrth had a surprisingly good eye for clothing and offered suggestions for a few items I'd missed. I asked her the question I should have asked Grigori. "Should I be really careful with these things?"

"Why?" the dragon arched scaled brows.

"So I can return them once we're done. I spent almost twenty-five thousand bucks. It's a freakishly large amount of money."

"Everything is yours," Aidyrth reassured me. "To do with as you please. Of course, if we ever have another task requiring such items, you can use them a second time. And a third."

I cocked my head to one side. "Why didn't Grigori ask if anything I had would fit the bill?"

"Would it have?" More eyebrow arching.

"Well, no, but he couldn't have known that." And then I remembered how he'd spied on me—for months—and shook my head. "Never mind."

Aidyrth drew a large gem from between two scales. "You will wear this tonight."

I took it from her, turning it this way and that as light flickered off its faceted surface. "Is it a diamond?"

"Aye, a yellow one. They're quite rare, and that one is nearly flawless." Her smile had vanished. "It's from my hoard and is only on loan."

A golden clasp affair was attached to the stone. I never wore jewelry, so I didn't have a chain. Before I could ask if maybe the dragon had something I could use to hang the diamond around my neck, she plunked a fine filigree chain on a nearby table.

"I will be warded and on the terrace," she told me and glided toward a set of double glass doors. Before she reached them, she vanished from sight.

Worried I'd lose the diamond, I ran the chain through its setting and secured it around my neck. Then I finished drying myself and gave my hair a lick and a promise with the hair dryer before doing it up in a French braid. Rooting through my purchases, I determined which outfit would have the splashiest effect.

The one I settled on was a lowcut black affair that clung to me like a second skin. Its silky fabric was slashed up one side, so nearly all of one of my legs showed. I'd begun to dress, but stopped after my stockings and underwear were in place. The suite had a small kitchen, and I helped myself to the fruit basket, crackers and cheese, and a miniature bottle of wine. Theoretically, each item would be added to my eventual bill.

As I sat at the table, eating and drinking, I marveled at how the 1 percent lived. Most people could only dream of this level of luxury, and I wasn't at all certain I'd want it as a constant infusion. It was unusual and special right now, but I'd tire of never doing shit for myself.

By nine, I was fed, dressed, and ready to leave for the casino. One argument I'd lost with Grigori was over footwear. He'd insisted I wear heels, and maybe he was right about my traditional running shoes not matching a designer gown, but I missed them. If I had to make a hasty getaway, running in heels wasn't practical. These weren't all that high, but I still risked turning an ankle.

To make certain I didn't fall on my face, I practiced walking back and forth in the suite a few times until the black leather high-heeled pumps didn't feel quite so awkward. I stopped in front of a full-length mirror assessing if I looked like a Russian playgirl. Close enough. The other role I could have passed for was a dominatrix. All I needed was a whip and leather gauntlets.

My final transit of the suite, I popped open the door to the terrace. The dragon's magic washed over me, solid and comforting.

"I'm leaving," I told her softly.

"I will be nearby," she reassured me, *"but tonight shouldn't be more than a reconnaissance."*

I hoped she was right. Not because I'm adverse to violence. I find it exhilarating, but my Russian princess doppelganger probably wouldn't. My only goal for the evening was to look like an easy mark. A pretty, not overly bright, heiress who wanted a good time and had a shit ton of money to schlock around.

I tucked one of my phones into an evening bag along with wads of cash and a wallet. After slathering on more lipstick, I left my home away from home only to return immediately for one of my new fur coats. Chicago was cold in late November. Not that I'd be spending much time outside, but wandering around in just an evening gown wasn't smart.

A different doorman greeted me by name—the phony one, of course. It kind of gave me the heebie-jeebies. Someone must have taken a photo of me, or maybe they'll pulled it off my ID from the info I'd given when I registered.

"Can I call you a cab?" he inquired.

"That would be perfect," I gushed with perhaps a spot too much enthusiasm in what I hoped was a credible Russian accent. Cabs should be old hat. I'd have to watch what came out of my mouth.

He offered me his arm and walked me to a waiting taxi with the back door standing open. "Where shall I tell the driver to take you?" the doorman asked.

"I'll let him know." I nodded pleasantly and pressed a five-dollar bill into his hand. Was it enough for less than five minutes of service? Who knew. He nodded his thanks and backed away.

Once my door was shut, I rattled off an address for the cabbie. Startled dark eyes met mine in the rear view mirror. "Are you certain?' he asked, obviously familiar with the location of an illegal gambling establishment.

"Quite." I leaned back against my seat.

He nosed the vehicle into heavy traffic, and I settled in to wait. His hesitation told me that patrons of The Gwen didn't normally frequent gaming houses, at least not ones that flew under the radar. When I paid him, I'd focus a bit of magic so he'd forget where he'd dropped me. Once I thought of it, I started the process from the back seat.

It worked. He didn't talk with me again. When we arrived, I paid him his twenty-dollar fare and tacked another twenty on as a tip. Before he could come round to let me out, I opened the door myself and stepped into a cold, windy night. A second downside of my dressy footwear was winter soaked right through their thin soles.

I trotted toward flashing neon advertising a fish restaurant. It was a front for the casino, and I had just the words to say once I got inside. My feet had turned to blocks of ice, so I sent a thread of power downward to warm them. This wasn't the best area of town, which was a nice way of saying it had totally gone to seed. Maybe wearing mink and diamonds wasn't all that smart.

No sooner had the thought formed than the stench of rancid body odor filled my nostrils. Two thugs with greasy black hair and stained flannel jackets jumped between me and the restaurant entrance.

"Where you going, girlie?" one asked. His breath stank worse than he did.

"In there," I said firmly and feinted sideways to get around them.

A hand closed around my upper arm. "No, you ain't."

"Yah, you're coming with us. We can fix you up good."

Irritation surged. I hadn't come this far to get mugged by a pair of lowlife fuckers. I could build a quick ward, which would give them quite the shock as I vanished. Or I could be less obvious—and more lethal. No one would miss either of these jokers. No one important, anyway. A quick glance around told me no one was within a couple of hundred feet of us. I started with the one touching me and sent a jolt of power up his arm straight to his heart. I was good at busting aortas, a skill I'd turned into an art form.

Gasping, he fell back, clutching his chest and eyes wide with horror before he crumpled to the ground.

"What'd you do to Nate?" the other one demanded as he fell to his knees next to his buddy.

"Nothing. I did nothing. It is the two of you who are the problem," I announced in broken English and hurried toward the restaurant. By the time he discovered his friend was dead, I'd be long gone. Besides, who would he report me to? What would he say? Me and Nate, we tried to mug the Ruskie, and she killed him. Yeah. That would never happen.

I felt like telling the one kneeling over his dying friend, "You pays your money and takes your chances," but I restrained myself. No one likes a Monday morning quarterback, and my use of such an American phase would blow my Russian cover if anyone were listening.

Ha. I'd hoped for uneventful. The night was young, and I'd already killed someone. Not that he hadn't deserved far worse than the quick, clean end I'd dealt him, but I hoped to hell it wasn't an omen for the remainder of tonight.

"I'll dispose of him," rustled through my mind. I didn't look up, but if I had, I'd have seen Aidyrth's generous wingspan floating against the gloom of a cloud-shrouded night.

After waving a hand skyward, I tottered toward the flashing neon sign. As I stumbled on my numb feet, I cursed whoever designed women's clothing to hell and back. Men would never put up with shoes that didn't offer warmth, protection, or balance, but they stuck us with them to show off our legs.

I was in a fuck-them-all mood when I pushed through the door and barked the words designed to hustle me out of the restaurant and into the game room.

CHAPTER 9

"Would the lady care for a cocktail?" a burly blond man dressed in a pressed white shirt and black trousers inquired. His chest and shoulders strained against the broadcloth fabric of his shirt. I suspected steroids. No one got that big on their own.

I waited to be escorted somewhere other than the restaurant foyer, but the maître d' didn't budge.

Oops. I'd jumped the gun. I was supposed to wait for just that question before responding with the code words. I flashed my most engaging smile and pushed my fur jacket off my shoulders to give him an eyeful of cleavage and bare leg. "An old fashioned, if you'd be so kind," I purred to cover my earlier faux pas. I had asked for the same drink, but not in response to his query.

He narrowed his eyes, assessing me while he raised a

hand in the air and snapped his fingers. A harried-looking, dark-haired cocktail waitress with her breasts spilling out of a totally inadequate sequined top hustled over with my drink on a tray.

This wasn't going exactly the way I'd been told, but I'm good at improvising. I opened my handbag far enough to give the man an eyeful of wads of cash before dropping five hundred dollar bills on the drink tray.

"Open a tab for me," I announced grandly, snatched up my drink, and flicked the fingers of my other hand in a get-on-with-it gesture.

"Where?" he asked. "Would you prefer the bar, or did you wish dinner?"

"She's got to be expecting someone," the cocktail waitress spoke up in a gravelly voice that suggested she smoked too much.

"You're still here?" The man shot her a pointed look, and she scurried away after tucking my money into a pouch suspended from her waist.

I'd figured five hundred bucks would seal the deal. This place was one step up from a greasy spoon. No way could the food here be expensive, and I hoped I didn't look like enough of a lush to swill that much booze on my own. No wonder the cocktail gal had been certain I was meeting someone.

Except she must know about the casino. Everyone who worked here probably did.

Meanwhile, two other couples had piled in behind me and were waiting for tables.

"What'll it be?" the maître d'—if someone presiding over a dump like this deserved such a grand title—demanded. I waited for him to snap his fingers again, but he didn't.

I lowered my voice. "I already told you. I want an old fashioned."

He pointed to the drink in my hand. "Yes. You seem to have one."

Another man strode to where we stood. Unlike the first, he was garbed in an expensive looking dark suit and pale-green silk shirt. Slightly taller than my six-foot height, he had a broad-shouldered build, a class-act haircut, a muted art deco tie, and polished shoes. "Is there some problem, miss?" he asked. His brown hair had been nicely layered and fell to collar level. The latest arrival was cleanshaven with strong bones in his face. A hawk's beak of a nose, square chin, and high cheekbones suggested Sicilian ancestry, but he might have been Slavic. Regardless of his ancestry, he was striking. Where Grigori's beauty was otherworldly, this man's sang to me, made me what to dip my fingertips into his hair and wrap my legs around his slender hips.

Whoa. Where had that come from? Sex hasn't been on my menu in years.

"Is there a problem, miss?" he repeated in a low musical voice.

"I hope not." I turned my most fetching smile his way and bent forward a bit to display the girls. "My English is not the best, but I was told if I came here and requested a particular drink…"

The first dude narrowly avoided rolling his eyes. "We got her what she wanted."

Behind me, the line was growing restive. "Serve her later," someone shouted.

"Yeah. We're missing the game," another chimed in.

"Go on into the bar." The dishy dude in the suit made shooing motions with one hand. "Playoffs are just getting rolling. They're up on the big screen."

Once they'd filed past, he turned to me. "Did you want the restaurant or the bar, miss? I'll escort you to a table."

My smile faded, turning to a frown. Either I'd received bad intel, or they were stonewalling me. Sinking into an even deeper Russian accent, I stamped my foot in a deliberate attempt to make my skirt separate all the way to crotch level. "I leave money, much money for drink. If restaurant or bar are only choices, I want my money back, and I will leave."

"How much?" the suit asked.

"Five C-notes," the gatekeeper told him.

"And she asked for an old fashioned." The suit eyed his employee. "You're an idiot, Brad."

"I am not," he protested. "She didn't get the question-answer order right. She could be anyone. You got to be careful, I tell you, and—"

"Enough." The suit didn't raise his voice, but the inflection in that single word could have etched grooves in stone. He offered me his arm. "Come with me, miss. Apologies for any misunderstandings."

"He will start tab for me, like I asked?" I didn't want to appear in too big a rush now things were finally falling my way.

"Already done." The maître d' nodded crisply. "Apologies."

"Mine too," I said in an attempt to be gallant. "English not easy for me." I left my drink on the front counter, tucked a hand lightly under the suit's arm, and walked beside him as we crossed to the other side of the room and through a locked door complete with a palm reader and retinal scanner.

"You didn't want your cocktail?" he asked.

I shook my head. "Ice had melted. Besides, I drink vodka. Straight."

He chuckled.

I bet an alarm lurked somewhere. Probably a silent one that flashed a bank of lights on someone's desk deep in the bowels of this building. I'd already broken one of my cardinal rules. After the scene by the main door, everyone would remember me. For one thing, my fancy duds stuck out against a sea of cheap cotton, wool, and denim.

"I didn't catch your name," the suit was saying.

"We have that in common," I murmured.

"Touché." He laughed, but it lacked warmth. Was he one of the mobsters who ran this joint? Horseracing was legal in Illinois, but onsite gambling wasn't. We reached the end of a brick corridor. A door, twin to the last one we'd passed through, stood at its end.

He stepped in front of me and stared pointedly. "I need to know who you are before I can let you in. It's a formality and won't be repeated your next visit."

I pursed my mouth in what I hoped looked like annoyance at having to deal with hired help and opened my bag. After rooting through cash, I offered a passport. He drew a penlight from a jacket pocket and shone it on the details in my fake Russian travel document.

How good was the forgery? Trusting Grigori dealt with the best, I hadn't taken the time to check. But this was a gangster. Surely he knew the telltale signs of phony identification documents.

"Irina Bukrov from Leningrad," he said as he handed my passport back. "Nice to meet you, Irina."

I tossed my head. "Princess Bukrov," I informed him haughtily.

"Thought they did away with all that nonsense," he murmured.

Closing my bag, I waited. I was done talking. Princesses didn't waste time with underlings, no matter how expensive their suit was—or how pretty they were. I stood tall and glared at him. After a pause long enough I considered telling him to forget it—this wasn't the only casino run by mobsters in this town—he got close to the retinal scanner and tilted his head so it could read his eye.

Good to know whose body parts activated things in here. I wasn't above snatching eyeballs—or thumbs or palms. I'd done all of the above to gain easy entry to places just like this.

The door swung open. I have to hand it to them. Whoever had constructed this had achieved a perfect sound seal. I couldn't hear a thing until the door opened, and then the typical sounds of a casino washed over me in a wave. Music, excited voices, the clink of chips and glassware.

"Point me to the baccarat table," I ordered him, still projecting a princesses-don't-take-shit-from-anyone tone.

I caught a flare of annoyance before he pointed across the room. "Walk a straight line, and you can't miss it." His lips spread in a leer. "May the odds be ever in your favor...Irina."

"The odds are never in one's favor in a place like this, but I like a challenge." Before he turned to go, I said, "Where can I find you if I require something?"

"Find one of the pit bosses," he said.

"Nyet. I want you."

He tossed a speculative glance my way. "Tell one of the boys to find Jake."

I tried to press a fifty into his hand, but he closed mine around it, said, "Place a wager for me," and left.

His upscale suit wasn't a ruse. He'd moved beyond where fifty bucks meant anything, and his loyalties lay elsewhere. Good to know both. In a spot where "fleece the rube" was a mission statement, him turning down cash was significant. Good old invisible cash. No one would have known about it except him and me, but it would have shifted the power differential between us, and not in his favor.

For the next few hours, I alternated between baccarat, blackjack, and five-card-stud. I'm not a bad poker player, but I'm far from pro quality. Eventually, I was close to out of cash. Time to pack in in for the night. I'd done what I'd come for. I had a good sense of the rhythm and flow of the place, of who worked here. Interestingly, all the dealers, pit bosses, and waiters were men. Women provided a nonstop floorshow with the occasional lap dance.

Occasional because no one seemed interested in them. Even more than legal casinos, this one catered to addicts, the ones who couldn't resist one more hand or one more spin of the wheel. Exactly what I was trying to mimic. In what I hoped was a credible performance, I checked my handbag and made a face before pushing myself up and away from the poker table.

"No more for me tonight," I announced and wove toward the door I'd used to get inside. I'd been pretending to slog vodka, but most of my shots had ended up on the floor. The place was dark and none too clean. No one would notice spilled hooch.

Before I reached the door leading to the tunnel that connected with the restaurant, one of the pit bosses hustled to me and grabbed my arm. "Not that way," he said gruffly.

"Let go of me." I yanked my arm back. "I came in this way."

"Yeah, lady, everyone does their first time. We have another entry to keep the restaurant and bar out of it."

I followed him back across the casino. It had to be maybe two or three in the morning, but the crowd hadn't thinned much. A door I hadn't noticed was off to one side of the raised dais where dancers bumped and ground their hips in time to music. The pit boss held it open for me. "Until next time."

I smiled. There was always a next time for those who were hooked on shit like this. Thank everything unholy I wasn't one of them. The damp chill of November in Chicago settled around me. I pulled my fur jacket closed while noting I'd come out next to a bank of dumpsters on the back side of the restaurant.

Setting a course for the front where I hoped to hell I'd find a nice warm taxi, I was lost in thought when a familiar voice called, "Irina."

Shit. Crap. The suit had found me, which meant the pit boss told him I'd left. Which also meant Jake had instructed him to do just that. Maybe the attraction that had speared me like a javelin was mutual, but I wasn't ready for a tryst. Not here and not tonight. After a nod in his direction, I kept walking.

He reached me and draped a heavy coat over my shoulders. "You look cold," he said. The garment was a soft wool, maybe alpaca or vicuna, and it smelled of expensive aftershave, spicy and thick with a bayberry-lime mixture.

The coat did feel good. My fur was more for show than

actual warmth, plus it stopped at hip level, leaving a whole lot of me clad only in silk. "Thank you," I murmured.

"Where are you going now?" he asked.

Oh-oh.

I gave myself a swift mental slap. Not oh-oh at all. This was a good thing. A smart little assassin would take advantage of it, not brush it aside. He'd sought me out, provided an opportunity for me to ingratiate myself with the group who ran this place.

"To my hotel," I replied.

"Would you like some company? Or maybe a late supper? The pit boss who saw you out told me you didn't eat anything."

I stopped walking. My feet couldn't possibly get any colder, and I'd only been outside for maybe ten minutes. "Do you take this level of interest in all your patrons?" I inquired.

"Nope. Only you."

I laughed at the obvious lie. If he'd said only pretty rich women, he'd have been nearer the mark. We started walking again. As we rounded the corner of the building, I spied two cabs, engines idling, in front of the restaurant.

"I have a car," he said. "And a driver. Let me treat you."

I looked away. "I shouldn't." To my credit I didn't ask treat me to what? Why do men always view their dicks as a gift from God? Except in his case, it might be true.

"Do you always do what you should?" The question hung between us. My performance in the casino where I'd blown over five grand was ample as answers went. I was actually damned proud of myself the money had lasted as long as it did.

"Tell you what," he said and extracted a cellphone where he tapped the display. "I've called my driver. He'll be here soon, so you can think about whether you'd like to see more of Chicago. With me."

It wasn't much of a choice. I'd positioned myself well, but I still dithered this way and that before I finally crawled into the back of an obnoxiously luxurious Mercedes limo and sank into soft leather that still had a new car smell. Did it ever go away in anything this expensive?

"Tell me about yourself," Jake murmured.

I turned to him. "You already know much about me. Who are you, Jake? Is this place your home?"

"I've lived in Chicago for ten years."

"And before that?" I adopted my most interested look, eyebrows arched, leaning toward him as I placed a hand on his thigh.

He shrugged and covered my hand with one of his. "Before doesn't count." The dismissal was abrupt and told me clearly anything personal was off limits.

Which meant I was wasting my time, but I gave it one last shot. "I understand," I murmured. "Truly I do. My life in Russia has been...interesting. No one can be trusted."

"Glad you got the memo on that part." His hand tightened over mine, and he urged it higher up his leg.

"Got the memo?" I tried to sound clueless.

"It means understand." He draped an arm around my shoulders trying to pull me against him.

I turned away and stiffened in his grip. "I do not want this," I said.

"Why'd you get into my car?" His breath was quicker, and I smelled his arousal.

"To maybe find a friend." I kept my words simple. "They are hard to come by. Lovers are cheap."

He unwound his arm from me and laughed. "I like you, Irina. You're a straight shooter. Means you call it like you see it. How about that dinner? You must be starving after losing all that money."

"Da. I am." When he wasn't trying to fuck me, he was engaging, and I smiled softly.

He tapped on the glass, told the driver to go somewhere called *Medallions*, and settled back on his side of the generous seat. "Tell me about Russia," he urged.

"Why?"

"I've always wanted to go there."

"Pfft." I rolled my eyes. "Then you are stupid. Or not well-informed."

"Why?" he shot back.

Lucky for me, I've been in Leningrad, Moscow too, and a few choice spots in Siberia. Doing my damnedest to keep my accent straight, I began to describe a day in the life of the average Russian. If he still wanted to play tourist there once I was done, maybe he'd drop his guard and give me something I could use in my quest to get closer to his bosses. One of them was a target. Maybe others too, depending on what I came up with. Grigori had offered us latitude in that regard.

The car rolled to a stop. I was still chatting up a storm as we got out and strolled into the restaurant. A shadow overhead reminded me Aidyrth had my back. I might be used to working alone, but I valued her knowledge, her wisdom, and her support.

We settled into a dark, quiet corner. People in this place knew Jake, were happy to see him. Maybe booze was the ticket. If he liked to drink, and started to trust me a little, it could smooth the way for a few disclosures. If he said too much, I'd have him exactly where I wanted him.

And the power differential would have shifted to my court.

What better person to trust than me? I'd be flying home in a couple of weeks, so any secrets he revealed would leave right along with me.

"It sounds so different," he was saying. "Maybe I could visit after you return home."

My eyes widened. Better and better. "Maybe so," I murmured. "My dacha, er country house, is large. The communists commandeered the chateau outside Moscow, so I am at the dacha year round."

"How long ago? I thought they weren't much of a problem anymore."

Catching myself before I gave away that I was far older than I looked, I said, "Long before I was born."

"Is it just you living there?" His dark eyes bored into mine.

"Me and my uncle. He is not quite right." I tapped my head to get the point about my demented uncle across.

Jake nodded. He hadn't ordered, but food began arriving along with a large bottle of wine. At least two liters. If he drank most of it, maybe I could pry something out of him. I could use magic to speed the process, but he'd be left with a squirmy, uncomfortable feeling that might derail any fledgling connection between us.

He was a man who trusted no one. Wariness streamed from the set of his shoulders; his bland expression had been carefully cultivated to give nothing away.

"Try these." He dropped a selection of hors d'oeuvres on a small plate and pushed it across the table.

"They must know you in this place," I said and cut what looked like a mini quiche into bite-sized pieces. I'd work on the escargot next.

He didn't answer but set about pouring wine. An easy grace to his movements reminded me of highly trained commandos, or black ops agents, people who'd honed their bodies to exquisitely crafted tools.

What was it about him that was so alluring to me?

Usually, I don't pay the slightest heed to men, but he was different. Sexual heat flickered between us, making me ultra-aware of arousal spilling across the table. I wanted him, pure and simple, but I'd let this play out a little. No harm in waiting. He'd want me more if he had to work a little to have me, and maybe by then he'd be more forthcoming with details I needed.

"Irina?" Jake tapped my empty wine glass.

I edged it closer to where a waiter had materialized and waited until he'd left to lift the goblet. "What shall we drink to?" I inquired.

"To being friends."

As our glasses clinked and we drank, I raised my gaze and looked Jake squarely in the eyes before I murmured. "Friends, it is."

CHAPTER 10

I was back at my hotel room by four thirty in the morning. Reinforcing the notion I wouldn't be an easy target for his amorous intentions had been an uphill battle. Over the course of dinner, I'd dodged his hands on my knees and thighs but had allowed him to lace his fingers with mine. No one values a pushover—or a slut.

Jake had offered the limo to drop me off; after several refusals I'd reluctantly accepted. It meant he knew where I was staying, but I could switch up my base of operations easily enough. He'd given The Gwen his seal of approval, labeling it one of Chicago's better places. I'd been certain he was going to make a pitch to walk me to my room, a thinly veiled euphemism for a roll in the hay, but his phone buzzed right before we arrived at the hotel.

After a speedy glance at his screen, he tucked the

device away. "Business calls, I'm afraid. Were you planning to return to the casino this evening?"

I shrugged. "Maybe. There are others on my list."

"Who gave you this list?" The question was bland, and he acted as if he didn't care, but my answer was important. Perhaps it had something to do with whatever text had flashed across his screen.

I probed lightly, a surface scan, to see what I could glean—and withdrew fast. A dark presence, one which hadn't been there before, had invaded his mind. Was he aware of it? Or was he an unwitting vessel? Such things were possible, but I'd never run into remote possession before.

"Irina?"

I offered a slight smile. "Sorry. Guess I am more tired than I thought. Thank you for a nice supper." Without waiting for the driver, I tried to push the door open. Yeah. Right. It was locked.

"You didn't answer my question," Jake said in the same neutral tone.

"Da. I cannot. Surely you understand. Could you please open the door?"

The dark entity was growing. I felt it reaching for me. Jake shook his head and winced.

"Are you all right?" I asked to shift him away from his fixation on ferreting out my source of information on illegal gambling operations.

"Headache. It will pass. They always do." For the first time, he sounded agitated as his pleasant persona slipped a notch. Reaching for the center console, he opened it and did something. The audible click of locks releasing was welcome. I could have chucked magic around, but with whatever was riding shotgun inside him, the more human I appeared, the better.

I pushed the door open and exited, shutting it behind me. I expected Jake to bound out after me. He didn't. Instead, the big black car accelerated smoothly into the mostly quiet boulevard. A doorman greeted me by name and held the door. I walked into a lobby that wasn't as quiet as I would have expected for this ungodly hour.

Aidyrth was waiting for me on the terrace, her power obvious the moment I opened the door to my suite and hung out the do not disturb card. I took a moment to snatch a warm jacket and slide my feet into warmer shoes —flat ones—before joining the dragon. Geez, it felt good to have practical footwear. I'd been teetering around on those heels for hours, and my calves weren't happy. Neither was my back or any of the rest of me.

Aidyrth had draped herself in a ward. She slit a hole and beckoned me through before sealing us inside. "No one can hear us," she reassured me, followed by, "What was that presence inside him?"

I shook my head. Unclasping the diamond pendant, I handed it to her and murmured, "I only noticed it right at the end. Was it there earlier too?"

She tucked her gem neatly away. "Aye. It grew more pronounced on your ride back here."

I zipped my coat and stuffed my hands in its fleecy

pockets. "This might be a stretch, but I don't believe he knows he's possessed—or whatever term fits. That one's not quite right."

"Why not?" Aidyrth skewered me with her spinning eyes.

"For starters, he might be wearing five thousand dollar suits today, but he grew up with nothing. All his posh manners are carefully cultivated, a veneer. He didn't come by them without effort."

"What does it have to do with him selling his soul to the dark side?"

I chuckled. "Oh, he did that all right, but it happened when he worked his way up the ranks in the mob he joined." I stopped to collect my thoughts. "Until tonight, the only marks I've had contact with, even the ones masquerading as mages, were purely human."

"And?" Aidyrth prodded.

"I understand them fairly well. Men like him have no use for anything they can't verify with their senses. As the dinner went on, he dropped his guard a little. He didn't let much slip, but I did get to know him enough to read between the lines."

I smiled wryly. "My off-the-cuff guess is his childhood was just as shitty as mine, except he only had his fists to bail him out. I had magic. It was quite the edge."

"I see." Aidyrth nodded. "My take, once I picked up on your date having a two-fold aspect, is someone keeps tabs on him. All the time."

"He wasn't my date." I made a snorting sound. "But you

may be onto something. He mentioned a headache, and someone texted him at a suspiciously convenient time. The headache showed up the same time as the text." I narrowed my eyes. "Does this mean one of his bosses—the one we're targeting—has power of his own?"

"Possibly. Or made a pact with one of Hell's demons. If it's true, it will make our task much more difficult. You will return to the same spot tonight. See what you can determine."

I'd come to the same conclusion. I'd hoped to move on to the next crappy underground casino, but it would have to wait. "All right, but I'm going to tone down my wardrobe, so I blend in better. No one else was gussied up."

I expected pushback, but Aidyrth didn't say anything. It saved me launching into all the benefits of me not being memorable—to anyone. "I'm going to catch a couple hours' rest. After that, I'll return to several shops and change out gowns for something else."

"No need for that. Just buy what you need," the dragon insisted.

I shook my head. A lifetime of frugal living was impossible to shake, and I wasn't certain I wanted to. "What will you be doing?" I asked.

"I will be gone for a short while, mostly to feed. See you around six tonight."

Before I could tell her good hunting—although god knew where she'd find food around here—she was gone. The local farmers would have coronaries if a dragon dropped out of the skies. Aidyrth like as not had her ways, though. I didn't need to know what they were.

The day passed uneventfully. I slept and cleaned up and ordered nachos and beer from room service. Exchanging the previous day's purchases had been even simpler than I imagined. And I felt much better about the assortment of warm woolen slacks, sweaters, and boots than I'd felt about my reincarnation as Cinderella.

Tonight, rather than leaving my pink-striped hair on full display, I braided it much as I had the previous evening. Six came and went. No dragon. When seven, and then eight, marched past, I grew worried and raised my mind voice. She didn't reply.

I didn't have backup instructions, but then I'd never asked for any. I was the original Ms. Work Alone. I checked my phone. No texts. No emails. Not that I was expecting such things from Aidyrth, but the dragon might have been in contact with Grigori. I tried to settle in with a movie but was too keyed up. At ten thirty, I tossed my newly resurrected cash supply into my bag, slung it over one shoulder, and headed out.

Now that I knew the drill, things went much smoother. I had the cab drop me in roughly the same place but walked around to the back. I'd raised my hand to knock on the nondescript door, but it opened on its own. Meant someone knew I'd arrived. Pausing for a quick moment, I scanned for an electronic camera. Sure enough, muted beams from several intersected in front of the door.

Geez. These people didn't take any chances. The door

was starting to close, so I scooted through. The same pit boss who'd escorted me out the previous evening met me. "Welcome back, Ms. Bukrov."

I nodded his way and headed straight for one of the poker tables. If nothing else, this assignment would sharpen my card skills. I played better tonight. Still had money left at two in the morning when I decided to pack it in.

There'd been no sign of Jake. Or Aidyrth, for that matter. I was decidedly concerned about her, but I had no clue about protocol for the Circle. Should I return for instructions? Keep the mission afloat on my own? Trust the dragon would return in her own good time?

I made my way to the exit, let myself out, and walked around to the front intent on a cab. Before I reached the taxi stand, Jake's limo—or one that looked a whole lot like it—rolled to a stop in front of me. Playing dumb was probably my best bet. For one thing, all black Mercedes limos were indistinguishable from one another.

I skirted behind the car and continued toward the taxis.

"Ms. Bukrov," an unfamiliar male voice called from the direction of the limo.

Decision time. Did I turn around, or keep on trucking?

Ignoring whoever it was ran counter to why I was here, so I turned slowly and peered at the limo through narrowed eyes. "Do I know you?"

"Jake asked me to pick you up," the man said.

I still couldn't see him, and invisible hackles rose on the

back of my neck. "That is nice of him." I tried for graciousness. "I am not getting into a car with someone I do not know."

"He would have called," the disembodied voice went on, "but he doesn't have your number."

The man's accent was pure New York. What the hell was he doing here? Did he really know Jake, or was this some kind of trap? Had someone—maybe the source of the dark power—intuited I wasn't what I appeared? Magic calls to its own, and any other mage would know what I was.

"Where is Jake?" I switched things up.

"Waiting for you."

"Da. But where?"

"A restaurant he thinks you'll like."

I nodded. "Fine. Tell me the name. I will get there on my own."

"Doesn't work that way." The man didn't sound nearly as friendly.

"It works that way, or no way," I informed him and turned back toward the idling taxis. At least there were a few people out and about. It lessened the odds of whoever was in the car making a scene.

A blast of magic hit me squarely between the shoulder blades with enough force to make me stagger. Shit. Fuck. How stupid could I be. I'd suspected problems and hadn't warded myself, a deficiency I remedied immediately. The next shot bounced off.

It also revealed what I was. Or at least that I was more than a Russian prima donna playgirl. Not the right occasion to tangle with this dude. I'd exposed myself, and it was past time to be gone. My heart had picked up a few beats; my throat was dry. Did I magic my way out of here? Or go the taxi route? Regardless, returning to The Gwen seemed unwise.

It was swanky enough, I could call them, have them package up my stuff, and send it elsewhere. Could they be discreet? While I dithered, the limo door opened.

Showtime.

Thanking all the gods I wasn't dressed in a silky nothing balancing on stilettos, I turned to see who'd emerged from the car. A swarthy mobster strutted toward me, dark hair greasy and slicked back from a low forehead. Lady luck was smiling on me. Sort of. He was one of my targets. I'd moved up the food chain without even trying.

My adversary's burly build was mostly obscured by a huge overcoat that probably hid more than fat rolls. My bet was he had a large bore weapon secreted within its folds. He was shorter than me, which was bound to piss him off. Short men loathe tall women.

Would he risk firing on me with all these people milling about?

So far, no one had paid us any heed. Residents of big cities learn to keep their attention to themselves. Safer for them that way. I had nothing to lose, so I probed him with magic. The same prickly nastiness I'd sensed in Jake rolled toward me, slapped against my ward, and tried again.

No reason to stick with my cover. It had already blown

sky high. "Had a run in with the crossroads demon, eh? How'd that go for you?" I taunted.

"Bitch," he growled and strode closer.

I held up a hand and jabbed him dead in the chest with power. "Stop right here. I'm leaving. So are you."

"You got that right. Except you're getting into that car." He jabbed a thumb at the limo.

"Really?" I arched a brow.

"Really." He mimicked my tone and reached inside the voluminous gray coat to withdraw a large revolver. Pfft. Like that was going to move me off the dime. I played at looking scared to buy myself a moment or two and probed the space between us assessing if whatever was inside this bastard would form an effective barrier against a lethal blow from me.

Before I was done, a shadow fell over us. Wings and a long neck and sinuous tail. Aidyrth. Good timing. Power rolled through the parking lot like a tidal wave. People yelped and squealed and grabbed their heads. Diversion in place, the dragon swooped low, curled her long red talons around the man's shoulders, and took off.

I heard him cursing in demonspeak, one of the more unpleasant languages with its preponderance of guttural phonemes, but not for long. Aidyrth said. "If I were you, I wouldn't squirm so much. I might let go."

When I glanced skyward, she'd vanished and her cargo along with her.

All around me, voices raised in disbelief as everyone took a stab at what had just happened. It seemed like as good a time as any to make my escape. I was nearly to the taxis when footsteps pounded behind me.

I scented the air. Jake. Fuck me. Had he been in the car the whole time?

Anger roiled through me twisting my stomach into a knot. I flashed around and dropped the Russian accent as I snarled, "You bastard. You set me up. Why?" My first glance at his face drove the breath from me. Someone had roughed him up, blackened an eye, maybe broken a cheekbone.

He'd reached me and jerked his chin upward. "What was that?"

"My friend." I left it at that. Let him wonder. I might be nonplussed someone had tortured him, but he wasn't my problem. Or my target, but I'd take him out in a heartbeat if he got in my way.

Snatching my arm, he pulled me toward a cab. I yanked out of his grip. "Nope. Not going anywhere with you. If you get moving, I might do you a favor and forget about you."

"You're one of...them, huh?" He tried to slit his eyes, but only managed it with the one that wasn't black and blue.

"If you're smart, you'll forget about me too." I scanned for the demon taint I'd found the previous evening. It was gone, so perhaps it was linked to the creep the dragon had taken out of the equation.

"Irina, or whatever your name is. I'm asking for a favor. I'll pay you."

Why was I still standing here talking with him? I should leave. Now. Instead of doing the smart thing, never one of my long suits, I asked, "What?"

"Take me with you. I need to drop out of sight for a while."

"What makes you think I can help with that?"

His broken face twisted into what was probably a smile. "Takes one to know one."

"Last night, you believed I was one more rube."

"Did I?"

The question hung between us. I made a snap decision, kind of a Shira specialty, dove into a cab, and gestured him in behind.

"Where to?" the cabbie asked.

"Hang on," I muttered. "You can start driving, though. Toward the rail yards."

"But lady, it's not safe, and—"

"Do it," I spoke over him.

Meanwhile, I trolled through my phone until I found exactly what I was looking for. A no tell motel, seedy, past its prime, and not the type of place anyone asks questions. After rattling off the address, we rode the rest of the way in silence.

I checked us in, picked up keys that were still keys and not electronic cards, and pushed open the door to 214. The place stank of smoke and stale sex. Once the door was shut, Jake sank heavily onto one of two swaybacked beds. "Not the type of place I'd have pictured you in," he muttered.

Not bothering to dignify his comment with an answer, I snapped up the ice bucket, visited the ice machine, and wrapped cubes in dirty washcloths for his face.

Once I'd done all I could, I said, "Why'd you pick me to bail you out?"

"It's temporary," he slurred. "I have a go-bag. Just need to get to it, and I'm out of here."

"Not your first rodeo," I observed.

He spat laughter and winced. "How'd you guess."

"Takes one to know one." I fed his words back to him.

"I'm outside." Aidyrth's words rolled through my mind. *"Behind your location."*

I rose and zipped my jacket. "Got to leave," I told Jake.

"Are you coming back?"

"Not sure. My, erm, friend is close."

His uninjured eye widened. "The, uh, the dragon-thing?"

I nodded.

He set down the bloody washcloths. "I want to see him."

Before I could say absolutely not, Aidyrth said, *"It's all right. I have to erase his memories anyway."*

"Okay," I said a bit too brightly. Revealing anything to anyone ran counter to all my years of solo operations. "By the way, it's a her. And it would be best if you didn't say a word."

He did laugh then, and groaned when the movement shot pain through his abraded face. "You've never worked for organized crime, sweetheart. Speaking only when spoken to is a cardinal rule."

I took a key, gave one to him, and we walked out the door, locking it behind us. Not that the cheap lock would keep anyone out, but we hadn't left anything in there to steal.

I deployed a strand of seeking magic. It took me right to the dragon, except we had to scale a barbed wire fence between us and the rail yards. I started to help Jake but decided against it. This was his choice. He could suck it up and deal with it.

Not waiting for him, I ran lightly to my bondmate. "Is he dead?" I asked without preamble. She'd know who I meant.

Scales clinked and clanked as she nodded. "Aye, but the demon within escaped my clutches."

"Tell me what that means," I demanded.

Ash and smoke plumed into the night, mingling with exhaust from train engines. "We accomplished nothing."

"Huh? I don't get it. He's dead."

"He wasn't our objective, except I didn't realize it until the demon who'd commandeered his body made a run for it. That's what we have to obliterate, and it won't be easy. Those aberrations have nine lives."

Jake had joined us. To his credit, he was staring pointblank at the dragon as if she were the most incredible thing he'd ever seen. "I can help," he said. "I know where the dark thing will go next."

"How?" Aidyrth and I asked almost in unison.

"Because it splits its time between three of my bosses. They had to do something, a ritual, to lure the spirit. I don't think it can enter just anyone. It wants me, but so far I've mostly kept it out."

The dragon dropped a taloned foreleg on Jake's head. Power blazed from her bright enough to light the night. When she was done, his face had healed, and she leaned down until she was eyeball to eyeball with him. Eh, leaning isn't exactly right. She telescoped her neck, which had the effect of lowering her head.

"If you double cross us," she hissed, "I will personally execute you. It will be long and slow and painful. Do we understand one another?"

He grinned. It shaved years off his appearance. And then he tipped an imaginary hat. "Yes, ma'am, we do." He shook his head, muttering, "An actual dragon. I'll be goddamned."

"I could be anything," Aidyrth informed him archly. "You can't always believe what your eyes tell you."

"Whatever you are is incredible," he said. I didn't interpret it as gallantry on his part. He truly meant it.

"I'm going back to The Gwen," I told him. "Tomorrow, I'll get you a couple of burners, and we'll take it from there."

"You know where to find me, but come early. I won't remain here much past dawn," he said and turned away, loping toward the no tell motel.

Once he was out of earshot, I murmured, "Do you think we made a mistake not wiping his mind and being done with it?" I might be attracted to him, but I was far from naïve, and I wasn't in the habit of leaving loose ends if I could help it.

Aidyrth snorted laughter. "Maybe. We might have tripped over ourselves, but I don't believe he'll come back to bite us. Besides, he has a role to play yet. I'm not certain quite what, but he will need all his faculties. Get on."

My eyes widened as I puzzled over her comments about Jake. "Get on? Do you mean onto your back?"

"Where else? Next stop is the terrace outside your suite. Tomorrow, we'll be moving."

I leapt onto her back, surprised how warm her scales were. Either that, or I was chilled through. "Not tomorrow," I said firmly. "We need to be out of there tonight. I'll figure out a less obvious spot to stay. Irina Burkov is dead. I'll use another of Grigori's identities for me. And maybe I'll dye my hair."

"Do you want to hear how he died?"

I didn't have to ask who. She meant the man she'd airlifted out of the square in front of the restaurant. "I do," I replied. "Every last gritty detail." Even if his death didn't count against our quota, reliving it through the dragon's eyes would be like a bedtime story for someone like me.

Death is where I live. I'd do well never to forget it.

CHAPTER 11

By the time noon the next day rolled around, I'd moved to one of several Hilton hotels in the area. It was nice, but not luxury personified. Between The Gwen and the Hilton, I stopped by the no tell motel. Turned out I was barely in time. Jake had already walked out of 214 by the time I landed in the parking lot just shy of seven in the morning. True to his word, dawn wasn't far off. Rather than riding the dragon, which was impossible to hide, I'd rented a car.

I pulled up next to him. "Drop you somewhere?"

His face looked as if he'd never sustained a beating. Aidyrth had truly healed him, not just covered up the worst of the damage. He slid into the passenger seat. "No. I'll get where I'm going on my own, but we do need to talk."

Dropping the car into gear, I selected a parking spot

near the far side of the almost deserted motel parking lot. Whoever stayed here probably didn't have vehicles. Once we were stopped, I opened the glove box and handed him two burner phones.

"I only need one," he said.

"Eh, take them both."

He nodded and dropped them into a jacket pocket. "Did you find the...the uh." He scrunched his face in a way that would have hurt last night and mumbled, "Don't know what to call it except the dark thing."

"Haven't even begun looking yet," I replied. "Could you point me to where your bosses hang out?"

"Don't you have other ways to locate them?"

"Yup. Sure do, but it will take longer."

He opened his mouth, closed it again, and finally said, "Sorry. I can't."

"Why the hell not?" I demanded. "They hung you out to dry."

He shrugged. "Maybe my loyalty is misplaced, but I'm going to have to start over. If I burn too many bridges, I'll have a tough time."

"You're not thinking straight," I told him.

"Of course I am," he bristled.

"I know all about starting over," I cut in. "What it means is not reaching out to anyone who knew you before."

"I liked you better when you were a Russian airhead."

His words made me smile. "I just bet you did." Pressing my advantage—if I had one—I added, "Since you're going to disappear, no one will know who told us about your bosses. Hell, they're probably already blaming you for the one Aidyrth killed last night."

He grimaced ruefully. "If it weren't for a bunch of witnesses who will swear up and down something grabbed Bruno and took off with him, they would be. As it is, they'll want a full accounting."

"You've been sidestepping them." The way I put it wasn't a question.

Jake nodded. "Yeah. They beat me up for nothing. I'd told them everything I could about you. Everything I knew, but they didn't believe me. I've proven myself many times over. I didn't deserve the whole brass knuckle routine. Besides, my sudden, unexplained healing will do nothing but raise questions. They'll think I'm in cahoots with something else in the occult realm."

I pressed my lips into a thin line. "I'm not surprised they didn't believe you. The presence inside Bruno recognized what I was, more or less. Since we'd had dinner, it assumed you knew more than you did."

"What are you, exactly?"

I shrugged. "It's not important. I kill people quietly and efficiently."

He arched a brow. "But not me?"

"That's right. Not you. You were a means to an end, one we haven't gotten to yet." It was a decent lead-in, so I asked, "About those locations?"

"Let me think about it. And I will. Otherwise, I'd just have stuck with no."

"Honor among thieves?" I joked.

"Something like that." He curled one hand around the latch. "I need to get moving. Put some miles between me and here before most of my brothers wake up."

"Feel like a trade?" I looked him square in the eyes.

"If you're offering sex for information, you've caught me at a crappy time. I'm still half zonked on pain killers even though I don't need them any longer."

"Not sex. Something you need more." I licked my lips, unsure I really wanted to go this route. It could spell the end of something I valued almost more than life itself: my privacy.

"What? I really do have to get moving, Irina, although I bet that's not your name."

"It's not. I have a place where you can stay. It's in Washington state."

He narrowed eyes. "What's the catch? Why would you do that for me?"

"Good question. I'm not exactly certain." I swallowed. "Two catches. The first in information. The second is Reggie."

Jake waved a dismissive hand. "I'll make sure he knows you and I aren't an item."

I snorted laughter. "He's a parrot. He wouldn't care, but he will need his dishes filled. And"—I paused for emphasis—"remember what Aidyrth said about hunting you down and dismembering you? If you fuck me over, damage anything of mine, or reveal the location of my home to anyone, I will see you suffer worse than a thousand deaths.

I'm good at what I do. I know how to hold you on the brink between life and death and how to haul you back and do it all again."

Jake hooted laughter. "Christ, woman, you make it sound like the best sex ever, except it's death instead of sex."

"Do we have a deal?"

"Maybe. I need to feel out just how bad things are. Is your number programmed into those phones?"

I shook my head and rattled off one of my burner numbers for him.

"Got it." He pushed the door open. "If you don't hear from me by the end of today, you won't hear from me at all, but thank you for your offer. It's one of the nicest things anyone's ever done for me."

Before I could respond, he was gone, moving with the easy grace of a big cat on the prowl. Why had I offered up my house? Christ. I could have put him in a hotel in any city in the world, but presumably he didn't need me for that. Anyone who works organized crime must have resources. He'd mentioned a go-bag. They always had IDs and cash.

Aidyrth was waiting for me at the Hilton. No spacious terrace here, so she was inside, wings folded in an attempt to make herself smaller. "How'd that work out?" she asked.

"If you know enough to ask, you know the answer," I sniped back.

"You got the question wrong," the dragon retorted. "Have you ever tendered your home to anyone?"

"No."

"Why him?"

"I've been asking myself the same thing. He's just a small-time hood, but something about him appeals to me. Damn if I know what. Anyway"—I shrugged—"my bet is I'll never hear from him again."

"Don't be so certain. I picked up something from him too. Otherwise, we'd have made certain he had no memory of us."

"Could you put a finer point on it?"

Scales clanked as she shook her head. "I trust my instincts, though. He's one of the pieces in play. Until we know more…"

"You said that before, but he's probably walking off the gameboard," I retorted.

"I don't think so. Meanwhile, I located last night's demon."

"Excellent news. Means we don't need Jake."

"He has a role to play," she insisted.

"Talk to me while I switch up my hair color," I said and proceeded to skirt around her bulk to the bathroom. While I worked on changing pink to dark brown, Aidyrth repositioned herself and swathed us in magic. I'd put out the do not disturb card, so I wasn't expecting a stray maid to interrupt. They're delighted when they get to skip a room. Besides, I'd just moved into this one a few hours before.

"Once night falls, we'll head to the northern outskirts

of town. There are deserted quarry sites with endless tunnels."

"Perfect spot for a demon to hide."

"More than one, I'm afraid."

"I don't know anything about them. Do they require a person's body? Or can they operate in whatever other form they have." Time to rinse the dye out. I bent my head over the tub and sluiced water over my head with the detachable shower arm. I'd picked temporary color; hopefully, the darker shade wouldn't totally ruin my pink tresses.

"Hell is real," she began. "Demons are Satan's minions, except they hold no loyalty to him or anyone else."

"How does a mortal talk them into, well into anything?"

Aidyrth's jaws lolled into a smile. "You've heard the phrase, sold your soul to the devil?" At my nod, she went on. "It's been around for an exceedingly long while. Demons are always on the lookout for mortals they can feed from. Human energy strengthens them, mostly because the mortals attracted to what they have to offer have dark, twisted souls."

I wrapped a towel around my dripping hair and got back into the clothes I'd worn the previous night. Dark, unobtrusive, they'd do fine for skulking around tunnels.

"So demons approach mortals, not the other way around?"

"Aye. Pickings have been thin since the tail end of the 1800s. No one believes in magic anymore, hence requests for devious interventions to vanquish foes dropped off as well.

"Tonight will be difficult," the dragon went on. "I've requested Grigori send another team along."

My head snapped around. "Huh? But we've scarcely begun."

"We're no match for half a dozen demons," she informed me. "We might hold our own, but we'd accomplish nothing."

"What about the rest of our assignment here?" I inquired. "Even after the demons are out of the way, we'll still have mob bosses from two other clans, or families, or however they depict themselves, to deal with."

"We'll take them out on our way to the quarry. For now, eat something and get some rest."

"But you didn't even ask me what I—" I clamped my teeth together. This wasn't Shira, the assassin, doing her thing any longer. It was Shira, part of a team that reported back to a still larger group.

"Aye?" Aidyrth raised scaly gray brows.

"Nothing." I let words about how this setup wasn't working for me roll through my mind and out the other side. I didn't have to make any decisions right this minute. I'd expressed doubts to Grigori, so if I went to him and told him this wasn't for me, it wouldn't come as a surprise.

"I'll return late this afternoon," the dragon said. Where she'd stood turned to empty space. I'm certain she picked up on my ambivalence and was leaving me to stew in my brand of indecision. Wise of her to go before I said something I might regret.

I'd just ordered a quesadilla and a beer from room service when one of my burners rang. I had to root around a bit to remember which pocket it was in. "Hello."

"We have a deal," Jake's voice said. "Where can I find you?"

Oh-oh. I'm suspicious by nature, and I didn't like the sound of that.

"I'll find you. Same spot as where we spoke last in, say, an hour?"

"I'm kind of in a hurry. I could swing by The Gwen."

"I moved. It's either where I said or nowhere."

"Okay. See you there." He hung up.

I stared at the phone. If I'd had hackles, they'd have been fluffed out the length of my spine. My food arrived; I ate mindlessly, more because I needed energy than because I was hungry.

Should I tell Aidyrth where I was going?

I rolled my mental eyes. I hadn't reported to anyone since I'd belonged to a gang as a streetwise twelve-year-old. Once I'd eaten everything the kitchen sent and inhaled the beer, I grabbed a warm coat and my keys and purse and headed for the underground garage and valet service.

Traffic was impossibly snarled. Even with GPS guidance to avoid the worst of it, I was still a quarter of an hour later than I'd said I would be, but he'd waited. Either my trade was too good to pass up, or he'd set a trap to inveigle his way back into his bosses' good graces.

He emerged from an older model Toyota with dings, dents, and a rusty patina. I kept a watchful eye as he walked toward me, said to hell with it, and scoured him with magic. He must have felt my scrutiny because he winced but kept coming.

"Was that necessary?" he asked as he slid into the passenger seat.

"Yeah. It was. For all I know, you cut a new deal."

The corners of his eyes crinkled; his jaw tensed. "If you don't trust me, why'd you come?"

"Because I might have been wrong. Did you?"

"Did I what?"

Fuck. He was being cagey. I draped a truth net over him. "Sell me out to your bosses?"

"I'm not like that. Figured when you said I could stay at your place, you saw through the corrupt parts to who I used to be."

His words passed my test. I dismantled my truth spell. "We're good."

"That poking, prickly shit was you doing something, huh?"

"Yup. I was testing the truth in your words. Meanwhile, you don't have to compromise yourself. Aidyrth found what we need."

"The dragon?"

I nodded. "Yeah."

"Okay then. Could have saved yourself a trip." He pushed the car door open.

"Wait. My part is still good. It's why I came. In case you

were on the up and up."

He turned toward me. "Why'd you doubt me?"

"I don't trust anyone. When you said you'd come by my hotel, it didn't sit well." I took a measured breath. "In my —our—business, we run on hunches, instincts. If I hit it wrong, I might not have a chance to recover."

"Brother, does that ring true."

I gave him my address and the code for the dude manning the gates. We settled on him being my brother from Chicago. Jake Teague.

"It's not so far off," he murmured. "Torvino is my last name."

"They know me as Suzanne Teague," I told him.

"But it's not your real name, either is it?"

"Nope. Travel safe," I told him.

Bending toward me, he kissed my forehead and then a cheek. "Thank you."

"Don't forget to feed Reggie."

He chuckled. "No worries on that front. Parrots have beaks. He'll probably peck me into submission if I fall short. When you come home, I'll cook you up a Bolognese like you've never had before."

I still felt the touch of his lips after he'd left me, and it took all my willpower not to run after him as he loped back to his car. Was I doing this because he was hotter than a two-dollar pistol? He was way more seductive when he wasn't trying to get his hands under my clothes than he'd been in the limo two nights before.

Nah. He was gorgeous, but his looks weren't it. There

were a whole lot of hot men in the world, and I ignored them all. So much so I couldn't actually recall the last time I'd been laid. I picked the attraction apart as I drove back to the Hilton, but didn't get any closer to an answer.

It seemed as if I'd barely fallen asleep when Aidyrth's voice rumbled through my mind. A glance at the clock told me I'd slept two solid hours. Should be plenty. I hadn't taken off my clothes, or my nice, flat, practical trail runners, so it took me exactly two minutes to grab my coat and run for the stairwell that would spit me out on the roof.

"Sorry," I told her. "I must have passed out."

"We're not late. Yet. Get on."

This time the invitation wasn't as much of a surprise. I welcomed the dragon's warmth as she spread her wings, shrouded us from casual view, and launched into the dank night air. At least it wasn't snowing. Or raining.

"Who are we working with?" I asked.

"Grigori and I'm not certain who else."

I'd given the whole group grope thing some thought. "Will my role be clear?"

"Aye, but we may well end up improvising."

"Will Grigori be pissed if I don't do exactly as he instructs?"

"Not so long as you don't place anyone else in danger." Aidyrth flapped faster, and the lights of Chicago flickered and flared beneath her wings. "He's not unlike any other commander. If what you do is successful, you'll have all the latitude you'd ever want."

I nodded to myself. I could live with that. I wasn't in the habit of failing, and I was good at what I did. If I hadn't been, he'd never have recruited me. "Anything I need to know before we get there?"

"The tunnels are tricky. If we get separated, make certain of your return route."

"What happened to taking out the other mob bosses on our way to the tunnels?"

"I decided it wasn't a great idea. We'll need all our magic for the task ahead."

A shudder ran down my back. I wasn't fond of enclosed places. Not exactly claustrophobic, but the specter of thousands of pounds of dirt above my head didn't exactly set well. "Will I have permission to kill as targets present themselves?"

Aidyrth puffed a trail of fiery ash into the night air. "Spare no one."

My mouth stretched into a vicious grin. I'd have rubbed my hands together if they weren't curled around the spines at the base of the dragon's neck. "We'll have a grand time."

"Focus on surviving."

Her stark words were like a slap in the face. They reminded me I was going toe to toe with a brand new adversary—a paranormal one. My norm was mortals, and they were a slam dunk. Demons would be slippery. Could I kill them the same way I mowed through humans? "Tell me how they die."

"What a predatory question."

"Judge all you want, Ms. Dragon. If keeping myself alive is the focus, I need to know how to kill those fuckers."

"This is why I chose you," she said and leapt squarely into a lecture on demon physiology, a joke because their bodies were fluid, but they had magical centers. Places that were vulnerable to attack. I'd had no idea demons could shapeshift, but apparently they could turn into anything, large or small.

"If we ever get back to the guild house," I said, "I need those books."

"Good you recognize it. Now, if they lead with fire, what do you do?"

The lights of the city had thinned out a while back. As we flew, she quizzed me on the basics she'd drilled into me. Mostly, I got the answers right, but I didn't feel ready as she circled to land.

"You'll do fine, Shira," she reassured me, "because you won't be alone."

I'd have laughed if the situation weren't so potentially deadly. I'd always viewed my solo status as a bonus. Get myself into shit; get myself back out. I missed working that way. It was cleaner, simpler.

Before I talked myself out of being a team player, I shut everything down and stared into the darkness below. Aidyrth's power was shrouded; mine as well. No matter if I worked by myself or not, the value of a stealth attack was undeniable.

We were about a hundred feet from the ground when the night exploded into fiery lights. Aidyrth flapped like a mad thing, and we circled, dropping back half a mile before her feet hit the ground.

"What was that?" I whispered as I slid off her.

"Don't know, but we almost flew into a serious downdraft, one strong enough to pull us out of the sky if we'd been any lower. I'll get us closer, and we'll figure out what we're up against." Her magic wrapped around me as she gathered me into a teleport spell.

"Are the others here?"

"Don't know that, either. Ssht. Silence until we have answers." Her spell faded, and I stared into an inky curtain. The night lacked both moon and stars; a mage light wasn't wise.

I needed answers. It was why I was asking questions, but I shut up and gathered my own power close so I'd be ready. I'd have liked it a whole lot better if I knew what I was preparing for, but I can punt when the going gets dicey.

Even though Aidyrth warded us, I added shielding to the mix. The harder we were to spot, the more time we'd have to react.

Timing is everything. A second often marks the difference between success and disaster. Telling myself not to think like that, not to envision anything other than victory, I crept forward.

The same eldritch lights that had warned us, flickered ahead. Time to slow way down, make a plan, and execute it. Except the dragon was still moving. I couldn't call her back, not with my voice or telepathy. Either would reveal our presence. After a long, undecided moment, I trailed after her cursing my skittishness.

I trusted myself, but I didn't completely trust my bondmate. Not yet. We didn't have enough miles under our belts. Presumably, she had more experience than me, but she was doing something I never would have: marching forward without sketching out the bones of an attack strategy.

I halted my interminable inner dialogue—again. That's what happens when you spend a whole lot of time alone: you talk with yourself because you're the only one there.

Two choices. Either I bailed or I covered my bondmate, which meant having faith in what she was up to. What it came down to was no choice at all. If I didn't trust her with my life, I had no business here. None.

She'd been there when Bruno had me in his gunsights. Hell, she'd picked me out of god knows how many mages to be her bondmate. Nothing had transpired to give me pause, so what the fuck was wrong with me other than my misplaced need to be mistress of my own ship?

Feeling like a fool, I rushed forward determined to play off Aidyrth's lead. She trusted me, was counting on me. I'd never bailed on a commitment. Tonight wasn't going to be the first time. I'd catch up with Grigori, float my misgivings, and see where they led, but that would happen later. Or maybe it wouldn't happen at all.

Red lightning forked across my visual field, followed by bursts of blue and green. Aidyrth had stopped, hopefully not because she'd tapped into my ambivalence. The next flash of brilliance illuminated boarded-up tunnel entrances, three of them.

The dragon extended a wingtip, and we glided toward the one on the right.

CHAPTER 12

Seeing in the dark is the least of my problems. My low-light vision is exceptional; it's part of my magic. We passed beneath creaking timbers and into a long rounded channel heading into the side of a hill and angling downward. The dragon had picked this one for a reason, probably because all the action was in one of the other entrances.

Smells of wet earth and decay grew stronger as we moved away from the entrance. Piles of bones, human and animal, lined the walls. Rats scuttled this way and that, the glow of their red eyes impossible to miss as they chittered their annoyance at our intrusion.

Aidyrth stepped on one; the crunch of its bones unmistakable as she kicked it aside. The other resident rodents scurried in all directions. "They'll stay out of the way now," the dragon hissed softly. "They're terrible gossips. If they aren't around, they can't tell anyone we're here."

Oh good. Speech was back on the menu. "What are we doing?"

"Coming around from the rear."

"Where's Grigori?"

"Close. Do not use power hunting for him."

I reeled in the seeking spell I'd been about to deploy. "Do you know what's going on?"

She twisted and lifted me in her forelegs until our heads were next to one another. "A gateway to Hell is nearby. I feel its pull. Whatever you do, do not get close enough to the vortex to let it suck you through. Hell isn't a pleasant spot."

I'd never envisioned it as a destination resort. In truth, I'd never believed it was real, but the same could be said for dragons. Gateways meant more of whatever had lived inside Bruno. I'd never laid eyes on an actual demon, but I'd felt its foul bleakness polluting Bruno's essence. The idea anything could corrupt him further was noteworthy since he was a warped piece of work to begin with.

The dragon set me down, and we covered maybe another half mile before she turned hard left and pushed on a recessed doorway I hadn't noticed. Made sense someone would have created methods to move from one passageway to another without going back to the beginning and starting over.

"Have you been here before?"

She cast a surprised look my way from beneath lowered lids. "Of course. I explored as thoroughly as I could once I identified this as the spot the demon had gone to ground."

The advantages of having a sidekick reared up and slapped me. Again. Her magic was stronger than mine, and far more versatile. For one thing, she could fly. And teleport.

"Quiet," her voice rolled through my mind. I took it as a rebuke and put a lid on my thoughts as we backtracked toward the tunnel entrances.

The same brightness that had lit up the night sparked from ahead. A guttural language, heavy on consonants, buzzed, growing louder as we moved nearer. Demonspeak. An enormous wolf fell in next to us. Silver with dark guard hairs, his shoulder was nearly as tall as mine. Amber eyes were hooded. I'd never seen more than hints of him in this body, but I'd know the feel of Grigori's power anywhere.

The space on his other side developed a liquid aspect before resolving into Mae, hawk perched on her shoulder. Her pale hair had been braided out of the way, and her aquamarine eyes glittered in the low light of the tunnel. I was glad to see her rather than someone I hadn't met yet, or god forbid Loren and that wolf of his.

In other circumstances, I'd have greeted Grigori and Mae, but not here. I tried to identify the suction Aidyrth had mentioned, but couldn't. Tough to avoid what I couldn't sense. One of my strong points has always been unshakeable concentration, but it had flown the coop. Along with my nerves of steel.

My heart raced, my palms were damp, and my stomach had formed a hard, painful knot making me grateful I hadn't eaten more. I hadn't puked in years, not since I'd accepted I was different, that not everyone could blind someone—or kill them with a stray thought.

Um, yeah. Way too many stray thoughts. I fused my attention dead ahead and stuck with the lights growing nearer. Shouts and squeals became louder, more obnoxious. We'd been gradually climbing, and finally reached a kind of plateau. If the vista spread before me hadn't been so surreal, it would have been terrifying.

Not much scares me, but we'd stumbled onto a ritualistic murder site. The brisk, coppery taint of blood was overwhelmed by the sour stench of fear and spilled entrails.

Two humans, almost dead but not quite, had been spreadeagled on the floor lashed to stakes driven into the dirt. Demons—the real deal with horns, tails, cloven hoofs, and red-scaled skin—hovered around the soon-to-be corpses with skinning knives. They were ugly as sin, and I could see where shapeshifting could be quite the boon. No matter how much a mortal wanted someone dead, facing off against a demon in his native form would take steel balls.

My stomach hurt worse, and I stifled breath that wanted to gush from me. Bile splashed the back of my throat; I swallowed it. The demons, half a dozen that I could see but there could have been more, were eating their victims alive. They'd carve off strips of flesh, stuff them into their mouths, and do it again.

Blood soaked into the ground forming a lazy river that flowed toward a deep gash in the ground. Was it the gateway Aidyrth had told me to avoid? At least so far, it wasn't posing much of a problem, but maybe the blood was keeping it quiescent.

Behind the action, other mortals waited their turn at annihilation. Suddenly the piles of bones in the neighboring tunnel made more sense. It had seemed strange so many bums would choose this precise spot to lie down and die.

The insidious power rolling from the demons grew stronger as they fed.

If we were going to do something, we had to move soon. The current odds were manageable. Six of them, five of us. Unless the cavalry raced to the rescue through the gently pulsing breach.

Should we try to close it?

Eventually, maybe. If we blasted power at the opening, we'd alert the demons. So far, they were so sunk in a feeding frenzy, they hadn't noticed us. We halted. Grigori waved a paw in a pattern that no doubt meant something to Aidyrth and Mae and her bird.

I was clueless, and voiceless. Telepathy would stand out like a flare.

Aidyrth swung me onto her back. Before I could protest I wanted my own legs under me, Grigori launched himself through the air and landed on the nearest demon.

He must have augmented his leap with magic; otherwise it would have been an impossible feat.

We bolted forward. Fire spewed from the dragon; I focused power at a demon's chest, willing his heart to burst. He spun to face me, blood dripping down his craggy face. Eyes like black stones with whirling red centers skewered me. Before he could suck me into an obvious drawing spell, I upped the magic pouring into his body.

"Die, you bastard," I shrieked.

Nowhere near dying, he sauntered toward me and the dragon. Piss on that. I angled my body to keep him directly in my gunsights and hit the ground lightly, never letting up the flow inundating him. Blue-white light from my power collided with red-and-black oozing from him. Hanks of his hide sloughed off and fell into the dirt, but his heart kept chugging along. Geez, what was it made of? Steel?

Aidyrth turned and poured fire over him. Maybe because I'd done a number on his protective hide, he turned into a torch, burning and sputtering and finally shrieking.

Good. One down. I started to withdraw my power, but Aidyrth shouted, "Keep going. We're not done."

I didn't question her, but I'd never found anything this tough to get rid of. How could he still be breathing? His body had mostly melted to a pile of sticky, stinking goo.

Mae's hawk flew past with an eyeball clutched in her beak. After crunching it down, she went back for another. I offered the hawk points. If the demons couldn't see, it would cripple them.

Smoke was thick in the tunnel; my eyes burned. "Enough?" I asked my bondmate.

"For this one."

Peering through the gloom, I tried locating my next target. Breath stung my abraded throat, and my chest ached from smoke. Out of nowhere, something knocked me flat and started dragging me across the slimy, blood-soaked dirt. I scrabbled at rocks, but nothing I grabbed onto held.

Aidyrth was turned away from me, shooting fire at another demon. I don't like to ask for help—not that I've had much of an opportunity, working the way I usually do—but somehow I'd gotten stuck in a tractor beam dragging me toward the maw into Hell.

I sent waves of power to chop through the invisible bands, but it made my situation worse. Somehow, whatever had hold of me was feeding off my magic, and I gained momentum. I had to get back on my feet. With a ridiculous amount of effort, I rolled into a ball and got my knees under me. Before I could spring upright, the force pounded me flat again. Grigori, Mae, and Aidyrth were busy knocking out demons. The hawk had another eyeball. I'd be damned if I'd bother them with my petty problems. I'd gotten myself into this mess by not being vigilant. I could jolly well get myself out.

No one likes a whiner, and Grigori had mentioned my first mission would be a test of my mettle. Guess I wasn't ambivalent about the Circle any longer.

The harder I fought, the faster I was hauled toward the

breach. I felt the vortex now, harsh and unmistakable with my name scrawled all over it. It went against the grain, but maybe I could outsmart the thing. Curling into a ball again, I went limp and cut the flow of my power. At least I'd stopped contributing to my own doom.

Would it think I'd given up? Or would it redouble its efforts? If it did, I was screwed. By the time I remounted a defense, it would be too late. Quietly, gently, I wound magic into a layered ward but held it close, not deploying it.

At first, I thought it was my imagination, but I was slowing down. Maybe the rift liked playing with its victims. I judged the distance between me and disaster. I'd slowed enough I might make it. My ward was very close to ready, but there'd be split seconds between when I launched it and when it fully protected me.

If the thing that had set its sights on me had quick reflexes, all my work would be for nothing. I slowed my breathing and put the finishing touches on the casting I hoped would save my ass. Counting back from three, I tossed my ward around me and sprang to my feet at the same time.

A protective layer snapped into place around me, and I loped away from the rift. Nothing tried to stop me until I was a good forty feet past where I'd fallen, and then it slammed into me with a vengeance. My ward absorbed the brunt of the blow.

I felt like jumping and cheering and fist pumping the air; I'd celebrate later. A quick glance through the smoky air showed Grigori rolling around in the dirt with his fangs buried in a demon's neck. The creature had lost its knife, but it was raking long, sharp nails down the werewolf's hide. Mostly, he couldn't penetrate Grigori's thick fur, but he'd carved gashes in the wolf's nose.

Aidyrth had immolated two more demons. Because it would be quick, I married my power to hers and pushed enough magic to stop their hearts. They were easier than the first one had been, maybe because they were already on fire.

A grunting shriek from Mae brought me spinning around in time to see two demons drive her to her knees. The hawk splayed his talons over one of the demon's heads and pecked his skull with enough force brains spilled out. I vaulted through the air and landed on the other demon figuring the force of the collision would knock him down. He swayed and let go of Mae, but he was still on his feet.

I had hold of his shoulders. First time I'd actually touched one, and my hands began to smolder. What the fuck? He didn't feel hot, but my flesh was burning.

"Never touch them," Mae shouted.

Power coursed from my abraded palms making them ache. The unfamiliar feel of Mae's magic mixed with mine. Between the two of us—and her hawk—we leveled the demons. They weren't dead, just sprawled on their bellies.

"We need Aidyrth," I said.

Mae shook her head and snapped her fingers. A wicked-looking spear jumped into her open hand, and she drove the point through one of the demons. Black blood geysered; Mae avoided it handily. The other demon scraped long, cracked nails through the dirt. In case he was thinking about getting up, I hauled off and kicked him in the ribs, wishing for stout leather boots.

The hawk clunk to him like a limpet, still pecking a tattoo against his skull. Grayish fluid joined hunks of white goop oozing through openings in the bone. Grigori was apparently tired of dicking with the demon he'd been fighting. Opening massive jaws, he closed them around the thing's neck and bit through bone, sinew, tendons, and whatever else was in there.

The demon's head rolled free. Aidyrth sidled near enough to stomp on it.

"Can we shut the rift?" I yelled.

The dragon shook her head. "Not worth the magic it would take, plus it wouldn't stay closed."

I kept a wary eye on the wound in the ground, expecting it to disgorge more demons. Apparently, they weren't team players. They must know some of their own had fallen, but no one so much as dropped by to investigate. The light that had flared from the breach slowed until it no longer pulsed like a hungry mouth.

Grigori shifted to his more familiar man form. The process was quick, and when he emerged he was dressed much as I'd seen him at the guild house. How in the hell had he managed that? I'd always thought shifters removed their clothes to avoid ripping them to shreds.

"Well done," he rumbled in his deep voice. "You especially, Shira. The assignment changed substantively, but you rose to the challenge. I will see you back at the guild house."

He draped an arm around Mae. Her bird joined them, and the three shimmered to motes of light. Guess I was the only member of the Circle who lacked the ability to teleport, but I could throw a pity party later.

Were we done? I scanned through dense smoke for more demons but didn't see any. The tunnel stank, reminding me of open pit graves with rotting corpses. I sidled to the two staked-out humans. What a wretched way to die.

Except they still weren't dead. One moaned piteously. Could a hospital salvage either of these men? I didn't believe so. They'd probably die before an ambulance arrived. A quick jolt of power from me stopped both their hearts. Mercy killings weren't exactly my style, but in this instance, I used my gift to end suffering, not create it.

"You did the right thing." Aidyrth had moved next to me without me realizing it.

I looked up at her. "There are others, " I said, wondering why they hadn't been clamoring to be cut loose.

She twisted her head atop her stalk of a neck and lumbered forward. I followed her, and then moved in front. About thirty feet up the passageway, three more men had been bound with chains. I sensed their life forces before I saw them.

Christ. One was Jake. What the fuck? Why hadn't he gotten out of Dodge when the getting was good. I fell to my knees and shook him, but he was nonresponsive. So were the other two.

"What's wrong with them?" I asked Aidyrth.

"Demon's breath," she said, "and remaining locked in place by those chains. Once we get them off and move the men outside, they should come around."

I fingered a length of heavy chain. It appeared to have been welded in place. Geez, where were bolt cutters when you needed them?

"Step aside," Aidyrth said and proceeded to hit the chain with focused bits of fire. The links clattered onto the ground. I stared at bolts that had been screwed into solid granite. This was far from the first time demons had held mortals here. Did they always knock them out? Maybe they preferred it when their fear was fresh. Anyone tethered here would be so unnerved watching the being-consumed-alive spectacle, they'd blow through all their adrenaline and end up limp as ragdolls.

And then they wouldn't be as much of a delicacy.

I still cradled Jake's head in my hands, willing his eyes to open. What was it about him? Why did I care? Me, who didn't give a damn about anyone except my parrot.

"Grab him," Aidyrth said. "I've got the other two."

I stood and utilized a magical assist to hoist Jake a couple of feet off the ground. Once I had him floating, I guided him the last quarter mile or so until the opening of the tunnel came into view.

Aidyrth was maybe a hundred yards away in a deeply wooded glen. I ferried Jake toward her before lowering him to the ground. He didn't seem any nearer to conscious than he'd been, but I'd wait until I was sure he could manage on his own.

The dragon started back toward the tunnels. I raced after her. "Did we miss someone?"

"Nay. I have other plans for this place. It shouldn't be allowed to remain."

"What can I do?"

"Watch and learn. We don't want anything splashy that will draw attention through satellite imagery, so we'll do this quietly."

I'm not sure why hearing her casually refer to satellites was so surprising. She lived in the modern world too, even if she didn't seem to fit there. Apparently, I had a whole lot of mental rearranging to do.

When she jostled my magical center, I joined my power with hers and followed along as she seeded power through the partially boarded-up entrance. When we reached the area with corpses, she channeled our skill deep into the earth. We set charges and beat a hasty retreat before they detonated.

Booms from beneath my feet were more vibration and localized heaving than actual noise. "Did we really wipe that unholy hellish spot off the map?" I asked.

"We did. Unfortunately, it's one of many. I wanted to send a message, but it won't make any difference over the long haul."

"Why not?"

The dragon turned to me, whirling eyes slowing and

softening. "Evil was here long before the rest of us. Nothing we can do will obliterate it."

"We have to try, though."

"Aye, we do."

I'd never considered wickedness in a global sense before. I'm not naïve. I understand bad things walk the earth, but what we'd fought today was larger than anything I'd envisioned. "I have a lot to learn," I muttered.

"Because you recognize it, you'll do fine."

Jake stumbled to my side. "Jesus. You're perennially bailing me out. Both of you."

"Why didn't you leave?" I asked point-blank.

"I tried." He shook his head. "It's a long story, but I'm on my way out of here now."

"Not that simple," Aidyrth said.

"What do you mean?" he and I asked nearly with one breath.

"You've seen too much," Aidyrth told him. "It places you in danger."

"What about them?" Jake jerked a thumb at where two other men remained unconscious.

"Do you know them?" I asked.

"Nope."

"Maybe we need to know what happened," I said to the dragon.

"Find out," she said. "I'll deal with the others while they're still out cold." Snatching them up, she spread her wings and took off into the night.

"Jesus." Jake's eyes were wide; wonder sheeted from him.

"You cannot say anything about any of this," I cautioned.

"Pfft. What makes you think I'd want to? They'd haul me off to the loony bin."

"Come on." I started toward a road with occasional headlights.

"Where are we going?"

"Somewhere we can sit inside and talk. You're going to tell me what happened."

"And then?"

"Depends on Aidyrth."

"What if I just walk away?" He arched both brows.

"You think we can't find you?"

After a long minute, he started to laugh. "Stupid of me, huh?"

As we walked toward hopefully another cheapy motel with a twenty-four-hour coffee bar, he turned toward me. "My life won't ever be the same, will it?"

It was an important question and deserved a serious answer. "I honestly don't know. If the dragon erases your memories of the bizarre stuff, then it will."

"Can she do that? Get rid of certain memories and leave the rest intact?"

I didn't know the answer to that one, either. Not exactly, but I fibbed a little with a murmured yes. He'd been through a lot; no reason to make it worse. What the fuck was wrong with me? Shira the straightshooter. Shira, the one where butter wouldn't melt in her mouth. Shira, who didn't give a crap whom she hurt along the way.

First, I'd eased the two mortals out of this life. And now I was downplaying mind swipes. A flashing sign for a Quality Inn dragged my attention front and center. "How about there?" I pointed.

"Works for me."

CHAPTER 13

Fortified with pastries and extra-large coffees from the motel's restaurant, we settled into another nondescript motel room. This one was quite a bit cleaner than the last, but Quality Inn is a national chain. Presumably, they have standards to uphold.

Jake wasn't overly chatty, so I didn't press things until he'd finished his iced croissant and half his coffee. The pastries were surprisingly fresh. I'd assumed they'd have a cloying day-old taste from stale shortening.

He placed his cup in front of him and wrapped his big fingers around it. I'd never noticed his hands before. They were calloused and looked as if he'd done hard time with manual labor. Not the prissy shit, but heavy equipment repair or something similar where brute strength ruled the day.

"After I left you," he began, "I was on my way to where

I have a go-bag stashed. I had to be careful, though. The shit in that bag was my ticket to freedom. If anyone followed me, they'd shred my ID documents, take the money, clunk me over the head, and no one would ever know."

"Kind of like being in the military where everyone's a trained killer," I muttered.

He nodded. "Decent analogy." A corner of his mouth turned downward. "We're good trackers too. Many of us hunted as kids. Not for sport, but so we'd have something to eat."

"Were you one of them?"

The question hung between us for long moments before he offered another terse nod.

"Why the hesitation?" I asked.

"I never tell anyone anything, not about me or about my business. Even something as inconsequential as that might be my undoing."

I understood. "The only way two people can keep a secret is if one of them is dead," I murmured.

"Something like that." Breath hissed from between his teeth. "Anyway, I was on foot. I'd considered a vehicle, but it's easier to keep an eye on things from ground level. I picked a circuitous route and stopped every so often, making certain I hadn't picked up a tail."

He was coming to the crux of how he'd been nabbed. I resisted the urge to feed him questions. We had time, some anyway, before I'd have to leave. Aidyrth and I still had targets to dispatch.

"I'm not certain quite how it happened"—Jake cleared his throat—"but one of our limos glided up out of literally nowhere. One minute, the street was empty—it was more of an alley than a street—the next, the car was just there. Running was out of the question. It would have made me look guilty and earned me a slug in the back of my head."

I spun my hand in a come-along gesture.

"I've always been careful not to paint myself into corners, but the minute whoever was in the car got a gander at my face, they'd know I had connections with magic on the other side of the fence line, if you get my drift."

"When they, erm, beat you up, they did it in front of an audience?" A tiny part of me recoiled in horror at the public spectacle aspect of this particular crime family's punishments.

"It's the family way." He tried to joke, but it fell flat. After another sip from his cooling coffee, he said, "A few of us are assigned to an internal police force. They keep order, usually by knocking miscreants around. Except I hadn't broken any rules."

He'd let go of his cup and curled his hands into fists.

"You assumed if you played straight with them, they'd do the same," I suggested. "And you're pissed they hung you out to dry."

"That's one way of putting it. I also feel cheated."

"You played by the rules, and they didn't." At his nod, I said, "You're ex-military, huh?"

His mouth twitched into half a smile. "That obvious, huh?"

"Maybe only to me. Go on. What happened after the car rolled up?" I tilted my cup back, disappointed to find it empty. The room had a Keurig, so I got up and added water and a pod to brew another cup.

"I turned around and faced the limo. One of the other bosses got out of the back seat and glared at me before making a crass comment about my face having made quite the recovery.

"I offered a noncommittal grunt and waited. He's not known for patience, and I sensed the darkness inside him." Jake grimaced. "I've never believed in this kind of crap. Always thought all those TV shows about paranormal shit were tripe."

"I'm still learning about the unseen world," I said in a show of solidarity and returned to the table with a fresh coffee.

"Says a lot since you're part of it," he replied. "The other boss, the one leering at me, ordered me into the car. I had to comply. Anyway, that's my last memory until I woke in the tunnel with you kneeling next to me. At first, I was convinced I'd died, and my mind had slipped a few cogs on the way out."

"No one questioned you about me or Aidyrth?"

"Not this time. Only before they roughed up my face, and then the questions were all about you. I can't see any of my bosses keeping a straight face and grilling me about a dragon."

He reached across the small table and placed a hand over mine. "Thank you."

"I haven't really done much."

"You've bailed me out a couple of times now. Hell, you suggested your place as a safehouse. It's above and beyond if you ask me. Not just thanks but many thanks. It's been a long time since anyone's done anything for me."

"I figured organized crime would have a brotherhood motif going."

He snorted derisively. "More like a watch-your-back one."

I angled my head to one side. "This is none of my business, but how'd you get from the military to where you are?"

"It was a circle. I signed up to get away from being poor and living in a crime-infested slum in Philly. The Marines gave me pride, taught me skills, and dumped me in the Middle East. It was worse than the inner city I was trying to escape, way worse. I did two tours and quit."

"Aren't there a bunch of perks for veterans? Like college on the cheap?"

"Yeah, and I went, but it always felt like I was playacting, like I didn't belong." He held up both hands. "It's enough. More than I've ever told anyone about myself, but you're easy to talk with."

He pushed to his feet. I expected him to make himself more coffee, or say it was past time for him to be gone. Instead, he walked to my side of the table, drew me upright, and closed his arms lightly around me. I could have ducked from beneath his embrace; I didn't.

When he dipped his head and touched his mouth to mine, I wrapped my arms around his back and kissed him. His lips were warm and firm against mine. Unlike in the limo that first night, he wasn't trying to "make" me. He was giving me choices. Himself too.

My tongue grazed his lips, and I bit softly, following each nip with a lick. He moved his hands. One upward, cradling the back of my head, the other down to the swell of my ass. When he pulled me against him, the bulge of his erection prodded my stomach.

His kisses grew more intense, more intimate. He swept the inside of my mouth with his tongue, and I sparred with it. Where my breasts were crushed against his shirtfront, the nipples pebbled into hard points. I hadn't been with a man in years. Once I pulled the cork out of the bottle, arousal swamped me, the intensity staggering and nothing like when I dragged out the box of sex toys I resorted to from time to time.

He made a low growling sound and strung kisses across my cheek to my ear and back again. I grabbed handfuls of his shirt and ground my body against his. In a very distant corner of my mind, I was aware if we were going to stop, it had to happen now.

Ripping my mouth from his, I asked, "Why?"

"Been asking myself the same thing." His voice had developed a low, sexy rasp. "Do you want to stop?"

There it was. Another choice, freely offered. "No."

"Do you know why?"

I shook my head. "I have a great toy box, but there hasn't been a man in my life for forty years." I winced. "Oops."

"I'm not going to ask how old you are. It doesn't matter." Moving one arm from behind me, he cupped a breast in his hand, pinching and tweaking the nipple through my top. Sensation crashed through me; heat slicked my thighs. I snaked a hand between us and curled it around the hard length of him. His cock was thick and long and captivating as hell. Suddenly, I couldn't deal with all the clothes between us.

Taking a step back, I said, "First one to be naked wins," as I dropped my jacket onto a chair and pulled my shirt over my head. My sports bra joined the pile of discarded clothes.

Jake just stared at me. "My god, you're a knockout. Men would fight wars over those tits." He dropped to his knees, threaded his arms around my waist, and took a nipple in his mouth while he fondled my other breast with his hand. The dual stimulation shot my heart into triple-time rhythm. Breath pounded from my chest and out my mouth in little panting gasps.

His hand ended up between my legs, and he lashed his mouth from one breast to the next, biting and sucking by turns. Between that and his palm rubbing my vulva through my jeans, I was lost. Sinking my fingers into his silky hair, I clung to his head while he tantalized my nipples.

Fingers busy at my waist, he undid my pants and slid them down my thighs, leaving only the nylon of my panties between his hands and my sex. I grappled with the sides of his shirt and tugged it over his head without unbuttoning it. Buttons popped off, flying across the room, but it didn't matter.

What did was the feel of his nakedness against me. Scars crisscrossed his chest, bullet holes, knife wounds, and a few I couldn't identify, but he was beautiful with coppery-gold skin, dark nipples, and muscles flowing beneath in an ever-changing pattern. I undid his belt and trousers. His cock fairly sprang into my hand.

The musky scent of him drove my arousal a few notches higher. I remembered that smell. Nothing like a male in heat to get a woman going. He stood and picked me up as if I weighed nothing. Once he'd laid me on one of two beds, he tugged off my shoes and then got rid of my khaki pants. Somewhere along the way, his clothes joined mine in a tangle on the floor, and he lay next to me on the bed, cradling me close as he explored my body with his fingertips. Every spot he touched caught fire.

The hot slick core of me needed him. It had been so long since a man had filled me to bursting, I'd almost forgotten the sweet urgency, the intensity, the sheer need.

I rolled us onto our sides and kicked a leg over his hip, opening myself to him, but he tossed me back the way I'd been and slithered down my body until his mouth was suspended over my sex. For the longest while, he breathed heat all around my distended nub.

My hips bucked. I grabbed his head, trying to force contact. I'd moved beyond thought. My body writhed from side to side, and I was moaning. I should watch it, this place probably had shit for soundproofing.

When his mouth collided with my clit, my body exploded. Forget about nuance, about long, lazy lovemaking. Driven by desperation, a climax rolled through me. The spasms had barely faded when he was on his knees with his cock seated at the entrance to my body. I reached for his hips, eager to draw him inside.

"Let me control it," he rasped and sank slowly into me, waiting as I stretched to accommodate his girth.

"You feel incredible, amazing," I panted.

He cupped the side of my face and lowered his mouth to mine. I tasted myself on him, salt and bitter, and wanted him with a fierceness transcending reason. He was fully encased in my body, and rocking gently before he withdrew slowly, teasing me with the head of his cock before sinking into me again.

Slow and nuanced gave way to feverish thrusting. He'd asked to be in charge, but I was lost in lust. Nails digging into his hips, I urged him to plumb me harder and faster. Another climax tantalized me before crashing over my head and drowning me in sensation.

Heat seared me as he painted me with gouts of semen. We strained against one another, heaving and gasping for air before he lowered himself atop me, gathered me close, and turned us onto our sides with his cock still buried inside me.

"That was special," he murmured. "Thank you."

"For me too," I told him. I didn't want to ruin anything, but I felt compelled to add, "I'm not a clingy kind of gal. Assassins don't let anyone get too close."

He chuckled, rich and low. "You think I don't know that? But we can be friends."

"We already are," I informed him somberly. "And I don't exactly have any, or I didn't before I met the dragon."

"Can you tell me about that?"

I shook my head.

"Figured as much." He kissed my forehead. "How about a quick shower, and then I'll get moving. I have a window here while the family regroups. I should be gone before it happens."

I untangled my limbs from his and draped my legs over the edge of the bed. "Are you still going to hang for a while at my place?"

He was on his feet, heading for the bathroom, but he turned toward me. "Is it all right if I do."

"Yes, of course."

"Then I will, but probably not for all that long. Just until I figure out what happens next for me. I can't go back to the family." He stopped for a moment, possibly getting his thoughts in order. "Maybe I could square things with them, but I don't want to. They found me guilty without benefit of a trial. I'm done with them."

Yeah. I wouldn't want to go back, either, but it wasn't my decision, so I kept my mouth shut. I watched as he covered the few feet to the bathroom. Such a stunning man with a gorgeous body. Broad shoulders, narrow hips, high ass, long muscled legs, and shapely arms. He wasn't slabbed with muscle like a hardcore bodybuilder, but his build was graceful, athletic. He moved with an easy instinctive gait that reminded me of wild animals on the prowl.

I heard the patter of water in the shower. I could have joined him, but I've kept my distance from men for a reason. I don't live the kind of life that lends itself to dinners at eight and domesticity. Instead of the bathroom, I went to the small wet-bar sink and wiped myself clean with warm water and towels. By the time he came out of the bathroom, swathed in a towel, I was dressed and sipping a cup of fresh coffee.

Nodding pleasantly, he got back into clothes that were dirty and stained. "Need to change these," he said, "and my shirt seems to need buttons, but I can skip it until I'm out of town."

"We're not done," Aidyrth's voice rolled through my mind. *"When will you return to the other hotel?"*

"An hour. Will that work?"

"Yes."

Jake's eyes narrowed. "You were just talking with someone, weren't you?"

"Yup. Aidyrth. How could you tell?"

"Something different kind of flickers around you. Same thing happened with Bruno when the darkness was inside him."

Intriguing. He sensed magic. Did he have any of his

own? It wasn't beyond the realm of the possible, but I had no idea how to check for such things. Obvious, in-your-face power, sure. But if he possessed magic, it was green, untrained, and buried under layers of denial.

Kind of like I'd been when I was only a kid and had blinded my first tormentor. I didn't believe I'd done it. And since I hadn't laid a hand on him, the only damning words were his. He said I'd done it. I denied the whole thing—and told the children's home people about him jamming his dick up my ass.

They hadn't cared for the message, so whether I was guilty or innocent, I was the one kicked out. It was my last orphanage. I hit the streets after that little incident and remained there.

"What should I call you?" Jake had walked close enough to lace his fingers with mine.

His words dragged me out of a spate of ugly memories. "Shira," I replied. "The Teague last name is the same."

He cast an appraising glance my way. His attention warmed me. "It fits," he said. "Irina didn't. Neither did Suzanne."

"Are you in the habit of deciding if people's names belong to them?" I'd tossed the question out lightly, but the easy expression left his face.

"Not deciding so much, as just knowing. I've never understood how it worked."

Hmmmm. More evidence of magic? Or wishful thinking on my part. This wasn't a time to explore any of it. I needed to get moving. I didn't have a car here, and it was a long way to the Hilton. I'd have the front desk call me a cab, but I still might end up late depending on traffic.

I squeezed his hand before letting go. "Safe travels," he said and smiled. Not a surface affair, it lit his eyes with warmth.

"Same to you." I wanted to kiss him, but if I did, we might not leave.

"I'll hang onto the burners," he told me. "See you, Shira."

I gathered up my jacket and the room keys, mostly so I wouldn't stand around like a lovesick puppy watching him walk away.

I gave it a few minutes before following him out of the room. My luck was running decently because there were a couple of taxis idling out front. I dropped the keys into a plastic bin labeled key-drop and flagged one of the cabs, my mind busy with what-ifs.

I wanted Jake to have power of his own, but it was selfish of me. So what if he did. It wouldn't suddenly change me into prime partner material.

No, but maybe he could join the Circle, and then at least I'd see him some of the time.

I rubbed my eyes, aware how tired I was. Whether or not Jake was part of the Circle, he and I could still carve out the occasional tryst. It wasn't smart, though. I'd only fucked him once, and he'd already taken up an oversized piece of real estate in my head.

My best bet was to forget about him. He'd said he

wouldn't be at my house very long, so if I stayed gone a couple more weeks, our paths wouldn't cross.

"Jesus," I mumbled, "have I always been this big a wuss?"

Yeah, I answered, *where men are concerned.* Irritation scoured a track through me. I wanted to scoop Jake up, run away, and stay gone forever, but my life wasn't like that. Nor would it ever be. Even if it were, his wasn't. We were cut from the same cloth: killers who'd always be on the fucking run. From everything.

"Hey, lady. You gonna get out, or what?" The cabby's strident voice surprised me.

"Um, yeah. Of course."

"Been idling four minutes. That's an extra five bucks over and above the fare."

I dug a twenty out of a pocket, chucked it over the divider into the front seat, and got out.

"What, no tip?" he shouted after me.

I didn't bother to turn around, just ducked inside the swinging glass doors and marched toward the elevators. Fuck the cabbie. Fuck Chicago. Just fuck everything.

As out of sorts as I ever got, I pounded toward my suite.

CHAPTER 14

Get a grip, one of my inner voices snarled.

Yeah, another chimed in. *Not like someone pissed in your Cheerios.*

No. The pissing in my Corn Flakes happened when I was ten and couldn't escape the fact I was different. Seventy years had passed; high time I got over it. Besides, given a choice, I'd take my magic over being a garden variety mortal any day.

My room was the same as when I'd left it. I did a quick check of some markers I'd left; they hadn't been disturbed. Meant no one had followed me from The Gwen to here. Not yet anyway. By the time they started seriously looking, I'd be gone. Unless I'd missed something, we were nearly done in Chicago.

Normally, I got in and out of job sites fast, but I'd never been tasked with crushing demons before. More accurately,

I'd never selected a job from the registry that looked like a setup for failure. From what I'd seen a few hours before, demon slaying required more than one mage.

It was moot. The registry was run by people like Jake's bosses, except they fell into more of a black-ops, less-organized category than mob families. Jake's group, and others like them, had their own assassins on payroll. The ones who posted to the registry were far less visible, and I'd never seen a non-human target on the list. It was a rare mortal who believed people like me existed.

I toed off my shoes and kicked back on one of the beds, not bothering to remove the bedspread. And then I jumped off just as fast. My clothes had to be filthy. I hadn't examined them, but I'd been sprayed with demon blood, brains, and other assorted goo. After stuffing everything into one of the plastic laundry bags conveniently provided by the hotel, I took a quick shower. Jake's scent was all over me, spicy and alluring. I hated to wash it off.

Geez, I was turning into a sentimental slob. Reminding myself of my earlier vow to steer clear until he'd left my house, I rinsed shampoo out of my hair and soap off my body. The water was tinged with the semi-permanent brown rinse I'd coated my pink tresses with. It left streaks on the towel too, and I reminded myself never to buy that brand again.

When I left the bathroom swathed in a towel, the dragon blew steam my way. It joined the mist wafting from the bathroom. Aidyrth was jammed into a corner, shoulders hunched so she didn't run up against the ceiling.

I hustled into fresh clothing and made myself another cup of coffee. Keurigs were ubiquitous in motels these days.

"How are you doing?" the dragon asked.

"Uh, fine. Why?"

"It was your first run-in with demons. Sometimes it leaves an...impression."

"Only that there's a shit ton I don't know." I climbed onto a bed so we were at eye level with each other. "Did I do all right?" It's not the kind of question I'd ever have envisioned asking anyone. If my target was dead, no matter how many blunders I'd made, success spoke for itself.

I was nervous as I waited for her assessment. I couldn't recall the last time I'd given a tinker's damn what anyone thought about me.

"It's a good question," she rumbled and turned it around. "How do you think you did?"

I scrunched my forehead. Did she know how close I'd come to being sucked into the portal? Should I fess up or pretend to be cool about everything? The weight of her whirling gaze raked me until I felt naked, exposed. Beyond her scrutiny, she was my bondmate. If I couldn't be honest with her, our relationship didn't stand a chance.

"I could have done better," I admitted and told her about my near brush with the vortex.

"Why didn't you call me?"

Because I'm stubborn when it comes to getting myself out of messes.

"I would have—if it had gotten any worse. They're not very bright, are they?"

"Who?" She raised a scaled brow.

"Demons," I clarified.

"They're smart in a feral, intuitive kind of way, but demons don't operate the portal."

"Who does?" I wasn't sure I wanted to know.

"Hell is its own entity, separate from Earth and other worlds, but it requires energy to maintain its integrity. Usually, blood sacrifices are enough. It was why the breach was located in the tunnel, and why demons were feeding it."

"Looked to me as if they were feeding themselves."

"That too. A win-win for all concerned."

"Except their victims," I said sourly.

"Aye. Back to the portal. It's sentient, and it felt the pull of your magic. One mage is worth buckets of human blood, so it set a trap to draw you in. It's intelligent in its own way, but when you made it appear you'd given up, it took your actions at face value."

"I get why it would avoid you or Grigori in full-fang mode, but why'd it pick me and not Mae?"

"You were closer." She shook a taloned foreleg in my direction. "Hell won't fall for that trick again."

"Noted." I crossed my arms under my breasts. "What's next?"

"You need to do a bit of footwork so we can plan for tonight."

I listened while she mapped out our other two targets. Also mob bosses, but from different organized crime families. Hopefully, demons had only inveigled their way into Jake's erstwhile group.

"I'll take care of it," I told her.

"Let me know when you're done," she said. "I'll take it from there."

"Does that mean we can leave here later tonight?"

"If we're done, we will return to the guild house."

I jumped down from my perch on the bed and settled on its edge to pull on my shoes. "What about me spending part of my time at home?"

She cast a peculiar look at me. "That will happen after you've learned more."

I propped my chin on an upraised hand. "I will never know enough to satisfy you, let alone myself, but I can't remain gone from home indefinitely."

"Why not? You'd have your choice of guild houses. They all have extensive libraries."

"Because I'm not willing to walk away from my other life. Not completely." Tilting my chin up, I said, "It was the deal we struck."

The dragon's jaws lolled. "So it was."

I'd readied more arguments, but she was gone. I had shit to do, but I took a few moments to have a good old-fashioned heart-to-heart with myself. I'd already decided not to return home if there was any chance Jake would be there. So why was I lobbying to go home tonight or tomorrow?

Was I just throwing my weight around in my new

partnership with Aidyrth? Or did I truly plan to show up, haul Jake into my bedroom, and not resurface for months?

What was it about him that drew me like a dowsing rod? He was striking, but there are lots of hunky men in the world. Try as I might, I couldn't come up with an answer. Not one that satisfied me.

I'd assumed I was immune to men. An inventive assortment of toys took care of my sexual needs. A man would only get in the way. He'd want to know all the nitty-gritty details about my work, which was impossible. I couldn't tell anyone what I did.

I could tell Jake. He'd understand, an inner voice piped up out of nowhere.

Was that it? I'd found a kindred spirit and didn't want to let him get away. Did him maybe having magic of his own play into the equation?

A glance at the clock told me I'd burned up half an hour in useless mental machinations. Time to get moving. I tucked my hair under a watch cap and zipped into a warm jacket. Rather than slinging my bag over a shoulder, I tucked my wallet and phone into an inner pocket to discourage petty thugs who might interpret my purse as an open invitation.

I left via a staircase that spit me out in an alley around the corner from the front of the hotel. What a difference fifty feet made. Where the hotel's main street side was crisp, clean, and orderly, the alley held a spate of smelly dumpsters cattycorner from me with bums digging through them.

I hustled away. There'd been a time when I'd done my own rooting through trash bins for food. It wasn't one of my more pleasant memories, but it left me with compassion for people who were hungry. I'd planned to take a taxi, but the day was pleasant with streaks of sun bouncing off wet pavement. It was cold, but not unbearable. Gloves would have been nice, but I didn't have any so I tugged my jacket sleeves lower.

My first stop was a smallish building tucked between two skyscrapers not far from Chicago's financial district. If Aidyrth was correct, one of our hits hung out here. I marched up steps in need of repair, slipping on ice, and assumed there had to be a rear entrance—or maybe one below ground. If anyone actually used the front door, they'd have chucked ice-melt pellets on the steps.

My only task was to determine if demons had gotten to our guy first. If so, it would change our approach dramatically. I reached for the door handle and tugged, not surprised to find it locked. No handy instructions posted anywhere. No buttons to press to get inside. I'd been planning to pretend to be lost, but that ruse fell apart if I couldn't enter easily.

Any other person who was lost would simply go next door and ply their questions about how to find whatever there.

The fine hairs on the back of my neck quivered; someone was watching me, but I couldn't let on I knew. I could scan for an electronic eye from the street, but unless I planned to return at night and take out their camera, locating it didn't matter. With a slight shrug, I slipped and slid back down the crooked steps and headed purposefully for the high-rise next door.

Its warm foyer was welcome after the perpetual chill, courtesy of winds raking Chicago's streets. A board off to one side listed the building's occupants. I pulled out my phone and made a show of consulting it as I stood in front of the board. It was unlikely whoever had been watching me from inside the other place had taken the trouble to get up and see where I'd gone.

After a few minutes, I pocketed my phone, trotted through the door and back to the busy street. Turning away from the building with broken steps, I walked to the end of the block intent on locating the alley running between this avenue and the next one over. Maybe I could approach from a spot where I wouldn't be a blip on someone's radar screen.

I gathered shadows around me, not quite invisible, but not far from it, either. This is why I prefer to work at night. A full-on ward eats up a lot of magic. I'd add to my partial one if I needed to. The alley was clogged with litter, but no bums were sleeping one off. Must be tough to be homeless here, and downright dangerous to pass out from too much booze. I bet at least a few drunks froze to death in drunken stupors.

I was behind the building I'd sought shelter in. Next one was where, presumably, Mr. Nasty hung out. A shiny black town car was jammed against a building on the alley's opposite side. Geez. What was it with mobsters and black cars?

The sound of a latch swooshing open stopped me dead; I filled in gaps in my ward and edged closer. Two burly men in topcoats lumbered down a longer set of stairs than I'd navigated in front. These were in better repair. The dude on the right was my target. How lucky could I get? He and his buddy were the only ones here—besides me.

I'm all about solutions. And opportunity. They didn't come knocking any more giftwrapped than this one. Intent on finishing him—and the other mobster—and exiting stage left, I sent lethal jolts of power at them both and waited for them to clutch their chests and crumple to the cobblestoned alley.

It didn't happen.

They turned toward where I stood, bodies changing by the second from men to demons as they pounded toward me. What the fuck? Why hadn't I caught the stench of sulfur and ozone? How had those bastards shrouded themselves?

I can't teleport, but I can move quickly. Redirecting my power, my next stop was the end of the alley. I could have gone farther, but not much. And I was still reeling from being duped—and what it meant. My heart pounded; my throat was dry, and I felt like puking.

Someone had identified me when I stood in front of the door. They'd intuited what I'd do next, which was downright terrifying, and set a trap to snare me. I smelled my pursuers now. What? Were they planning to run me down in full horn-and-scale-and-tail mode in the middle of East Avenue? The sidewalks were full of people.

I jettisoned my ward before leaving the alley and broke into a full-out sprint, dodging people as I passed them. Annoyed shouts of "watch it," and "slow down, girlie," followed me. No one said jack shit squat about what was behind me. Great. I was the only one who knew they were there. It was how they could get away with running after me.

What felt like a whip with a long tail snapped against my back, nearly flattening me. The next strike, the tail wound around my ankles, working on tripping me. If I fell, I was done for. Instead of running in a straight line, I feinted from side to side. A cop yelled at me. I kept on going. Let them think I was crazy. All that mattered was getting away.

I risked another short hop. It gave me a couple of blocks' cushion, but that wouldn't last.

Demons can ward themselves—and they're as quick as I am. Good to know. A cabstand was only a few feet away. Not at all sure a car would provide an escape, I dove into the front taxi and rattled off an address down by the rail yards, hoping against hope I hadn't signed the driver's death warrant.

We lurched away from the curb, and I girded myself to hop out of the cab if demons teleported into it. Maybe they were as handicapped as me in that regard, but I couldn't bet on it. Or anything. Raising my mind voice, I called Aidyrth and told her where to meet me. I'd picked the first chintzy motel where Jake and I had gone to ground.

The dragon didn't answer. Had she heard me? I'd find out quick enough.

After asking if I was all right, the cabbie didn't say a word until he pulled into the motel parking lot. It looked even shabbier in the fading afternoon light than it had after dark.

I counted out the fare, handed it to him, and went to the office, intent on renting another room. The twenty-five bucks was cheap enough, I'd never miss it. The same clerk sat behind a grill of windows. He grinned, displaying a couple of broken teeth. "Like it here, huh?"

"It has its charm." I grinned back and pocketed a key. I didn't remain in the room long. The adrenaline had subsided, leaving me wrung out. Once night fell, I made my way across the fence and into the rail yards and hunkered down to wait.

Aidyrth thumped heavily to the ground about five minutes later. "Demons are on the warpath. What did you do?"

I told her, followed by, "In my defense, it never occurred to me they'd masquerade as mobsters. Can they teleport?"

"Yes. They're also master shapeshifters, but you knew that part. How do you think they insert themselves into men's lives to tempt them?" Smoke wafted from her mouth before she continued. "If they held onto their real forms, people would run shrieking for the hills."

I'd had time to think during my short stint in the room. Standing as tall as I could, I said, "If this was my operation, I'd be on my way out of here."

The dragon cocked her head to one side. "Really? How well do you think that would work for you?"

"No one's been able to find me before." Defensiveness rose in a hot tide; I squelched it before more words came out. Ones lauding my competence. I'd gotten myself into this mess because of ignorance; better not to compound it with more of the same.

"You've never pissed off supernaturals."

"Yeah I have. Vampires, but they go to ground in the daytime." I stopped long enough to blow out a measured breath. "If leaving won't cool things down, then we have to kill more of them. Enough so they go back to the old home place, fire-and-brimstone-central."

Aidyrth turned her head to the side and shot a stream of fire-laden ash skyward. "That's the spirit, except we can't do it from here."

"But they're here, we're here... I don't understand."

Rather than explaining, she asked, "Whatever possessed you to take a shot at them while you were alone?"

"I told you—or maybe I didn't—one looked exactly like our target. I assumed it was a stroke of fortune. He was there. I was there. I figured the other fellow with him could be cannon fodder, collateral damage, so I went for it."

I shrugged. "Figured I may as well. I absolutely did not scent demon on anything, or I'd have been more cautious."

"Interesting. I can always sense them, but our powers are different. Perhaps this is my fault for sending you out on a scouting expedition."

Breath puffed from my mouth, making clouds in the still night air. "I absolutely do not care whose fault anything is. What do we do next? You said we can't fight from here. Will we be taking a field trip to Hell?"

"In a manner of speaking." She flapped a wing. "Get on."

It was tempting. The temperature hovered in the mid-teens. With the ever-present wind, it was more like single digits. "Where are we going?"

She angled her long neck, winding it around until her head wasn't too far above mine. "You'll have to trust me. I have no idea who's listening, and mind speech isn't a hedge. It can be intercepted as readily as someone eavesdropping outright."

It was all the answer I'd get, so where was my hesitation? I rocked from foot to foot, no closer to mounting the dragon than I'd been a minute before. "Will it just be us?" The previous night, Grigori, Mae, and her hawk had been part of the lineup.

Aidyrth nodded. "If I were following the rules, I'd request backup, but in this instance I'm not convinced more of us will matter."

"What rules?"

"The ones governing the Circle that you've yet to absorb."

There it was again. My almost total lack of knowledge about not just the Circle but everything magical beyond what I'd scoped out for myself. Maybe this whole Circle of Assassins gig had been a bad idea. Probably a whole lot of the mages would be like Loren, who'd be convinced I didn't belong.

I wasn't inclined to have to prove myself over and over again.

"Get on," Aidyrth repeated. She hadn't raised her voice, but its meta-message was unmistakable. Sort of a do-this-or-we're-finished note.

"I need to know more," I insisted, damned if I'd fold like some chickenshit poker player.

"Do you trust me?"

"So far. You've never given me reason not to."

"I've known about you far longer than you've known about me. I went to a lot of trouble to locate and entice you to join me. I was cautious, took my time. If after all that, I chose badly…"

She didn't finish her thought. She didn't have to. This was one of my prime motivators for working alone. I didn't want to let anyone down. My fuckups were mine and mine alone. No ripple effects to trip anyone else up.

When I finally climbed onto her back, my ambivalence must have been bleeding out all over the place. She hadn't said another word. Neither had I. Was our partnership doomed after whatever came next was over?

I had no idea how I felt about that. I wasn't in the habit of feeling much of anything. Not that I didn't have feelings, but I was a master at subverting them, shoving them off to one side until they stopped nagging. It was why my reaction to Jake had been such a surprise.

I'd tried to chalk it off to lust incarnate, but it ran deeper than that.

Still silent, we'd been airborne for a while. A retreat to my solo status would be a relief, but it would leave me with a sad, broken place. And I'd miss Aidyrth. We hadn't traveled many miles together, but I really liked her.

No need for decisions. Not yet. First, we had to make it through a demonic bloodbath. The reminder cut through all the mental baggage dogging me. I dropped my reservations into a pit, slathered magic over them, and instructed them not to bother me.

Aidyrth was flying in a slowly descending circle, which meant we were landing. Not much in the way of lights glittered below, so we must have traveled quite a way from Chicago. I started to ask where we were, but didn't. Location didn't make any difference; what we did once we were on the ground was what mattered.

CHAPTER 15

A large, flat field stretched around us, sloppy with mud. Dead ahead, openings into the ground had been boarded over. It looked like a horizontal version of the deserted mines outside Chicago. From what I could tell, the place had sat empty for a long while, perhaps years.

"Can we talk yet?" I murmured from a spot I'd returned to after walking a broad circle around the jagged holes. Resident rodents poked snouts between wooden slats and chittered at me, annoyed I'd disturbed their nesting ground.

"We have to, no choice," she said into my mind. *"This place was a copper mine. Mortals abandoned it after demons set up much the same type of operation you've already stumbled across. The gateway is still here. I'm banking on no one from the other side keeping an eye on it."*

"*Where are we?*"

"*Canada.*"

Wow! We'd traveled a long way in a short time. Aidyrth must have mixed teleport magic in with her normal method of flying. I wished I could fly, but I'd settle for being able to teleport.

"*We're going down there?*" I angled my chin at one of the holes. They all had barbed wire around them. *Keep Out* signs and ones warning *Danger* flapped in a staunch, icy wind.

"*We are. This will be as quick as we can make it. We kill whatever we run into, and then we leave.*"

I probably shouldn't have questioned her, not after my reluctance to get onto her back, but following blindly isn't my style. "*I'm not seeing how this will fix anything. All it will do is piss them off more. Besides, there are two of us and*"—I faltered since I had no idea what kind of numbers we'd face—"*god knows how many of them.*"

"*We have to do something. They nearly had you.*"

Her loyalty warmed me, made me feel both grateful and unworthy. "*I agree about striking back, but we have to do something that will truly send them packing. Can we bomb the place?*"

"*Drop explosives into Hell?*"

I nodded, waiting. It had been an off-the-cuff suggestion, but I favored explosives if I had to wipe out something big and I didn't want to be too close when it happened. It wasn't as elegant as looking my targets in the eyes and watching the light fade from them, but C4 was extremely effective.

"Is that something you can construct?" she asked, back to softly spoken speech.

"Yup. Sometimes getting the raw material takes a while, but I have contacts."

"Grigori might balk. Blowing things up has never been a Circle strategy."

"Do we have to tell him?" I winced. "Eh, that didn't come out quite right."

"We do."

"Help me understand why we could engage in a stealth suicide message and drop into Hell from where we are, kicking demon ass along the way, but we can't do something like bomb them, which would be a hell of a lot safer."

"We're warriors. A bomb is cheating."

I snorted back laughter. "Nothing is cheating if it gets the job done."

Aidyrth might have been smiling. "I told Grigori fresh blood was a good idea. Back onto me. Our next stop will be the guild house. You can pitch your case. If he's in agreement, he might have ways to procure what you require."

I cast a last glance at the holes in the ground. This place held a deserted air, but something about it got my hackles up. "How many spots like this are there? Portals into Hell?"

"Many. Why?"

"You picked this one because you figure no one is watching it?" At her nod, I went on, "Do they post guards or something?"

"They used to, more to prevent Hell's denizens from leaving than to keep anybody out. No one volunteers to enter."

Despite the raw, sour feel of the place, I was curious. "Can we teleport from down there?"

"Aye." Fire streamed from her open jaws; she understood what I was suggesting and welcomed the chance to snuff out a life or two—or ten.

I took a running start and flew through the air, landing on her back. *"Long as we're here—and no one's expecting us—we might take a peek around. See what we face. It'll help determine the best placement for explosives."*

Her power rose around us, linking with mine. Instinctively, I built a ward; it meshed seamlessly with hers. The iced-over mud frittered to nothing, replaced by rocks lining a low-ceilinged passage. The same dank smell was worse here. More rodent than rot, with dregs of residual evil that burned my nostrils.

I was almost crushed between Aidyrth's back and the slimy roof of the tunnel. It wasn't a position where I could do anything except cling to her, which made me worthless. Moving slowly, I slithered backward until I could let myself down quietly, the soles of my running shoes slipping on the rocky surface.

We moved forward, not making any noise. Aidyrth's clawed rear feet did a far better job navigating on the loose, rock-laden ground. I'd dropped behind her, mostly because the space was too narrow for me to take the lead.

She wouldn't have liked it, anyway.

Putrid smells thickened as we moved along a gradually downward-sloping path. Abandoned mining equipment littered alcoves. The damned rats were worse than a herd of geese with all their squeaks. I visualized piles of garbage, animating them as I went.

It did the trick. Convinced a feast had materialized, our rodent honor guard dove into my illusion. Rats aren't the smartest. By the time they figured out they'd been duped, we'd be long gone. The tunnel had widened a little; I fell in next to Aidyrth. Stones had yielded to dirt as we reached the end of the road for the copper mining operation. Someone had piled bricks to ceiling level at the end of the corridor we'd been walking along. We'd reached the culmination of men's incursion in this spot; silly of them to think bricks could keep ghouls out.

Not just bricks. Crosses hung from several places, and someone had splashed blood around. No longer crimson, it had mostly flaked off, but I could make out sigils against evil.

The prickly feeling against my skin had intensified, and a sucking sensation wafted through the barricade. Suddenly, it made sense. Probably, a few hapless mortals had been swept into demon traps. The wall definitely cut the drawing sensation.

I employed my extremely limited teleport ability and ended up on the far side of the wall. The tunnel was lower here, narrower. Shit. Aidyrth probably wouldn't fit. Bouncing back to her side, I murmured, "Tight quarters ahead. Wait here. I won't be long."

Before she did something like order me not to go, which would not have sat well, I bounded back through. The downward cant to the path intensified. I wasn't exactly slipping and sliding straight downhill, but close to it. More rocks formed a ring, one I'd have to walk through.

Not trusting the looks of the thing, I probed gently with magic, keeping my touch light. How far was I from Hell's actual entrance? I added a wrinkle to my ward to keep me from being propelled forward. The farther I went from the bricks, the beefier the drag. Smaller rocks rolled in constant motion, subject to the inexorable pull, but they covered the sound of other rocks I loosened.

Not that I've ever wondered how a magnet felt, but now I knew.

The current question wasn't how much farther I should go, but whether I could cross the circle without alerting someone. It seemed benign enough, and I didn't sense anyone, good, bad, or indifferent, anywhere close to me. Besides, if I was going to return here, or to another gateway like it, I'd have to get closer than this to plant any kind of explosives and have them be more than a petty annoyance.

It decided me, and I ran lightly through the circle. The rocks in it gave way, pelting me as they bounced off my warding. Was this an environmental distraction? Or was I living on borrowed time because I'd tripped an early warning system? Hanging around to find out wasn't wise, but I was past the rocks, so I sprinted downward, determined to locate a spot to plant ordnance.

The passage necked down; the dirt under my feet turned to piles of rocks, most of which weren't solid, teetering and wobbling as I continued past them. I slowed to avoid twisting an ankle. The place had been pitch-black, so dark I'd been using my psychic vision to navigate. Light flickered ahead, and I halted my forward motion fast.

It was tougher than it might have been; small boulders tipped and tilted, threatening to send me on my way. The guttural hum of voices speaking the same nasty language I'd heard the other night pricked the edges of my hearing.

Excellent. I done what I set out to do. This was close enough. Time to go. I turned and started up the steep incline, still trying for stealth. It was impossible. Rocks rattled and rolled under my feet, and, for every step forward, I slid back two. After five minutes, I was back to where I'd begun. The relentless pull of Hell made escape far harder than I'd imagined it would be. Clearly, this hadn't been one of my brightest moves. The voices were louder now, definitely louder and not my imagination. Sweat dripped down my sides despite the cold; my heart thrummed so fast I figured any demon worth his salt could locate me. They're drawn to anything with a pulse, not unlike Vampires.

Deepening my warding, I ducked behind a large boulder and quieted my mind. It wasn't easy. I was terrified. Being trapped underground is one of my worst nightmares. The scratching of claws on stone moved nearer. Damn I wished I understood their language. Was this a routine inspection on their part, or had they heard me and come to investigate?

Once I hid in a swampy cave in Thailand for three days, pinned down by the drug runners I'd been hired to wipe out. The filthy water had taken a toll—and I'd picked leeches off constantly—but I hadn't been especially worried. If I'd been caught then, a nice clean bullet through the brain would have ended me. If I were apprehended now, they'd torture me as they sucked every last morsel of power from my bones.

My line of thought wasn't helping. I cleared my mind, and then did it once more. My heartrate stabilized; the cool, detached mindset that had seen me through many dicey situations descended. I glommed onto it.

Demon stench, a combination of months' old stale sweat and rotting flesh, surrounded me as three of them passed by yammering at one another and pointing. Okay. It appeared they'd determined someone had been here, but if they'd sensed me, they wouldn't have walked past and on up the hill.

I'd had such a fuck of a time with the same steep incline, I kept my eyes glued to where they walked. Granted, their physiology was different: clawed feet and a forked tail for balance, but they were to the right of where I'd been. Less loose rock and the faintest of paths.

Should I follow them? It would make things simpler to move past the stone circle that had obviously sounded some kind of alarm. The more I considered it, the better I liked the idea. Otherwise, my next trip through the stones would trigger the same alarm. If the demons convinced themselves their system had malfunctioned, or been activated by a stray gust of wind, having it go off a second time would kill their theories.

They'd be back in a trice, hunting me. It was maybe half a mile from the stone circle to a place I could handily teleport to where Aidyrth was waiting, probably impatiently at this point. Even if I took off on a dead run, they'd catch me.

No time to think this to death. Either I followed my instincts—or not. My feet began moving before I was aware I'd come to a decision. I did my damnedest to travel silently, but I dislodged the occasional rock as I traversed the slope.

Each time a rock clattered down, breath caught in my throat, and I halted. One stray rock could be accidental; two or more in close proximity would be suspect. Finally, I reached the path I'd missed before. The demons were so far ahead, I couldn't see them. Reaching them in time to tag team their crossing of the stones would take some doing on my part.

Being quiet and rushing require two totally different approaches. I did the best I could, but I was panting by the time the demon in the rear came into view. Damn. I was nowhere near enough to make it. Not at the rate I was managing. Any quicker, and they'd hear me for certain.

Did I have enough power to keep up my ward and jump

myself closer? More importantly, if I used magic to close on them, would they feel it? Warding is power turned inward. It's meant to be unobtrusive, unnoticeable. Transport spells were more of an in-your-face affair.

While I thought, I clambered upward. This might be a natural shaft, or maybe demons had built it. Mortals hadn't. Anything with this level of cant wouldn't work for a mining operation. Heavy equipment couldn't navigate it. A side benefit of movement was terror no longer consumed me. It was there, all right, but no longer front and center.

I tested a tiny jump. It only bought me about three feet, and came remarkably close to dislodging an entire rubble pile. That settled things. No jump spells. Not until the terrain leveled off. I couldn't exert the level of control I'd need to ensure I didn't make enough of a racket to wake the dead.

The rump of the last demon was still in sight. Meant I hadn't lost ground, but neither had I gained any. After far longer than it had taken me to traipse down the slope, I crested the steepest segment. The demons were strung out about a hundred feet ahead of me. The lead monster had nearly reached the stone circle.

His jabbering and pointing ramped up a few notches as he sashayed from this side to that grabbing rocks in the circle and shaking them. I edged as close as I dared. I've never liked it when my options neck down to a single choice. But I was there. I'd wait until this bunch were well and truly gone, and then I'd make a run for it.

They move faster than you, my inner critic reminded me.

I didn't bother answering. Slipping into a small declination in the wall, I waited for the demons to shut up and go back to demon central, or Hell central, or whatever they called home.

It didn't happen. Instead, they hunkered on the far side of the stone circle. One drew something bloody and dripping out of a fold in his scales and proceeded to munch on it. One of his companions held out a hand and barked something that had to mean, "Pony up, bud."

The one with the prize skinned his lips back from his teeth and growled. The third one stepped between them. At first, I thought he was intent on playing peacemaker. Instead, he ripped a chunk off the prize. The first demon yowled his displeasure and lunged for the one who'd stolen from him. In the process, the remainder of the chunk of flesh went flying.

Demon number three made a dive for it and popped the whole thing into his mouth. Never mind it was far too big and hung over his jowls as he chewed furiously.

If I hadn't been in such a crappy position, I'd have laughed. They reminded me of a pack of wolves squabbling over a carcass. Good news for me, though. Their attention was a million miles away. After blowing out a breath to steady my resolve—I had to get out of here, sooner rather than later—I left my protected position and threaded my way across what remained of the stone circle while the demons rolled around in the dirt pummeling each other.

I'd have been wiser to move slower, but freedom was so close I could taste it. I shifted from a walk to a trot to a full-out sprint. Fifty feet to where I could jump out of this hellhole. Forty. Breath seared my lungs. I expected to be set upon from behind at any moment, but I didn't want to take precious seconds to check.

Thirty feet. Twenty. I said to hell with caution and launched my jump spell. Driven by desperation, surely it could go twenty feet farther than usual.

It did. I rolled out into the frozen ground, drained as if I'd run a marathon. Twice.

"You stink of demon. Where are they?" Aidyrth demanded.

"Half a mile within," I gasped, working around lungs that believed no amount of oxygen could compensate for what they'd gone through.

"Stay put," she barked and vanished.

I blinked at the spot she'd been. What the hell? I didn't have much choice but to stay put. Not being able to teleport was a huge impediment. If she didn't come back, I'd be stuck first figuring out where in Canada I'd ended up and then negotiating travel arrangements home.

Chill from the ground rose, sinking into my bones. I'd begun to shiver by the time I dragged myself to my feet, wrapped my arms around myself, and focused power to warm my frozen fingers and toes.

How much time had elapsed? I'd been so occupied first getting my breath, and then not freezing to death, I hadn't kept track. Should I go after Aidyrth? Should I try to reach Grigori with telepathy?

I shelved that notion. Aidyrth had made it clear we

were out here as rogues. Moving nearer the bricked-up hole, I prepared to jump back inside. Maybe she'd gotten stuck. I wasn't certain what I could offer beyond moral support, but I couldn't let her languish in there by herself.

Booming rolled toward me, along with sharp cracks, rumbles, and an ominous roar. Fire shot past the space between the top bricks and the opening. Aidyrth's bulk formed next to me, wings spread. I'd never used magic to propel me upward, but the same process that sent me forward should work.

It did, kind of. I got close, but the dragon had to catch me with her forelegs and toss me onto her back. We sped away. Heady with the knowledge we'd escaped, I asked, "How in the hell did you fit in there?"

"I didn't. It's why it took me so long, I had to do everything remotely."

"Everything, as in you blew the place to bits?"

She puffed gouts of smoke and ash. "Aye. I cheated, but those three will never bother anyone again."

My mouth spread into a grin. I was glad they were dead. Ugly, mean, misshapen fuckers. "Do you know their language?"

"Aye."

"Teach me the basics before we go out again. They were chattering like a pack of crows, and I'd have given a whole lot to know what they were saying."

"But your magic will translate anything."

Whoa. News to me. "All right. Then please teach me how to do that."

"Certainly."

We'd only been in the air for maybe ten minutes when we shot through a jagged gap, flew through gray mist, and emerged in the guild house courtyard.

"Neat trick," I murmured.

"Not a trick at all. Grigori set up specialized ley lines to enhance our access to the various guild houses. In case someone is injured, it could spell the difference between solid healing or a mage being saddled with ill health—or worse."

We landed with a *thunk*, and I jumped down.

The dragon lumbered toward the same spot we'd received our orders before, a grove of white oak trees a little way distant from the courtyard. I followed, eager to present my let's-bomb-the-fuck-out-of-them strategy.

Even if Grigori didn't agree, I might just do it anyway.

CHAPTER 16

It took a while before Grigori materialized, but that was okay by me. I took advantage of the time to settle my thoughts and develop the seeds of a presentation.

"Glad you're all right," I told Aidyrth.

"Aye. I was worried about you too, but so long as I maintained a link to your energy, I knew you were alive."

"There's something else I'd like you to teach me," I told her and grinned crookedly. "The list is long."

"Growing longer by the moment." She grinned back.

"I understand there's been an alteration in our plans." Grigori strode into the grove and added a layer of magic to better conceal the rest of our conversation. He shook his head. "Who would have thought Chicago would be overrun with demons."

"Not overrun," Aidyrth corrected him, something I wasn't ready to tackle—yet. "They appear to have infiltrated the various groups in charge of the city, though."

"Don't let the cops hear you say that," I mumbled.

"Suppositions aside," Grigori said. "You ran into demons. What we did in the mine didn't discourage them."

"Far from it." I did speak up then. "They have my name etched into their brains."

Aidyrth detailed our jaunt to Canada, ending with, "It wasn't nearly enough. Ending those three wasn't the wisest idea. It will only rile them up more, but I couldn't resist. They were on the young side and easy pickings."

My eyebrows shot up. Another tidbit I didn't know. "They're harder to kill when they're old?" I inquired.

"Much like us," Grigori replied. He stopped there, but he had to be wondering what rock I'd crawled out from under.

"Shira has an idea that could save us time," Aidyrth said and focused her attention dead on me. Grigori did the same.

Showtime.

I swallowed around a big dry patch in my throat, aware I was on the verge of a major case of nerves. It was ridiculous. The worst thing that could happen would be he'd laugh in my face, and we'd do what he wanted. If that happened, it would offer a snapshot into my future with this group. When he'd recruited me, I hadn't been certain I was cut out to be a soldier in any army. Even an elite paranormal assassin one.

Nothing about that had changed.

"Did you change your mind?" Aidyrth asked me.

"Not at all." I blew out a breath and started talking. "I understand this isn't how you usually handle things," I told Grigori.

He flapped a hand my way. "Skip the caveats. What are you considering?"

"Whenever I've accepted a major job—and remember it's always been just me—I've employed two strategies that had a big impact from a distance."

"For instance?" Grigori pressed. He seemed irritated I hadn't actually ponied up anything specific yet.

"Poison or explosives. Both can be planted ahead of time. Poison takes care of itself. Bombs run off remote detonators or timers. I wasn't thinking it would be practical to use a toxin since I have no easy way of getting to the demons' central kitchen—if they even have such a thing.

"But bombs could work. It was what I was doing beyond the mine boundary in the last spot Aidyrth and I went. Checking how close I could get without being noticed."

"Hell is a big place," Grigori said.

I tried to pick up an inflection, but I didn't know him well enough to read the nuances in his speech.

"It is," I agreed, "which is why I figured we could select four likely spots, plant a big honking bunch of C4 in each of them and detonate them at roughly the same time. Obviously, we won't wipe everything out, but we'll create enough chaos, they'll be years digging themselves out."

I turned my hands palms up. "Means they won't be bothering us for a while, and we can get on with projects like the Chicago one, unimpeded. Killing mortals is a walk in the park by comparison."

Grigori chuckled. "You've done this before? Employed ordnance?"

"Yup. Several times. Getting hold of what I need is the rate-limiting step. Once I have it, I know how to build a bomb and attach it to a remote. Or it could run off a timer. That would mean—"

"I know what it means," Grigori cut in. "Timers are better. One of us would have to be close to depress a remote switch."

Aidyrth blew a plume of smoke upward. She'd switched her spinning gaze to Grigori as both of us waited for him to bless this project—or not.

"How long would it take you to construct the bombs?" he asked.

"Really?" I tried not to squeal, but it was a losing proposition. I'd been certain he'd look down his nose at me and sneer. Since he was still asking questions, he was seriously considering this.

"How long?" he repeated.

Oh yeah. He'd asked me a question. I creased my brow as I reconstructed what I had in the basement of my house. Everything but the actual explosive was simple to procure. I had the makings for two good-sized bombs, already. "Depends how easily I can come by the C4."

"What exactly is that?" he asked.

I wasn't certain how much detail he wanted, but he'd tell me to shut up if I gave him too much. "I use the same mix the Army does. It's 91percent explosive, bound with a plasticizer to make it more stable and a thickener that has a few elements including motor oil. The only stuff that's challenging to come by is the actual explosive. It's a nitroamine and closely controlled."

His mouth spread into a smile. "Thought you dropped out of school."

"Doesn't mean I couldn't find what I needed in libraries. But the Internet has been a huge boon. Nothing I can't research there so long as I keep my hacking skills in fighting shape."

"If you agree," Aidyrth addressed Grigori. "I will determine where to plant the bombs Shira builds. Once they're ready, we can assemble teams to sneak them into position."

"It's doable," he agreed, "and I'm warming to the idea."

I asked the same question I'd asked the dragon my first trip to this guild house. "Where are we? Remember, I don't teleport. The bombs are reasonably stable once they're built, but I don't want to risk moving them by magical means."

"How have you transported them?" Grigori asked.

"By car. Which leads me to my second point. It would

be good if these four locations were somewhere that didn't take too long to get to by vehicle."

"So, not in Siberia?" Grigori raised a russet brow.

"Something like that," I replied.

His expression turned somber. "This is why I've stuck with magic, rather than blending technology with it. Your explosives would probably survive a teleport, but it's an unknown."

"We could test it," Aidyrth ventured. "Loop a few bands of power around a small bomb and see if we can move it without it exploding."

"We'll work on it," Grigori said and turned to me. "The main ingredient, the one that's hard to get, let me know if you run into problems."

"It's expensive. I can cover it, but..."

"How expensive?"

"Depends who has it. The markup varies wildly. You never did say where we were. How can I reach either of you once I'm back home?"

"Is that where you're going?" Aidyrth asked.

"It's where my supplies are. And a makeshift lab in my basement."

"We are off-world," Grigori said and rattled off a string of numbers.

"What's that?" I asked.

"My cell phone, but you already have it." One corner of his mouth twitched.

Before I could protest, say he'd never given it to me, I remembered he was who'd hired me—for a hit in Cuba.

Except he'd been the target, and the whole thing had been an elaborate ruse. "So I do," I murmured.

"I will see you home," Aidyrth said, "and then I'll work on my part of things. Where will you be?" she asked Grigori.

"The guild house in Nevada."

"Location?" I looked from one to the other of them.

"I'll show you," Aidyrth said.

I felt her gather power. We'd come to a decision, but work lay ahead. A whole lot of it. I kind of enjoy making explosives. There's a simplicity to it that appeals to me. I needed to take stock, figure out precisely what I'd require, and put out feelers to a couple of different dudes. Hopefully, they didn't know one another because I planned to amass enough plastique to blow half of North America to smithereens.

"Thank you for trusting me," I told Grigori.

"I'm still somewhat ambivalent, but if this works, it will add another layer to our toolbox."

"Some won't trust it," I muttered, thinking of Loren and his wolf.

"That would be their problem. Now get moving." Grigori turned away in clear dismissal.

Aidyrth draped her spell around me, and we were gone. I'd never told her where my house was, but she didn't ask. Maybe she could find it by scent. As we shot through blackness, I remembered Jake. "Uh, probably should tell you Jake may be at my place."

"Really? Why?"

"I offered it to him before the demons shanghaied him. Remember? You even asked about me doing that. He needed a spot to go to ground, where no one could find him. My house is perfect for that. Besides, I didn't know when I'd get back there, and my parrot could do with some attention."

"Mmph. Is there room for me inside?"

"Yeah. Extra-tall ceilings. Large rooms, but you'll really enjoy the deck. It overlooks Lake Washington."

Did dragons swim? I had no idea. I felt certain they could swim, but whether or not they liked water was a big unknown. "Can you tell if Jake has magic?"

Christ. Where had that come from? I needed to monitor my brain better, ride herd on what slipped out of my mouth. "Sorry. Never mind," I mumbled.

"You must suspect he's more than strictly mortal," Aidyrth observed. "Or you wouldn't have asked."

"True, but it's all right. You don't need to answer."

"I know, but I will, anyway. I have ways to tell if someone has magic, but so do you. You sense magic, right?"

I thought about it. "If it's strong enough and in my face, sure. But before I figured out I wasn't like everybody else, I spent a lot of energy trying to be normal. Didn't realize I was running from the truth until I accepted I could do shit most people couldn't. During all that denial, I shielded my power, so it wasn't very visible. Maybe he's doing the same thing, except he's a hell of a lot older than I was, which means he'd have gotten better at it."

"What made you ask the question about him in the first place?"

I shrugged. "He could sense telepathy between us, and he noticed an alteration in Bruno and some of the other mob bosses when demons were in the driver's seat."

"Some mortals are sensitive to alterations in auras," Aidyrth explained. "It could be as simple as that, or he might have power of his own. If it's true, why wouldn't he want to claim it, hone it into something he could benefit from?"

I knew the answer to that one. In spades. Because I'd been there. Except I'd been a kid, and no kid wants to be different. "Depending on what you come up with," I replied, "we can ask him."

"Should I aim for the lake or inside your house?" Aidyrth asked.

"Inside. It will save power since you won't have to ward us."

Her transport casting broke into pieces, replaced by the familiar walls of my living room. I jumped down from her back. Reggie's outraged squawks buffeted me until he flapped to my shoulder and dug his talons in deep while rubbing his beak against the side of my head. Geez, maybe he liked me more than I'd suspected.

Jake had been sitting at a desk I have set up on one side of the living room. He bounded to his feet, a warm smile on his face. "Great to see you. Both of you. I had a feeling right before you arrived. Was sorting what it meant, and then there you were. Poof." He snapped his fingers.

Aidyrth draped a silvery net over him, saying, "Be still. I won't hurt you."

I winced. I'd figured she could do something unnoticeable to evaluate what stuff he was made of. To Jake's credit, he maintained an easy stance, but his smile faded replaced by a confused expression, forehead furrowed as he tried to figure out what she was doing.

The webbing she'd deployed began to glow before it merged with the air.

"What was that all about?" Jake asked.

"Shira wanted to know if you held magic of your own. You do, but you already know as much. Correct?"

He nodded slowly. "Not the type of thing I bandy about. And I've never had enough to do much more than sense events a few moments before they happen or get an eerie foreboding if something isn't right."

"How?" I asked.

"Romani father, witch mother." He shrugged. "What's the big deal all of a sudden?"

"You could do more with it," I blurted and wished I'd had the grace to keep my mouth shut.

"Maybe, but I never wanted to. After the demons showed up, I was damned glad I'd played my cards close to the table. And I made a point of never drawing their attention my way."

"Not why we're here," Aidyrth announced and gave me a small shove. "Get moving. I'll check back in once I've accomplished a few things, but before I go, do you have a tiny bomb I could practice with?"

A surprised look played over Jake's rugged features. "Bomb, is it? I'm pretty good building them. Picked up the skill in Iraq and Afghanistan."

"Great. Maybe you can help me," I said, still mortified I'd suggested he was remiss for not taking advantage of his innate power.

"Love to."

I headed for the kitchen and the trap door to the area below the house. Once I moved the throw rug and lifted the door out of the way, Aidyrth said, "I'll wait up here. Hurry, though. We all have a lot to do."

Originally an unfinished basement, my underground lair had concrete floors and walls. I'd had a few issues with seepage when lake levels were high, but a sump pump kept things under control. I hit a switch, and a bank of fluorescents winked to life. The few windows were high in the walls; I'd covered them with blackout curtains from an Army surplus store.

Jake eyed my workbench and whistled. "Fancy."

"Gets the job done." I kept my words terse, businesslike, to counteract an overwhelming desire to throw my arms around him and crush him against me. He looked relaxed. The hunted, haunted look had departed, leaving nothing but charm.

After pulling out a few drawers, I collected what I needed and took a clod of plastique I'd already assembled, cut it down by half, and attached it to a detonator. Careful not to disturb anything, I carried it upstairs. "Here you go. This one is small. It would maybe wipe out a modest house." And then I pointed out how the detonator worked, explaining this was a positive contact rather than a dead man's switch primed to blow as soon as whoever had hold of it relaxed pressure on the button.

To be on the safe side, I withdrew the detonator wire and showed Aidyrth exactly where to plug it back in.

"Got it." The dragon tucked everything between a couple of scales. I felt the bite of her magic, and then she was gone.

Reggie hadn't left my shoulder. He pecked lightly at my head. "Missed me, huh?" I joked and looked in the fridge to see if Jake had bought anything I could chop up for the parrot. Sure enough, I located kale and cucumber and had moved them to a cutting board when Jake climbed the ladder and strode into the kitchen.

"How many bombs are we building?" he asked, a jaunty note to his question. Guess he enjoyed constructing death as much as me.

"Four. Thanks for picking up food for Reggie."

"I had to look up what parrots eat. Luckily, he and I like a lot of the same things."

I turned from my chopping board and glanced his way. "Any problems here?"

"None. I bought an old beater. It's in the driveway. Figured the management here might give me grief over it, but hasn't happened yet."

"It won't," I said and finished Reggie's meal. Once I'd plopped it onto a board for him, he flew over and dug in.

Jake threaded his arms around me. "I really am glad to see you. I wasn't sure I would before I left."

Now was a good time for honesty. "You wouldn't have except the demons haven't given up, and we needed a way to discourage them in large numbers."

"Ergo, C4?" Jake raised a dark brow.

I nodded. "Ergo, C4."

He felt so good against me, all planes and angles and graceful muscles. His dark hair had fluffed out, framing his face. Sliding his hands down, he gripped my ass and snugged me against a swelling hard-on.

I tried to pull away, but my heart wasn't in it. What I wanted was to take up residence in his arms and never leave. "We can't," I murmured.

"Work first, then," he agreed but didn't loosen his hold on me.

Conflicting feelings slapped me this way and that. I wanted him, but I wasn't a good bet for anything. Certainly, not a relationship that had depth beyond the occasional tryst. Except he wasn't one-night-stand material. Not for me. He was like a drug. The more I had of him, the more I'd want. I did not need that level of complexity in my life.

Meanwhile, my nipples had formed stiff peaks, my thighs slicked with heat and need, and my breathing quickened. My body was making its needs abundantly clear; it was my mind jumping through hoops.

Jake kissed my forehead and let me go. "I've imagined

you coming home so many times," he murmured and smoothed hair back from my face. "We can take it slow. I've been kicked back here, but you've been working. You need time to unwind, and—"

I shook my head, almost undone by his unexpected kindness and understanding. "I have to make four bombs, and then I need to help deploy them and oversee the operation. It was my idea. I can't farm it out to anyone else."

He nodded. "I understand. Do you have a source for C4?"

"Sometimes," I replied cautiously. This was Jake, but I didn't want to say too much about anything.

"I could help with that," he told me. "Just say the word."

My eyebrows shot up. "You have a reliable discreet source?"

"You bet." He snorted. "Everyone who peddles that crap is discreet, or they wouldn't stay in business."

Talk about stating the obvious. I started laughing. He joined in. Whatever tension had hovered between us evaporated. We were still chuckling when he tugged out his cell phone and tapped out a text.

Regardless of sexual tension sharp enough to cut with a knife, I'd found a friend. They'd been few and far between in my life, and I was grateful for his support and his help. I stammered through a bunch of thank-yous before he gathered me close again and held on tight.

"Ssht. It's okay. I understand."

We were in the middle of an endless kiss that lit my heart and soul with fire when his phone buzzed. He dragged his lips from mine. "Playtime's over," he murmured before clicking accept on the display and saying, "Yup."

CHAPTER 17

Turned out Jake's supplier was a whole lot simpler to deal with than my list of them. Cheaper too, but it made sense since he tapped into his military connections. We tag-teamed chores, and I cobbled dinner together while he ran out to meet someone.

A couple of hours later we were in my lab, knee-deep in building explosive devices. "You're more than just another pretty face," I joked.

"I could say the same about you." He grinned. "Never in my wildest imagination did I think I'd be hunkered in a basement with a Russian gambling addict building bombs."

"Except she never existed," I pointed out.

"True enough. These slabs of plastique are huge." He tapped one of them with an index figure. "What are you blowing up?"

"Better if you don't know."

"I'm good enough to help, but you don't trust me?"

I shook my head. "Trust is nowhere in this equation. You're better off not knowing. No one can dredge what's not there out of you."

"Mmph. You already said you were going after demons." He laid out wires for the timer for one of the devices. I'd attach them when the countdown began.

"Let's talk about you," I said, not wanting to say one more word about demons or Hell.

"Eh, not the greatest topic. Why?"

"You told me you grew up in a slum in Philadelphia. Seems like an odd spot to find a witch and a gypsy."

Jake snorted. "Not so odd as all that. If my folks had been more visible, they'd have been castigated, run out of polite society."

"For their magic?" I felt confused.

He shook his head. "For being so odd. Dad ran a gambling operation and was constantly on the move. He had such a foul temper, I was glad when he wasn't home."

"Not sounding very magical," I murmured.

"He used his ability to stay two steps ahead of the cops. They never did bust him." Jake thinned his lips into a sour expression. "If he hadn't been drunk all the time, he'd probably have done a whole lot more with that side of himself."

"What about the witch half of things?"

"Ma was always after chicken blood and dead cats and powdered bone fragments for something or other she was working on. People came to her when they wanted someone to sicken—or die. Usually, her work ran true, but victims who escaped her net were always after her."

"How'd they track the spell to her?"

"People talk." He shrugged. "She was the only openly practicing witch in the area. Eventually, something freaked her, and she ran off. Never told us where she was going and never came back. I was mostly by myself after that."

"Did you have siblings?"

"Yeah. Lost track of them. They were gone before I hit ten."

"That much older?" I was digging for more, but his face had developed a closed-off expression. I felt for him, except I'd had it worse. Maybe. Who could say if a lack of parents was an improvement over useless ones. We worked in silence for the next couple of hours.

"Looks like we're ready," I said, surveying our handiwork. "You made this go faster than if I'd been by myself."

He reached toward me but stopped. "What comes next?"

"Aidyrth will either contact me or come back here. Then some of my associates will place the devices, and—"

"Not what I meant. What comes next for us? Or is this the end of it? I have plans in place, and I'd meant to be gone in a couple of days, anyway. I didn't think I'd see you again."

Damn it. This was not a discussion I wanted to have. Not now when I felt so uncertain where he was concerned.

We worked well together, he and I. In and out of bed. But he'd asked the question and been fair with me, so he deserved more than some schlocked-up excuse.

I turned my three-legged stool so I faced him. "I'm almost eighty years old. From the looks of things, I'll live a few hundred years. Magic enhances lifespans. I've been alone mostly because I'm not a good bet as a partner. Or even a friend. I haven't been able to be honest with anyone about who I am or what I do. If I can't be upfront, what's the point of any relationship built on lies?"

"You've been candid with me," he said softly.

A soft smile formed. "You caught me at a weak moment."

He shook his head. "Not at all. You caught me when I was vulnerable and stepped in. Without you, I'd have had far less commodious digs to plot my next moves."

I blew out a breath. "I like you. Probably more than I should, but it doesn't change anything."

"Why not?"

"I'm still gone at the drop of a hat. And I just signed on for…" Biting my tongue in the nick of time, I stopped.

"Can't say, huh?"

"About the size of it."

He angled his head to one side, catching my gaze with his. "Is this secret thing something I could do too?"

"I have no idea. They came to me."

"Because you're an assassin." At my nod, he went on, "I come with a decent set of transferrable skills."

"They wouldn't assign us to work together. I have zero

control over my assignments. It was a sticking point for me. I'm used to picking and choosing my gigs."

"I'm not, and I'm up for a new gig. This one could be right up my alley," he persisted.

"This is more than a new gig. It's a forever commitment." I figured I could tell him that much.

"Sounding more and more interesting," he replied and added, "The mob is the original lifetime commitment."

"Except you ran away," I pointed out.

"Yeah. I did."

Aidyrth picked that moment to plunk down on the kitchen floor. I felt her distinctive brand of power about the time a heavy *thunk* rattled the ladder leading downward.

Jake bounded up the ladder. I heard him say, "I bet you're part of the cadre Shira can't tell me about. Is there a way I could sign on?"

Muffling a groan, I mounted the ladder and joined them in the kitchen. I'd expected to catch hell from the dragon. Instead, she'd bathed Jake in the same paranormal evaluation she'd conducted earlier, except deeper.

"Maybe," she said at length, and reeled in her spell.

"Maybe is better than an outright no. What's next?" he asked and added an engaging grin that diluted his savage side. I wasn't fooled, and I bet Aidyrth wasn't, either. We all had a feral aspect, or we'd have picked different lifepaths.

"If we want you, someone will find you." Aidyrth was all

business. She'd wooed me, but then Jake wasn't her presumptive bondmate.

"Good enough." He nodded brusquely.

I'd expected him to press the issue. He didn't. Maybe between the military and the mob, he'd figured out what don't-call-us-we'll-call-you sounded like.

"How are things on your end?" I asked Aidyrth.

"We're set to go. The miniature bomb transported fine, and we established an account for you to draw against for your expenses. Details are back at the guild house."

"Do you need me for anything else right now?" Jake asked.

Reggie chose that moment to fly from the living room and perch on Jake's shoulder. He stroked the bird's feathered head.

"Probably not," I said. The words cost me because I didn't want him to leave.

"Then I'll get out of your hair." He grabbed a jacket off a hook, slung it over a shoulder, and trotted toward the front door. The easy grace of his movements reminded me once again of a majestic beast on the prowl.

I caught up with him outside on the front stoop and threw my arms around him. "Thank you. I hope our paths cross again. Truly I do."

He held me close for a moment before letting go. "Me too, Suzanne." And then he was in his car and driving away, leaving me feeling bereft. It was ridiculous. I was in the middle of my first operation for the Circle. I still had to prove myself; I couldn't afford to get sidetracked.

Shutting the door on everything but right now, I returned to the house. The parrot flew inside with me. I hadn't realized he'd followed us out.

"Let me get the materials," I said after securing the door.

"Do you want him in the Circle?" Aidyrth asked.

I'd started down the ladder, but I climbed back up and looked at her. "Is it a possibility?"

"It is. He's untrained, but he has potential. And discipline."

"What about a bond animal?"

"That part has a way of working itself out. Does he understand it's a lifetime commitment?"

I nodded slowly. "It's the one part I made clear once he started making where-do-I-sign-up noises."

"So he's unaware you and I are bondmates?"

"Yes. Unless he's used the power he claims is minor to look beneath the surface."

"It's not all that minor. I'll talk with Grigori. See what he thinks."

Recognizing the Jake-topic was closed—and rightfully so since we had a long few hours ahead—I scurried back down the ladder and carried the devices up one at a time. Once they were scattered across the kitchen counters, I returned for the timers, matching each up with its device.

That's the thing about homemade anything. Each one is slightly different. No assembly line to smooth out production kinks. "The timers are set for a one-hour countdown," I explained. "Should be plenty of time to place them and put some distance between ourselves and the bombs before they go off."

"Grigori assembled two other teams, along with himself and us," Aidyrth said. "We will meet them presently. You'll have to teach them how to attach the timers."

"We could wire them now, but I don't want to risk the countdown mechanism activating by accident. I could cut the wires, but then I'd have to build a new timer."

"Understood. We will do this in several trips. I'll take two of the devices, return for the last two, and then return a third time for you and the timers."

Reggie squawked like a crazed thing as magic flooded the kitchen, and the dragon vanished in a cloud of haze and glittery streamers. I tossed the dishes from dinner into the dishwasher and changed into clean, warm clothes. I felt Aidyrth return and leave again while I was getting dressed.

The same nervous tension that pushed me to the top of my game traveled from the soles of my boots to the tiptop of my head, sluicing first hot and then cold. What if I'd miscalculated? I had no idea what stuff Hell was made of. A remote possibility existed that the underworld was impervious to C_4.

"Don't be stupid," I mumbled. "C_4 wipes out everything in its path. Organic. Inorganic. It's an equal opportunity destroyer."

Feeling a bit more settled, I refilled Reggie's feeder bins and told him I'd be gone again. "Gone. Gone," he squawked as I turned off lights and checked the doors and windows to make certain they were locked. His chant reminded me of a kid complaining about desultory parenting. He'd bonded with Jake damned quick, probably because he'd been here twenty-four seven for a few days.

I stroked a fingertip over the crest of a wing. Not much point in apologizing. My life was what it was. I'd be here even less than I had been, and the bird needed to get used to the new normal.

Yeah. Big talk. A real hard ass wouldn't have assumed responsibility for a pet in the first place. I tucked the timers into pockets and settled in to wait.

I sensed Aidyrth before I saw her, and she didn't waste any time. Spell still simmering, she scooped me and the timers into it, and we were off amid a fresh flurry of squawks from the parrot. I expected us to emerge at the guild house. Instead, we plopped down on a high mesa dotted with sagebrush. Dawn was just breaking, adding a pinkish glow to the eastern horizon.

No wonder the transport spell had been so fast. "We're in Nevada, right?" I asked, certain the cold, dry air and desert was familiar.

"Aye. Come this way."

Empty space stretched on all sides of us, but I didn't question her. Grigori had mentioned a guild house here. If that's where we were, it had to be shrouded in layers of invisibility spells. Made sense because while the hinterlands in this state were virtually uninhabited, the occasional miner, trail buff, or climber intent on conquering peaks with no names wandered through.

I felt a jolt as we passed across some sort of magic-infused barrier. The desert yielded to manicured grounds studded with various species of cactus. A rustic lodge sat in the middle. No gates. None needed since the place was well hidden. Grigori and Mae were in the courtyard along with a slender blond man I hadn't met before. Mae's hawk quorked a greeting, and Mae raised a hand.

"Well met, sister."

"Good to see you." I smiled warmly. I liked her, and she was a solid warrior.

The blond man turned to face me. Delicately built and barefoot, he was clad in leather britches and a tunic. Longish copper hair was braided tightly against his head, displaying pointed ears. The power wafting around him had a spicy smell.

I offered a hand. He shook it. "Thanks for trusting me," I said.

"Grigori requested volunteers. They were one shy, so we agreed to help." He made a clucking sound; a lithe black panther glided to his side and wound around his lower legs. The deep rumbling sound had to be the big cat purring.

I moved to a table where the devices had been laid out and extracted the timers. Asking everyone to move closer felt presumptuous. I was the newest kid on the block, so I matched up timers to bombs and started talking, explaining how to attach everything and arm the timing mechanisms.

"It would be best," I went on, "if the explosives detonate at roughly the same time. These have my particular power stamped all over them. Someone helped build them, but the predominant magic in the mix is mine. I do not want a batch of demons dicking with the timer on a bomb that hasn't yet exploded and tracking the mess straight to me."

Heads nodded; hands reached for the devices.

"This should go smoothly. We worked the details out while Aidyrth was ferrying things back and forth," Grigori said.

Voicing doubts isn't like me. Usually, I keep them to myself, but words rushed out despite a need to prove myself to the Circle. They may have chosen me, but they were under no obligation to hang onto me. As far as that went, neither was I under any requirement to remain. It might be a forever commitment, but surely mages had left the Circle over the long years of its existence. Hadn't I been dithering back and forth about whether their group grope was a good fit for my mostly solo skillset?

"One thing I'm not certain of," I began, "is if C4 will make a dent in Hell. It blows everything else in the universe to bits, but Hell might be different."

"It's not," the blond man said.

"How do you know?" I twisted to face him.

"I ran a test with the small bomb. Not the whole thing, just a tiny bit of it."

"How'd you get it to explode without a detonator or a timing device?"

He smiled, adding to his otherworldly appearance. "I gave it a push with fire and air."

"Okay. How did you not get hurt?"

"Shira." Grigori's tone was sharp.

I held up a hand. "Sorry. Getting off topic."

"We need to be gone," he informed the group. "You all have your locations. Set the explosives, double-check the timers are still set for an hour, and return here."

The others shaded to nothing, making me jealous of their ability to travel paths closed to me. I tucked the last incendiary device under an arm and fell into Aidyrth's spell.

The next part was almost too smooth. We popped out in a passageway so low the dragon needed to hunch to fit. The same sulfur and ozone scents that had assailed me last time I'd pushed closer to the nether realm were thick and acrid. I found an alcove near floor level and had the timer plugged in and activated in no time at all. An hour was a long time, though, so I draped a combination of don't look here and invisibility spells around the bomb before giving the dragon a thumb's up.

Once we were well clear of the place, I said, "Is there a way I can learn to transport myself?"

"I don't see why not." She detailed a method of mixing elements that never would have occurred to me. I'd have to practice somewhere the stakes weren't quite so high.

From long habit, I set the countdown timer on my phone, so I'd know when the deed was done. At least for our device. Everyone was waiting for us in the cactus garden except Grigori. At first, it didn't concern me, but when my phone indicated less than thirty minutes remained, I grew worried.

"Where was Grigori's target?" I asked.

"Not sure," Aidyrth replied, followed by, "Tell me where each of you went." After Mae and the man whose name I didn't know told her, she said, "It leaves two possibilities."

"How could you not know for certain?" I muttered.

"Because I scouted locations, and he selected them," she answered.

"We have to check on him," I told everyone.

"We could take one of the spots," Mae offered.

I shook my head. "I need to check both. If something went wrong, I might be able to fix it. Worst case, I can disable the bomb since I built it."

Aidyrth didn't wait for me to quit speaking. She whisked me into a travel spell that felt different. "We'll check the farthest possibility first," she informed me.

I looked at my phone. Twenty-two minutes. "Your magic seems different. Why?"

"This was a key spot because it's quite close to the seat of the demons' power, which is why Grigori grabbed it for himself. We're warded to within an inch of our lives."

"How long to get there?"

"How long do we have?"

"I'm not sure," I told her. It's twenty-one minutes before ours detonates. Grigori's could be a couple of minutes sooner."

"Or later," she inserted.

"Probably not later. He left before we did."

"Aye, but he had farther to travel."

I bit back a snark-laden comment about having it her

way. She was worried about the werewolf. So was I. This whole shebang had been my idea. If it ended up killing the Circle's leader, no place would be far enough for me to run. Mages like Loren would mark me for death and not give up until I was no more.

"We'll find him." Aidyrth tried for reassuring. Clearly, she'd been inside the turmoil my mind had become.

Another peek at my phone. Twenty minutes. By the time we broke through to Aidyrth's first pick, the twenty was down to sixteen. Shit. If he wasn't here, there wouldn't be time to check the other option.

Don't think like that, I admonished myself. We'd make time. Somehow.

I gave it the space between two breaths to be certain we weren't about to be mobbed by demons. Darkness surrounded us, unremitting and heavy; demon stench was thicker than it had been where we'd left our bomb.

I tried a seeking spell, but Aidyrth had us and our power sewed up tight within her ward. Desperate, I drilled a small hole in its weave. The moment I did, Grigori's voice exploded in my head.

"Go. I'm finished."

CHAPTER 18

"*L ike hell we will,*" I told the dragon and started deeper into the passageway. It was hot down here, uncomfortable enough I began to sweat in bake-oven temperatures.

"*Silence. Remain within my ward,*" she instructed and sealed up the rent I'd created.

I wanted to tell her it was the least of our worries. We were all on the verge of dying down here, anyway. I'd stopped watching my phone. The countdown would march on without my attention glued to it. I took a few deep, centering breaths with firm instructions to focus on now.

The flicker of flames reflected off the walls, revealing a dogleg in the corridor. I crept forward, aiming for silence. Fuck. Double fuck. Grigori had been lashed to a metal stake with iron chains set next to a huge firepit. They'd caught him mid-shift, so his limbs had fur and claws. The metal had chewed flesh from his bones.

Because I knew what to look for, locating the bomb was easy. It sat off to one side. Apparently, he'd set it up before the demons mobbed him. It didn't appear anyone had discovered it, or they'd have been hunched over the alien object trying to pull it apart.

Maybe, just maybe we'd caught a break.

There is a way to disconnect the timer, but if someone clips any wire except the green one, the thing detonates prematurely. It's counterintuitive. Anyone who's ever done any electrical work would go for the black wire first. Or the blue one. Red and green are usually the last to go. The demons were still intent on Grigori, circling him, baiting him. I had no idea what it meant for a shifter to be stuck between forms, but it couldn't be good.

He'd said he was finished, but I got it. He was running out the clock. It was why he'd told us to leave. The demons had probably heard his mind speech but chalked it up to him being half out of his mind with pain.

I couldn't risk telepathy, but I had to get to the bomb. I didn't have wire cutters, but a focused shot of magic should do the trick. Could I make it thin enough it didn't fry the wire next door?

Guess I was about to find out.

Gliding away from Aidyrth, I circled back a few feet until I reached the rounded, rocky wall. I employed a few flickers of magic to power my psychic senses to find my way, but I muted them as much as I could. Achieving a balance point was tough. One where I didn't risk stumbling —and making noise—because I couldn't see and moving so slowly I didn't reach the bomb in time.

Sweat was pouring down my body and dripping into my eyes but I couldn't take time to brush it aside. Stupid of me to swathe myself in winter outer clothes as if our destination were the North Pole.

The bomb was near enough, my heightened senses caught the whirr of the electronics. Ten more steps. Five more. I first thinned and then discarded my warding. No way to demolish the wire with any accuracy if I were shooting through a barrier.

It was turned so the LED faced the wall. I twisted it ever so slightly so I could reach the wiring harness and see the readout. Three minutes. My lungs were on fire, and I understood I'd quit breathing in my quest for silence. To avoid gasping, I sucked air slowly and found the wire I needed by feel. Sometimes being the architect is a good thing. In this case, it meant I didn't require additional light. With one hand on top of the device and the other stretching the green wire away from the red, black, and blue ones, I gathered the thinnest, most focused beam of power I'd ever managed and sent it at a spot an inch behind my hand.

Whatever was happening in the cavern had dropped away. The sum total of my focus was six inches in front of me. My aim was true. The green casing melted, and the wires frayed but didn't break. I gave them a yank, but I was down to under two minutes now. When jerking on them didn't complete the break, I sent another jolt of magic. Some of it slopped, but I stopped it with a hand, burning myself in the process.

Eh, small price to pay.

I felt like cheering when the remaining bits of cable snapped. The LED blinked out. So far, no one had discovered me, but one problem was under control. At least now we had time to rescue Grigori.

Or to try. His situation wasn't ideal.

I'd begun to retrace my steps when a burst of frantic demonspeak froze me in my tracks. Of all the times to not understand a language, this one wasn't it. I needed to know what they were suddenly so fussed up about.

At least, they weren't paying any attention to me. I scuttled back to where I'd left Aidyrth except she'd moved. Risking still more power, I activated our bond-link; it was either that or chance not finding her. Her warding was so good, she was effectively invisible. Crap. I hadn't exactly tossed caution to the wolves, but every time I used magic, I upped the probability of discovery.

She'd retreated farther into the tunnel beyond the dogleg turn. Scooting through her ward I whispered, "What happened?"

"They're torturing Grigori for information about the Circle." She hesitated. "You won't like this next part."

I didn't think I could be much more keyed up after my near miss with the C4, but my stomach tightened into a knot. And not because of my burned hand.

"Not sure how it happened, but Jake is here. He crept

past me and was headed right for you and the bomb when one of the demons noticed him. That activated the bunch of them, and they jumped him."

Goddammit to hell. Somehow, he'd tracked me. He'd been trying to help, but maybe he'd been in a hurry. Maybe he didn't understand the finer points of warding. Maybe...

Fuck everything.

Second-guessing the whys wouldn't help him.

Raised voices had grown louder. "Can you understand them?"

"Aye."

She stopped there. With good reason. We had to do something. Create a diversion. What had the other mage said about using fire and air to detonate clumps of C4?

Yeah, but how big had the clumps been. Would this whole fucking shitshow come down on our heads if anything exploded?

I climbed up Aidyrth's back, and then shinnied up her neck ripping the crap out of my pants in the process, but I wanted to be right next to her ears. She obligingly angled her head.

"The other mage said he'd detonated small bits of C4 with magic. What if I get some of the bomb material and planted it in a few key spots? We could set them off and create enough of a diversion, we could grab Grigori and Jake and get the hell out of here."

Aidyrth was quiet as she considered my Hail Mary suggestion. It wasn't as if we had many choices. We couldn't waltz into the middle of a demon pack and demand they release our companions. They'd laugh themselves silly. I figured the dragon was bombproof. I couldn't see them tying her up, but I was just as vulnerable as Jake.

"Do it," she said. "They're still busy with Jake, trying to figure out how he and Grigori slot together. You'll have to get yourself out of here, though. Between breaking through Grigori's binding and defeating however they'll have bound Jake, I'll have my talons full. Remember what I told you about how to teleport?"

I did, but I'd have liked to have run a few experiments from a nice safe location in the dead of night. Whining was off the table, so I mumbled, "Yeah. I'll work it out."

After I'd jumped down from my perch on her back, I retraced my steps to the bomb I'd hoped never to see again. C4 is a lot like modeling clay, so I'd placed the material into metal buckets to contain it. When I work with it in my lab, I wear gloves. No such luxury here. The shit stung like mad when it contacted the open wounds on my right hand, the bite of chemicals so harsh it stole my breath. I kept going, making mounds the size of golf balls. Should be plenty big.

Maybe too big. I wasn't much of a judge of the proper amount of plastique to create a diversion and not bring the cavern roof tumbling down on us all. Not that I cared if the demons ate it, but I had a vested interest in getting out of here along with Aidyrth, Grigori, and Jake.

Still shaping the chunk I'd carved off into balls, I crept forward, hugging the wall and warded to the nines. My fingers were growing numb. Maybe there were good reasons I'd always avoided touching the stuff. Now wasn't a time to gawk at Grigori snarling as he strained against his chains or Jake trussed up like a Christmas goose and suspended over the fire. His clothing had begun to smolder, and his face was a mass of bruises. I hoped he was unconscious, but a fat little demon poked him with a pikestaff, and he grunted. Meanwhile, a crew of red bastards had gathered round, intent on turning him into their next meal.

Would they even wait until his flesh was cooked? If the scene in the mines outside Chicago was any representation, the answer was no. Maybe I should have pushed the timer forward an hour and bought us time that way, and then I remembered there wasn't a way to tamper with the mechanism once it was set.

Jake twisted, fighting the cords binding him and cursing. No time to waste.

I made it to the far side of the cavern and a few feet down an interconnecting tunnel before I planted the first glob of plastique. I'd have to remember precisely where each one was, so I added a small beacon.

Risk piled on risk, but I'd never have the precision I needed without something that called to my magic like a lodestone. After leaving two globs in the tunnel, I placed the remaining eight around the periphery of the chamber, taking care but working as fast as I could.

Every demon snort and shout brought me up short. Every time a nostril flared or a head turned my way, I froze.

They'd have to be able to smell me, except maybe they'd confuse my scent with Jake's. Maybe. Surely, they could sort male from female.

After what felt like forever, I was winded and my heart felt like it wanted to escape my ribcage, but I was back to Aidyrth. "The first one will be a crapshoot," I said softly.

"Not so much as all that. Ybar said two parts fire, half a part air, wait a few seconds and add another half part air."

Great. I had proportions, but one critical element remained. "How much is a part?"

"Start small." She dropped a foreleg onto my shoulder. "I have been planning how to execute my part. The moment the first charge blows, I will move quickly." Her talons squeezed hard enough to hurt. "We will make this work."

I shut my eyes for the briefest of moments, hoping to hell she was right. Jake's grunts and curses had yielded to a shriek. I smelled burning hair and flesh and hurried to the vantage point I'd selected at the end of the dogleg curve. Power pinged off the farthest beacon, lighting it for me.

It wasn't much light, just enough to flag its location. I pushed fire and air, waited five seconds and added more air. Time dripped by so slowly, I feared it had stopped. Or Ybar had gotten it wrong. Or the C4 mix he'd had was slightly different from this one. Made sense. Each batch was unique, and—

A low rolling boom expanded exponentially accompanied by cracks and the roar of a major earthquake as the tunnel where I'd planted the explosive fell in with a resounding crash that shook the dirt under my feet.

Aidyrth swept by me.

We had a plan, but dirt was cascading down. The demons had abandoned their victims and run for the disturbance, sheets of dark power rolling from them in waves. I'd never get a better opportunity, so I activated the other glob I'd left in the tunnel.

Unfortunately, the fuckers were close enough to see my beacon flash to life. One grabbed hold of the plastique, shouting at it in demonspeak. I saw the whitish clump in his hand just before it exploded, blowing him to bits of gristle, bone, and blackish tissue. Because I'd aimed to shave the latency, I'd added more fire this time. It had the desired effect. Rocks rained down, followed by dirt and a gush of water stinking of sulfur.

The cavern was so full of dust and grit, seeing anything was a struggle, so I checked with magic. No one would notice my seeking spell in the midst of all this chaos. Breath whooshed from me. They were gone. The dragon, Jake, and Grigori.

Should I activate the remaining pods?

Maybe the ones farthest from me. I needed line of sight to work, which meant I couldn't retreat beyond where I stood. Not until I was done. Feeling frisky—or desperate—I sent power to activate four more clods of plastique. Once they started going off, I fled in the opposite direction while mixing power in the way Aidyrth had said would get me out of here.

It took several tries. The ground heaved and rocked under my feet. Boulders rained down from the tunnel walls, narrowing my path to less than twelve inches. Shit. I had to get out of here. Sooner or later, one of those fuckers was bound to hit me. If I were unconscious, any chance of escape would evaporate.

The right side of the tunnel collapsed inward. I couldn't stand upright any longer, so I sank to my knees and crawled. My hands were trashed from burns and the chemicals, but I had to keep going.

Or did I? Maybe what I needed to do was stop and focus every shred of my attention—and my magic—on teleporting out of this shithole. I forced myself to slow down. To think.

When I did, the answer I needed was there. I already knew how to move myself short distances. If I added the information from Aidyrth, I should be able to get myself out of here. A Volkswagen-sized boulder crashed in front of me, followed by another just behind. I was effectively trapped.

Unless I could make this work.

"Breathe, goddammit," I shouted above the din and tossed all my remaining magic into escape.

The cave flickered and reformed several times as I changed up elements. Finally, when I was so frantic my throat was nearly swollen shut, the cave walls flickered and stayed gone, leaving me floating in a black void.

Where was I? Why hadn't I returned to somewhere familiar? What had I done wrong?

I slammed my palm against my forehead. I hadn't visualized where I wanted to go. Even for my short, two-block hops, it was a required element. Was I too late? Did I have to feed that information into the spell at the front end? If so, I was truly fucked.

Or was I?

Nothing said I couldn't start over now that I had a blueprint for how to do this. The question was if I had enough power left to make it work. Maybe, if I didn't ask too much of spell number two, I could milk enough juice out of my dwindling stores.

Problem was I had no idea what the hell-cave had been close to. My heart rate was escalating again. I forced a series of measured breaths to slow it down. Anxiety worked against me every time. I'd discovered that as a young, reluctant magic-wielder.

Either I aimed for home or for the guild house in Nevada. I had the coordinates even though I wasn't certain precisely where in the state it was. Once I was calm enough to take another run at things, I opted for the guild house. It was where Grigori had told us to go afterward.

I ran through the steps twice in my mind before loosing my spell. The same latency I'd dealt with before plagued me, but I rode it through. For all I knew, the new spell had taken off, but my environment—the floaty, dark place—wouldn't have altered since it was the path to all destinations.

With little warning, the darkness shattered around me, leaving me tumbling end over end. Land was a long way down, but I could make out the Nevada guild house as I dragged the last of my power into a buffer to shield my fall.

We'd done it. Aidyrth and me. I couldn't wait to high-five the dragon.

My arrival wasn't as elegant as I'd have liked, and I scrambled up after landing on my butt. Grigori, back in human form strode to me and inclined his head. "You displayed courage and tenacity. Aidyrth chose well when she selected you."

His words warmed me.

"Where is she?" I looked around, but he and I were the only ones in the courtyard.

"Jake is gravely injured. She moved him to our main guild house where our healers will do what they can."

A weight settled on my chest; breathing became a struggle, and I staggered back a step. He had to be all right. We'd gotten him out of there before the demons had begun carving him to ribbons.

Grigori gripped my arm hard enough to make me gasp. "Go inside. Clean yourself up, and I'll take you there."

"But I want to go now. I have to see him. If he hadn't been watching out for me, he'd never have been there, and —" To my horror, my eyes flooded with tears.

The werewolf shook me, not hard, but enough to get my attention. "Your hands are blistered and cut to hell. Your face is abraded. Go clean yourself up. Five minutes won't matter one way or the other."

"But—"

"That's an order, Shira. Now go."

I'd make it as short a five minutes as I could. Turning away, I loped for the house feeling like a truck had run over me. It wasn't my injuries. They were superficial. It was my power being run down to bedrock that created this hollow, beat-to-crap feeling.

I ducked into the first bathroom I found and yelped as hot water hit my torn-up hands. The face staring back at me might have belonged to a stranger. A cut had opened along one cheekbone; dirty streaks covered me from forehead to neck. After my hands were clean, I ran cold water, cupped them, and drank until the raw places in my throat calmed down.

A few more swipes got the worst of the grime off my face. When I ran back outside, I was feeling slightly better. Still sucking fumes, but no longer at risk of falling on my face and not being able to get back up.

"I'm going to walk you through how to teleport." Grigori was all business. "I'm guessing you ran into problems. It took you a while to get here."

Much as I wanted to learn, Jake's situation was precarious. "Walk me through it as you put it together, please. We have to hurry."

"He's still alive, Shira. Aidyrth's been checking in."

The tears that had escaped before were shockingly near the surface. I blinked them into submission, said, "Teach me," and paid close attention as he provided details I'd missed. I've never been a crier, not since I was really little. What in the hell was wrong with me?

By the time Grigori was through, and we were

established in a journey channel, I must have looked flummoxed because he asked, "What?"

"It's a miracle what I did worked at all."

"Not really. This particular casting is quite robust. That you managed a complex teleport—and by that I mean one that began in an off-world location—with so little instruction is the miracle here." He offered a rare smile. "Keep the faith. Jake crossed your path—and mine—for a reason."

"I have no faith. This isn't as arrogant as it sounds, but I've always only believed in me."

"You drove that point home in Havana." His smile expanded a notch. "It sounds odd coming from a fellow assassin, but the good guys usually win."

I smiled wanly and hung on. Jake was still alive, or he had been a few minutes ago. At least I'd get to see him before he— I stopped and wiped my mind absolutely clear. Even breathing the word *dead* could be bad luck, and I'd be damned if I'd jinx this any worse than it already was.

What had he been thinking, following me? Sneaking after me, more like. It would be my very first question. After I told him how unspeakably grateful I was he'd retained solid footing on this side of the veil.

CHAPTER 19

Grigori brought us out in a place quite different from the first guild house I'd visited. Beyond a far more casual architectural style, this place had tropical vegetation and a balmy climate. For the first time since leaving my house, I stripped off my jacket. Not that I'd needed it in Hell, but I hadn't exactly had extra time to layer up or down. I was glad to rid myself of it; the garment stank of demons and sulfur and the sweetish reek of C4.

"Come on." Grigori motioned me forward. We crossed gardens fragrant with tropical flowers I couldn't identify and walked up broad stairs and into an airy foyer.

Aidyrth must have been expecting us, or set some kind of marker to alert her when we showed up because she hustled forward and raked me from head to toe with her prickly brand of dragon love. Not that I'd admit it to anyone, but I rather enjoyed being fussed over and cared about.

"You're all right." Smoke puffed from her jaws, swirling around Grigori and me.

"Baptism by fire." I tried for a smile but fell short.

"I was worried," she went on, "when you weren't right behind us, but I was the logical one to bring Jake here. My power is stronger. It shortened his journey, which may well have saved his life."

"So he'll pull through?" My heart was in my voice, which cracked, but I didn't care.

"We believe so," Aidyrth said. "He's with the White Fae. They're talented healers."

"What was wrong with him?" I asked, certain demons must have beaten him and broken something critical.

"Not what you might think," Grigori said carefully.

I narrowed my eyes and looked at him. "What's that supposed to mean?"

He exchanged a pointed look with the dragon. "May as well tell her," Aidyrth said. "She'll find out soon enough, anyway."

"Find what out?" I'd moved from relief Jake was out of danger to being pissed they were treating me as if I were a child to be shielded from some awful truth.

"Jake's father was Romani," Aidyrth said, as if that explained everything.

"Yeah. So what?" I offered a blank stare. "I already knew that. And his mother was a witch."

"Gypsies possess what power they do because they bargained with the devil," she said.

"Pfft." I rolled my eyes. "That's an old wives' tale. Something gypsies have circulated to make themselves look tough."

"Except in this case, it's true," Grigori spoke up. "Jake probably could have accomplished what he set out to do if his demon blood hadn't sounded a klaxon warning to the others. They apprehended him because they noticed him. Something he hadn't bargained on."

"What did he set out to do?" Sheesh. I was the original twenty-questions girl today, but Grigori and Aidyrth were spewing riddles.

"Obviously, he wanted to help us, well actually you," Aidyrth replied. "From what I've been able to piece together, he returned to your place after we left and tracked us to the guild house. By the time he got there, everyone had left. He couldn't figure out where we'd gone, probably because four magical directions were still floating in the ether. Instead of doing the smart thing, which would have been leaving, he concealed himself and waited."

"To make certain I got back," I murmured caught between wonder I meant that much to him and irritation he'd appointed himself as my babysitter. The two emotions were at odds with one another, leaving me confused.

"Probably." Grigori nodded.

"So he must have overheard us talking when you didn't return to the rendezvous point," I guessed. "But how in the hell was he able to follow us?"

"Hell keeps an open door for its own," Grigori said. "Jake has sufficient magic to teleport. I have no idea if he's ever tried before, but somehow he made it work."

"Does he know he's part demon?" I asked.

"He isn't, not exactly," Aidyrth said. "Romani blood is fired by demon magic. It's in a class by itself, but some of the Rom don't have any power at all."

"Most of them don't," Grigori broke in. "And fewer with each passing decade."

Something about Aidyrth's words alerted me. "You knew about the demon link, didn't you?"

She nodded.

"Why didn't you say something?"

"I answered your questions. You never asked what kind of power he had, only if he had any."

"Don't blame her," Grigori told me. "It's a topic we usually skirt because we loathe demons."

I raked a hand through my tangled hair. "Let me make sure I have this right. Jake's magic comes courtesy of demons, but he isn't one."

"Some of his magic," the dragon corrected me. "You're forgetting his mother's contribution, which was likely more significant."

"I thought witches were mostly playacting at magical endeavors," I protested.

"Most of them are," Grigori replied, "but some have genuine power."

Aidyrth cocked her head to one side. "He's awake," she announced. "And insisting on leaving. It's a good sign."

"And the wolf?" Grigori asked.

I rolled my tired shoulders back. "What wolf?"

"The one who contends he's his bonded one," Aidyrth sounded pleased. "I'd have preferred another dragon, but my kind rarely leave Fire Mountain."

I paid out a bit of seeking magic, hunting for Jake. My power was coming back online, but it would take food and rest before I was up to snuff. "I'm going to go see him," I said. "I won't stay long, so I don't tire him out." And then I remembered the dragon had said he was intent on getting out of here. I had a feeling the wolf who'd staked a claim to him might have other plans.

"Shira."

Grigori's words stopped me, but if he told me to wait I'd argue the point. "Yeah?" I half-turned toward him.

"You've proven your worth to the Circle today. Thank you again for saving my life."

"You're welcome, but it was Aidyrth and me working together. Neither of us could have done it alone."

He nodded. "Which is precisely why the Circle is constructed as it is." He flapped a hand my way. "Go see your friend. Give him hell for complicating a complex mission."

"Why do I have a feeling you beat me to it?"

The werewolf snorted. "I would have—if he'd been awake to listen."

My heels clicked over tile floors as I made my way to an airy room at the far end of one of many halls. The place was organized in wings spiraling out from a central core.

Warm breezes drifted through many open windows and doorways. Unlike the first guild house, this one appeared to be a place to rest and recharge.

A pair of female Fae, wings neatly folded, cream-colored robes brushing the floor bustled about the room. Delicately built, they stood just over five feet, perhaps a few inches more. Silvery hair had been braided out of the way, and it matched two pairs of silver eyes.

Jake sat on the edge of a bed, bending to put his shoes on. "I'm fine I told you," he said irritably. 'Thanks for patching me up and all, but—" He stopped midsentence and stared at me.

"Shira. Thank Christ you're all right. I felt you down there. I was heading for the C4, to dismantle the bomb, but they grabbed me, and—"

"Hush." I crossed the room to him and sank to a crouch. "Never do anything like that again. Promise."

"Absolutely not, I won't promise." His face settled into a mulish expression I'd come to recognize.

"Well then, at least tell me what you're up to."

"If I can." He grinned crookedly. "In this instance, once I understood the problem, I was the logical one to help. So I worked it out as I went—until a couple of demons nabbed me. I still have no idea how they knew I was there. Usually, my disguises are bulletproof."

A low growl snapped my attention to the far side of the bed, and I rose to my feet to peek over the edge. A sable-colored wolf was stretched out on the floor, fangs bared. At least eight feet long, he was formidable—and gorgeous. Ha. This must be Jake's potential bondmate. Did he know?

Jake had his feet under him and had pushed upright. He swayed slightly, but altered his stance until he was steady and walked around to the wolf. "Hey, buddy. Not sure why you're here, but apparently I needed all the help I could get, so thanks."

The wolf showed more fang and growled.

"He's beautiful," I murmured. It earned me an approving woof, but I wasn't certain if I should say more. It wasn't my place to explain the inner workings of the Circle of Assassins, not that I knew all that much myself.

Grigori chose that moment to show up and shoo the Fae healers away. Once they were gone, he closed the door and moved forward.

Jake narrowed his eyes. "I think I know you, but I can't place it, not precisely."

"We were prisoners together in Hell," Grigori said smoothly.

No matter how practiced Jake was at hiding his reactions to things, surprise washed across his battered face. He opened his mouth, probably couldn't figure out how to couch what he wanted to ask, so he shut it again.

Grigori nodded. "I was partially in my other form. I'm a werewolf, but it's not why I'm here. You'd asked Shira about becoming part of her new organization. I'm going give you much the same pitch I handed her. You showed ingenuity, courage, and grit. You'd make a good addition to the Circle of Assassins."

"Shira said it was forever." Jake was facing Grigori squarely.

"It is, but you are still at a point where you can walk away. I will erase your memories of us all, though, if you decide this isn't for you."

"Including Shira?"

Geez, Jake was quick on the uptake where I was concerned. The same mix of happiness and concern roiled through me.

"Including Shira," Grigori agreed.

The wolf growled again, louder this time.

Grigori snarled back; the wolf rose to his feet and padded to Grigori. "No one made you any promises," he told the wolf. The beast whined and sank to a sit, jaws lolling. At least his fangs weren't showing any longer.

Jake looked from me to Grigori to the sable wolf. "How does he fit into things?"

I settled in as Grigori sketched out the basics about the Circle of Assassins. He provided more history than he'd given me, but then I'd had Aidyrth to fill in details. As Jake listened, his interest was obvious. No longer invested in looking like Mr. Cool, he leaned forward, absorbing every word. Even the ones about the Romani link to demonic aspects of his heretofore mostly unused magical ability.

"So," Grigori finished up, "if you accept, you will become part of the circle. Arrow will be your bonded one. It's how things work. The animals pick whom they want, much as Aidyrth did with Shira. Your task will be learning how to work with him.

"Think about it," Grigori went on. "I'll be here if you have questions, and—"

"I don't need to think about it. I'm in. It sounds amazing." Jake extended a hand, intent on sealing the deal.

"Are you certain?" Grigori pressed. Power flowed from him, encompassing Jake as he tested his words and his resolve.

Jake held himself still under the werewolf's appraisal. "Very certain. Wise of you to check, though."

"Why's that?" Grigori withdrew his spell.

"Demons are the enemy, or one of them. If my ability is partially underwritten by them, it would make me suspect."

"And also potentially very strong." Grigori clasped Jake's hand.

Meanwhile, Arrow was on his feet and padding toward the men. He pushed his big head between them and growled, "Come with me. We have work to do."

I laughed. "Get used to it. The bond animals own us, but trust me it's good to be loved." I met Jake's direct dark-eyed gaze. "I'm going to fall on my face for a few hours. I'll find you before I go home."

Grigori let go of Jake and dropped a hand into Arrow's thick neck ruff. "Come on. Let's give them a few minutes."

"But he's mine," Arrow protested.

"Not contesting that," I told the wolf. "How about if you get to know Aidyrth while Jake and I talk?"

The suggestion must have appealed to the wolf because he left the room with Grigori. I wound my arms around

Jake and smoothed fingertips over the healing places in his face. "It's a lot to get used to," I murmured.

"You're kidding, right? This is like a fantasy come to life. I get to do the things I do best with a wolf partner." He shook his head as disbelief spilled from him. "I'm worried this is a dream, and I'll wake up and none of it will have been true."

"It's true, all right," I said. "Took me quite a bit longer to decide this was what I wanted. I came within a hairsbreadth of turning Grigori and Aidyrth down. And even after I said yes, I harbored doubts."

"Do you still?"

"Small ones, but they're fading by the minute."

He cradled the side of my head and kissed me, slow and sweet and full of hope and promise. When he raised his mouth from mine, he said, "I understand we won't necessarily be working together, but I hope you'll give us a chance."

The same flicker of joy speared me. "I will. Who else would have been dumb enough to wend their way through untried magic to try to save me?"

"I'd have beat you to the C4 if those fuckers hadn't grabbed me."

"You probably would have, and maybe we'd have figured out we'd need tiny globs of it to help spring Grigori." I held onto him tighter. "As it was, I had to make a second trip back to the device. You'd probably have known how big those pieces needed to be too. I was flying by the seat of my pants."

He tucked my head into the hollow between his neck and shoulder, and we stood locked in one another's arms as minutes ticked by. Apparently, we'd taken too long of a break because Grigori strode into the room.

"Time's up," he said briskly and tapped me on the shoulder. "Jake has a wolf to get to know, and you need sleep. Aidyrth's waiting for you in one of the outdoor bedrooms so she can watch over you."

We untangled ourselves, and Jake kissed me once more. "See you soon," he said.

"Sounds good to me." I floated out of the room listening to Grigori and Jake chatting behind me. Jake was asking good questions, probably ones I should have asked, and Grigori was providing answers.

I found Aidyrth easily by following my link to her. She'd settled in the sun, wings folded. A pallet had been laid on soft grass next to her. I didn't need an invitation to stretch out. I needed a shower, but it could wait until I woke up.

"Rest." The dragon breathed steam. "I'll watch over you."

"You need a break too," I told her.

"I'll be fine. Dragons don't require sleep in the same way as you. I'm glad Jake will be part of the Circle. He's a natural addition, unlike many who've joined us over the years."

"Is everyone who ever said yes still here?"

"Nay. Of course not. Grigori says it's forever, but he doesn't want those who do not wish to stay."

"So? They're either dead, or someone erased their memories," I murmured.

"Something like that. We need to return to that last hotel in Chicago to gather your things, but later. Grigori called them and extended your stay with instructions not to disturb your room."

I fought the sleep that hovered, intent on claiming me. Somehow, we'd pulled victory from the jaws of defeat. When we'd been in that cavern, I wouldn't have given us better than 20 percent odds of success, yet we'd prevailed. My last doubts about the Circle finally melted away.

It was a lot like what Jake had articulated. I was living a dream with a dragon sidekick and maybe, just maybe, a man to fall in love with. The orphaned street-kid I'd been had finally found safe harbor. Eh, maybe not safe. I'd be bored with safe, but I'd found a rich and satisfying life.

"Thank you for selecting me and sticking it out," I murmured. "I can be bitchy and insufferable."

She didn't contradict me, but she did say, "Thanks for giving our bond and the Circle a fair chance."

"I almost didn't."

"I know. I know everything about you."

I tried to articulate how much it meant, her knowing me to my bones and not rejecting me, but the words tangled on my tongue.

"Rest, Shira. Everything will still be here when you wake." The dragon puffed more steam over me until I finally fell asleep.

You've reached the end of *Shira*, first of the Circle of Assassin books. Read on for a sample chapter from *Quinn*, next in the series. Unlike Shira, he was one of Grigori's earliest recruits who left the Circle behind. While *Shira* is fresh in your mind, please take a moment to leave a review. They mean so much to authors, and they're a way to let other readers know what you loved about a book. Until next time.

BOOK DESCRIPTION, QUINN

The only constant in my long life is murder. Assassin for hire, to put a finer point on it. I'm an earth wizard. Usually, we're on the peaceful side. Not sure what happened to me, but I never fit in with my kinsmen. They'd have chased me out of the fold—for obvious reasons—but I saved them the trouble. I left on my own. The same way I left the Circle of Assassins because it was too tame for my taste. Or maybe too structured.

Along with my bondmate, an oversized eagle, I've been playing fast and loose with the rules forever. Of course, the rules have changed, but I've rolled with the punches. Never found a policy I couldn't manipulate to my advantage.

There's an old saying about life coming full circle. It's about to snatch me up and spit me out. I can run, but there's nowhere far enough to hide from what I am or the Circle of Assassins.

My first home.

My first nemesis.

Grigori said I'd be back. How in the hell could he have known?

QUINN, CHAPTER ONE

Automatic weapons make a hell of a racket. My ears ached. Worse, they'd be ringing for days. Depressing the trigger of my Kalashnikov I fired another burst in the general direction of the Taliban commando unit. It had been mighty quiet these past few minutes, but I didn't trust those bastards as far as I could see them. It's not accidental the Brits have never won a war against them. For that fact, neither has the U.S. Mountains are high and wild and inhospitable in this remote locale with a million places to hide and stage counterattacks. No matter how rough things got, local militia had an ace in the hole: they wore their enemy out until they gave up and went home.

I'm not in the habit of giving up. Period. My ace in the hole is I have magic. I'm an earth wizard. Not too many of us left, not because we died out but because we got tired of dealing with mortals and made a run for other worlds.

They're not perfect, either. I know. I've shopped them, and I always end up right back here slopping around in mud and blood and guts. Afghanistan could be the posterchild for human quirks. In the past few decades it went from being run by Russians to the U.S. training the Taliban to overthrow them to the Taliban spiraling out of control and giving the U.S. hell's own time.

I never take sides. I'm for sale to the highest bidder so long as what they're asking me to do doesn't run aground on the few scruples I have left.

More firepower rained from the two men with me on this mission. Spaced fifty feet on either side, they were solid fighters. The mercenary world is small. We all more or less know each other, but not too well. It's not that kind of club.

"Quinn." My earphone crackled with static along with my name.

"Yup. What?"

"Think they're dead?" Rafe asked.

Breath hissed from between my teeth. It was the question of the hour. "No. But any survivors are long gone."

"How? I'd have killed anything that dislodged so much as a pebble," he growled.

"Another of their infernal underground tunnel systems. How else."

"What do you want to do?" a different voice joined the discussion. Leon had clearly been listening in.

More hissing breath as I considered his question. "Move in. Sweep for survivors. Search for anything that looks like a tunnel entrance and drop grenades."

"Works for me," Leon agreed.

Rustling from both sides alerted me my companions were on the move. I paced myself to their stride, and we arrived at a five-hundred-foot granite wall. It's broken rockwork offered virtually unlimited paths upward to still more crags above. Bodies littered the ground. I never bother to count, and I didn't now. Dead was dead, and these poor fuckers weren't dressed for the minus twenty temps. Maybe we'd done them a favor, all in all. Dragging out my phone, I snapped pictures to provide proof we weren't out here with our dicks in our hands jacking off.

A spate of curses from Rafe brought me at a run. He stood over exactly what I'd been certain we'd find. A hole in the ground leading god only knew where. "Got it," Rafe mumbled as he pulled pins and dropped grenades. By the time they detonated, we were a hundred yards away, running over talus blocks and sucking dry cold air. Our work was done, no reason to tarry.

"Fuck me. Bird's still there," Leon shouted and fist pumped empty space in front of him.

"Sure is a pretty sight," Rafe chimed in.

I'd given it fifty-fifty our ride wouldn't be disturbed. Not great odds, but better than even in my business. Of course, I didn't actually need the chopper. I can teleport.

Saved a lot of explanations, though, since I'd be the logical one to come back with another bird.

It's where not being BFFs came in handy. None of the dudes I worked with asked very many questions. Or any at all about the times I'd bailed them out. Rafe and Leon hadn't worried about the chopper being stripped for parts —or blown up—because they had faith I'd come up with another exit strategy on short notice.

Leon headed for the bird at an easy lope.

"Hold up," I yelled. "We don't want any ugly surprises."

"Like it exploding when you hit the ignition?" Rafe arched dark brows. Not that everyone I work with is a clone, but men in this trade all have the same look. Roughhewn with lots of muscles, they've lived through nightmares and keep coming back for more. Truth was they didn't do well in polite society, and they knew it. Kind of like snarling watchdogs; necessary, but no one wants to get too close to them.

The occasional woman is drawn to this life, but not many. Too bad because there's nothing quite as fierce as a cornered bitch.

I understood all of it too well. Assassins are born, not made. We only feel alive when adrenaline is pumping, and Death's dank breath stinks up the joint. I bit back a snort as I went through the chopper from stem to stern with Rafe and Leon helping. Death was actually a woman, and she wouldn't have appreciated my reference to stinky breath.

"Clear," Leon yelled. Rafe echoed the word.

I'd just yanked the door open when the rat-a-tat-tat of an automatic rifle jerked my attention away from the chopper. More rifles joined the choir. Damn it. I could deal with one, or even two, from the air, but not the dozen or better filling the night with their death chant.

"Fuck. Not home free yet," I shouted. Feeling naïve and gullible—and pissed—I dove for a boulder pile This attack made perfect sense; I should have expected it. The Taliban hadn't bothered to boobytrap the chopper. Why go to the trouble when they could kick back and wait for us to return to it.

Leon zigged and zagged before jumping next to me. I scanned for Rafe, but didn't see him. Rather than wasting magic, I relied on our communicators. "Dude. Make a run for us."

Bullets peppered the rocky ground. Bits of broken granite blew everywhere, deadly as shrapnel.

"Nah," Rafe's crusty voice crackled against my earpiece. "I'm good where I am."

"Hold your fire," I cautioned. "Let's let them burn up more ammo."

"Copy that," Rafe muttered.

For the next quarter hour, we hunkered as bullets splatted around us. I sent a thread of power outward intent on eavesdropping. Maybe I'd hear something helpful, like if they had enough ammunition to last all night. It had been dark for a couple of hours, and the temperature was dropping—if that were even possible.

The Taliban had always drawn its ranks from small

remote villages. Driven by faith, they were fearless fighters and as tough an adversary as I'd come across. I'd fought them before—many times. I'd been approached a time or two about switching sides, but some of their activities rub me the wrong way. Human trafficking for one.

"Christ. Colder than a well digger's ass," Leon mumbled and dragged a hood over his helmet.

Cold weather gear was a dreamboat these days, compared with the ratty woolen coats we used to have that always smelled like rancid sheep fat. I'd have called him a pussy if I weren't so intent on deciphering a conversation in Dari and Pashto.

I held up a hand. "Ssht."

"No one can hear us," he protested. "Not with all this racket."

It wasn't why I'd silenced him. A trio of the rebels were arguing—in two languages. They hadn't counted on us going to ground. They'd assumed they'd smoke us out and make short work of us. Ha. I'm not in the habit of being easy pickings for anyone, and certainly not for this bunch of dicks.

"You need to get out of there," a familiar voice buzzed through my head.

"What do you see?" I asked my sidekick. Some would call him a familiar, but he's been my partner in the assassin trade for hundreds of years. He's an eagle, but only in a very distantly related sense. In the days he was hatched, they were far larger, true birds of prey. His given name is Roland, but I saddled him with Gwaihir after *Lord of the*

Rings became popular. It amused him—after I told him about Tolkien's tale—and he hasn't said not to call him that. Not yet, anyway.

"Men are moving toward you," the eagle squawked.

"How many?" I screwed my mouth into a scowl. Counting wasn't the sort of thing he excelled at.

"Too many."

Not the answer I'd hoped for, but I trusted my bondmate.

"We've got problems," I told Leon, assuming Rafe would hear too.

"How do you know?" Leon shot back. "Nothing's changed."

I keep Gwaihir a secret. It's why he was in the air and not down here with us. After a small shrug, I said, "Instincts."

"You've got to do better than that, dude," Rafe protested.

No. I didn't. Since no answer would satisfy him I didn't offer one. He didn't push it, either.

Thoughts collided as options bounced around. We couldn't take the chopper. She'd be shot down before we got off the ground. It only left one option, and it wasn't something I could talk about. I located Rafe easily and crafted the underpinnings of a spell to move us all out of here.

"What you thinking, boss?" Leon nudged me.

"Going to have to trust me," I mumbled and sent a wing of my casting to scoop Rafe into it. Was it worth wasting ammunition? So far, we hadn't fired a shot. The same phalanx of boulders protecting us meant we'd have to move beyond their shadows to use our weapons. I was still listening to the three men haranguing each other. Since I'd established a link, I rode in on it and opened the dirt beneath their feet.

At first, they probably figured it was another quake. The ground was riddled with fissures from volcanic disturbances. By the time they realized this was something different, that they'd be sucked through layers and layers with rocks sealing their egress, it would be too late.

So much for those three. Were the others worth killing? If I told my comrades-in-arms we were going to open fire, they'd be all over it. Murder has a seductive aspect, particularly when the target is fighting back. Makes it easier to justify. Not that I've ever required an excuse to snuff out a life.

Leon elbowed me again and angled a come-on-already look at me out of clear blue eyes. He was right. We'd overstayed our welcome. One of the sheltering boulders exploded, peppering me with rock fragments.

Clock just ran out.

I tightened the wing of my spell draped over Rafe and ignited it. The shithole countryside dropped away, and we catapulted through blackness. No worries about Rafe and Leon. Something about the vibrational force of teleporting rendered mortals unconscious.

We were headed back to Camp Leatherneck Marine base in Helmand province. The CO would be irate about his chopper. Or not. Far from the first aircraft lost in combat, it wouldn't be the last, either. Besides, I hadn't completely given up on it. Our mission had originated at Leatherneck, but I wouldn't bring us down inside the base. I could do a little bit of memory alteration with my buddies, but not for everyone on the base who saw us wink into existence out of thin air.

Too many balls in the air when I wasn't certain who'd seen what. People would compare notes, though, and it made modifying memories a total crapshoot. Gossip ran rampant in spots like Camp Leatherneck. It was the kind of place that turned humans into alcoholics—or addicts. Drugs were cheap and plentiful in the Middle East. The Marines had a sporadically enforced policy about illicit drugs tucked away somewhere. I had vague memories of signing it along with a spate of other hush-hush agreements.

It's a dirty little secret the military hires mercenaries to do certain aspects of their wet work. Places where it would be inconvenient to admit U.S. involvement have made me a wealthy man. Except I was set for life long before the war in the Middle East.

Once I made the mistake of asking an Army commanding officer if he had second thoughts about training the Taliban. He'd turned on his heel and left the supply tent. Eh, when you're as old as I am diplomacy isn't a driving force.

My spell, which had been chugging along on autopilot, was running down. Not dissimilar to the barren region we'd left, I dropped us a few miles outside the Marine installation on a high, windswept mesa. A squawk from above told me the eagle had anticipated my moves and beaten me here. Shit. He was worse than a wife, not that I've ever had one. Women are a complication I don't need. I settled Rafe and Leon with their backs leaned against substantial rocks. They had GPS equipment and could figure out where they were once they came around. I expected to be back before then, but plans have a way of derailing. While they were still out cold, I mucked around and planted a memory of us making a run for it.

And then, I deepened their trances to make it believable we'd covered the miles between where we left the chopper and here. Because they were sitting ducks, I swathed them in invisibility and ripped a page out of the small notebook I never gave up carting around.

I've kind of made a transition to the digital age. Sort of. But this was simpler than relying on electronics.

Gone back for chopper was all I wrote and crumpled the paper into Leon's hand. He'd find it and not worry about where I was.

Gwaihir squawked again, and I loped toward him. He flew to meet me, landing heavily on my shoulder. It's always a shock something made mostly of feathers could weigh a good forty pounds. Images flooded my mind of the incoming troops he'd warned me about.

"We're going back," I said.

The eagle pecked the side of my head. His version of a love bite, it always drew blood. "Hurry," he urged.

"Why you bloodthirsty bitch."

"Not your bitch," he retorted in a stock answer to my comment.

The exchange made me laugh. We were friends, companions, buddies, mates. All of the above and more. He'd become my bondmate long ago when I was part of the Circle of Assassins. Long story short, Grigori and I butted heads once too often. I could have given him a run for his money, challenged him for control of the Circle, except I had less than zero interest in piloting a rowdy crew of supernatural assassins.

And so, the eagle and I had left sometime during the 1700s. We'd been on our own ever since despite Grigori's parting shot that I'd be back. Not only was it never a consideration, but I wasn't even tempted. I knew what I had there. Likeminded companionship, but at what cost?

Grigori ran the Circle with an iron hand and single minded purpose. He picked the jobs and parceled them out. He wasn't unreasonable. If I wasn't up for a mission, he offered it elsewhere, but the lack of autonomy grated. The first time I left was for a month, the second for a year, and the third far longer. I hung around for another hundred plus years after returning, but the writing was on the wall. I knew I'd leave, and so did Grigori.

He tried to talk me out of it over flagons of well-aged brandy one winter evening. Ironically, that conversation made up my mind. My leave-taking was amicable, as those things go, and I occasionally ran into him or his operatives. I'm not a bridge burner. That door is still open, but it would take a whole lot to entice me to sign back up.

Different terms, for one thing. A world where I picked my assignments, sought them out on my own. I wasn't a neophyte, and I didn't require protection from the baser aspects of my nature. I could burn down the world leveraging earth magic—if I wanted. I didn't. Everyone has a niche. I'd found something that was as good a fit as I was likely to come by, and—

Another peck reminded me it was time to get moving.

Returning on my own had advantages. The primary one was I could chuck as much magic around as I wanted. I might come up short if I faced a hundred ragtag Afghanis —those dudes were tough as knotty oak—but my bet was the vast majority had decamped.

Didn't matter. I'd kill until the fire raging inside me retreated. It never withdrew for long, but I'd learned to control it, turn it to my advantage so it worked for me not against me.

"Coming?" I asked the eagle to determine if he'd share my transport spell or cast his own.

"Still here, aren't I?" Talons dug into my shoulders treating my layers of cold weather gear as if they weren't even there. Blood trickled down my back and chest. I diverted a shot of magic to seal the wounds.

Holding an image of my destination firmly in mind, I wound fire and air into a teleport spell. It would take a little longer, but it freed up earth and water to weave into a wave of destruction.

I'd hit the fucking ground on all fours, running for all I was worth. They'd never know what hit them, and maybe I'd get my chopper back. If they hadn't stripped it for parts. Most of the Bell AH1-W's components weren't interchangeable with the Sikorskys— carryovers from the Russian occupation—favored by the Taliban,

Rather than ripping the Bell to shreds, they'd be smarter to fly it back to Taliban central. It pained me to admit it, but my current adversaries weren't short on brainpower. If they'd been inept, their regime would have caved, outsmarted by western forces.

Training them had been one of the U.S. military's dumber moves.

"I'll take stragglers," Gwaihir announced.

"Eat a few eyeballs for me."

The bird huffed laughter. "I can save you some."

"Nah. They're your favorite. Pay attention, we're almost there."

Power crackled between my raised hands as I prepared to lay a sheet of death a quarter mile wide in my wake. But first, I had to make the transition from teleport channel to terra firma. For a split second I'd be vulnerable, and it would be a pain to have to regroup if someone caught me half in and half out of teleport mode.

The eagle's weight shifted as he spread his huge wings. Seeing him airborne would be enough to send the superstitious jerks ranged against me into a tailspin. Viewing me unshielded, power bubbling around me, ran a close second.

More than ready, I channeled Death's presence. I was her agent, doing her work, even though she'd been horrified the time I'd suggested as much. And I'd been exasperated she refused to dive into the nitty-gritty delight of eliminating marks who were a waste of good air.

We'd agreed to disagree, but one of these days we'd have a rematch, she and I. The deep gray of my journey channel exploded, leaving me in roughly the spot I'd left. No more phut-phut-phut from rifles, but I didn't let that stop me. Everywhere I sensed life, I sent power chasing after it intent on finishing what I'd begun.

ABOUT THE AUTHOR

Ann Gimpel is a USA Today bestselling author. A lifelong aficionado of the unusual, she began writing speculative fiction a few years ago. Since then her short fiction has appeared in many webzines and anthologies. Her longer books run the gamut from urban fantasy to paranormal romance. Once upon a time, she nurtured clients. Now she nurtures dark, gritty fantasy stories that push hard against reality. When she's not writing, she's in the backcountry getting down and dirty with her camera. She's published over 90 books to date, with several more planned for 2021 and beyond. A husband, grown children, grandchildren, and wolf hybrids round out her family.

Keep up with her at www.anngimpel.com or http://anngimpel.blogspot.com

If you enjoyed what you read, get in line for special offers and pre-release special reads. Newsletter Signup!

ALSO BY ANN GIMPEL

SERIES

Alphas in the Wild

Hello Darkness

Alpine Attraction

A Run for Her Money

Fire Moon

Bitter Harvest

Deceived

Twisted

Abandoned

Betrayed

Redeemed

Cataclysm

Harsh Line

Warped Line

Cracked Line

Broken Line

Circle of Assassins

Shira

Quinn

Rhiana

Kylian

Coven Enforcers

Blood and Magic

Blood and Sorcery

Blood and Illusion

Demon Assassins

Witch's Bounty

Witch's Bane

Witches Rule

Dragon Heir

Dragon's Call

Dragon's Blood

Dragon's Heir

Dragon Lore

Highland Secrets

To Love a Highland Dragon

Dragon Maid

Dragon's Dare

Dragon Fury

Earth Reclaimed

Earth's Requiem

Earth's Blood

Earth's Hope

Elemental Witch

Timespell

Time's Curse

Time's Hostage

Gatekeeper

Shadow Reaper

Rebel Reaper

Untamed Reaper

GenTech Rebellion

Winning Glory

Honor Bound

Claiming Charity

Loving Hope

Keeping Faith

Ice Dragon

Feral Ice

Cursed Ice

Primal Ice

Magick and Misfits

Court of Rogues

Midnight Court

Court of the Fallen

Court of Destiny

Rubicon International

Garen

Lars

Soul Dance

Tarnished Beginnings

Tarnished Legacy

Tarnished Prophecy

Tarnished Journey

Soul Storm

Dark Prophecy

Dark Pursuit

Dark Promise

Underground Heat

Roman's Gold

Wolf Born

Blood Bond

Wolf Clan Shifters

Alice's Alphas

Megan's Mates

Sophie's Shifters

Wylde Magick

Gemstone

Lion's Lair

Unbalanced

STANDALONE BOOKS

Branded, That Old Black Magic Romance (paranormal romance)

Edge of Night (short story collection, paranormal and horror)

Grit is a 4-Letter Word (nonfiction)

Heart's Flame (post-apocalyptic romance)

Icy Passage (science fiction romance)

Marked by Fortune (post-apocalyptic coming of age story)

Melis's Gambit (historical paranormal romance)

Midnight Magic (paranormal romance)

Red Dawn (post-apocalyptic paranormal romance)

Shadow Play (historical paranormal romance)

Shadows in Time (Highland time travel romance)

Since We Fell (contemporary romance)

Warin's War (paranormal romance)